THE NEW GIRL

ALISON STOCKHAM

Dear Tilly

Thanks for all you do for
writers, readers + the book
community!

B

Boldwood

x

First published in Great Britain in 2024 by Boldwood Books Ltd.

Cover Design: 12 Orchards Ltd.

Cover Photography: Shutterstock and Pexels

A CIP catalogue record for this book is available from the British Library.

Paperback ISBN 978-1-80426-008-1

Large Print ISBN 978-1-80426-007-4

Hardback ISBN 978-1-80426-009-8

Ebook ISBN 978-1-80426-005-0

Kindle ISBN 978-1-80426-006-7

Audio CD ISBN 978-1-80426-014-2

MP3 CD ISBN 978-1-80426-013-5

Digital audio download ISBN 978-1-80426-010-4

Boldwood Books Ltd
23 Bowerdean Street
London SW6 3TN
www.boldwoodbooks.com

To my daughters – for reminding me always, what is most important

1

'Was it really that awful? It was supposed to be a romantic trip away. What went wrong?'

'So awful. Honestly, it was...' Anna shuddered. 'I could just feel the pressure of what it was supposed to be and it made it so hard to actually relax. It was like I was watching myself playing the part of the thrilled, surprised wife being pampered by her thoughtful and loving husband.'

She wrapped her hands around her cup of coffee as she sat opposite her friend, Kate. They'd taken the corner booth at the local coffee shop that they always met in. It was halfway between both their offices, and they met for lunch once a week without fail. Fitting it in was difficult around their commitments with work, with Jon and the church, but the weekly lunches were a lifeline for Anna. She could be wholly honest with Kate. Or, at least as honest as she could be with anyone. She looked into the cup as she blew air out of her cheeks. The holiday had been horrendous. Jon had whisked her away on a romantic trip to Italy, her favourite country. He'd booked a glorious hotel in the centre of Rome, a stone's throw from the stunning Spanish Steps, and they'd spent time just meandering around the city hand in hand, drinking in the architecture, the history and the wine. It should have been wonderful. It was supposed to have been a break from everything, from the stresses of setting up their own printing business, to the emotional turmoil of their as yet unsuccessful attempts to conceive. A reset. A fresh start.

'What happened?' Kate asked, looking pained on Anna's behalf. She knew almost all there was to know about Anna and Jon, having been his friend first, being part of the same church community and having been the one who'd introduced them to each other.

'I got food poisoning.'

'Oh. That's not good.'

'Oh, that would have been OK. It wasn't so bad. A day at most and I was fine. It was probably some off wine or something. But I was sick and tired. And Jon...'

'...thought you might be...'

'Exactly. I tried to tell him I wasn't pregnant. I *knew* I wasn't. Stomach pains and clammy skin are not signs of having conceived. But he wouldn't listen. You could practically *see* the hope shimmering in his eyes. He was all "well, you know, it might be, maybe we should test." *We*, like it was him trying to read instructions in a language he didn't understand, though they're basically all the same. Him, trying to wee on a stick whilst still feeling really shaky.'

'Oh, honey.'

'Yeah. And I knew it would be negative but the only way to stop him hoping, to stop him running away with himself in his head, was to disappoint him. Again. Like I've been disappointing him for years now.' Anna hung her head, looking at her jiggling feet.

'No,' Kate said firmly. 'You know that you are not a disappointment to him. The situation maybe, but you? Never. He loves you.'

'Does he?' Anna said bitterly.

In the aftermath of the negative test, they had barely spoken to each other. Not properly. Just surface level chat. The previous days of spending time trying to just enjoy each other's company in beautiful settings, the romance, the *joie de vivre*, had been replaced by two people who seemed to have nothing to say to each other. He touched her, she flinched. Terrified that he would immediately move from disappointed to trying again as he had done before. Like she was nothing more than a baby machine, who, if you just kept trying, would eventually produce one. Not like she was a human being who had to have time to process things, to emotionally deal with things before being able to move forward.

'Yes,' Kate insisted. 'Look. I know he can be intense about the whole baby thing. He's wanted to be a dad his whole life. But...'

'I know. I know it's all he wants. And his first wife and their baby who... And now me?'

'It's not all he wants. Just sometimes, I think he finds it hard...'

'I find it hard too.'

The weekend would have been the perfect time to try again. Jon had clearly spent a long time planning the surprise, whisking them away one Friday afternoon. He'd picked a beautiful boutique hotel with rooms that were spacious and luxurious, and you could just be in and feel amazing. It was quiet despite being central and every day they'd enjoyed breakfast in their room on their balcony overlooking the city as it woke up. And yet, Anna had been on edge. She had known the expectation and she had struggled to make it feel less forced to her. He wanted a family so much. She wasn't sure it was the cure-all he thought it was. She didn't know if she could have a baby. *Another* baby.

'I know, hon, I know.'

'Do you?' Anna snapped before apologising. Kate nodded her acceptance, acknowledging that she, in fact, did not know. 'I know Jon lost a child when his pregnant wife died in that awful car crash. I know it was horrific for him. But... I lost my baby too. And I had nine months of feeling it growing inside me. Nine months of feeling like I was going to be a mother, feeling like I already was, and then? Nothing. No baby. I was not a mother any more.'

Kate reached across and squeezed Anna's hand.

'Hon, I know it's hard to talk about it... I... How...' Kate tried to ask with trepidation.

Anna shook her head. She'd never told Kate the whole story. It was too much. It was bad enough that she felt her best friend was sort of on Jon's side, or was at least neutral. She didn't think she could cope with Kate knowing everything, and the possibility of her then taking a step back. Anna didn't have many friends as it was. She couldn't lose Kate. She also couldn't undo the past; she could merely try to survive it. So she pushed all of it to one side and locked it up in a box that she refused to open. But the hinges of that locked box were straining now. All these years later, although in all intents and purposes she was happy, it kept coming back up to haunt her.

'We sort of rescued each other. We saw the same pain in each other. Now? I wonder if we're just making that pain worse.' Anna chewed her lip. She needed Kate to tell her she was wrong, to tell her that her marriage wasn't in trouble. That the only solid part of her life was in fact still strong, weathering everything life could throw at it. She looked up at Kate, trying not to look too desperate.

'Oh, come on now,' Kate said, as brusque as Mary Poppins. 'Now you're just being melodramatic. You two are meant for each other. Obviously you have both experienced trauma, and that could be a bad combination, but you two, you heal each other. Like you said, he is a good man. You are a good woman. I know you're not the most confident. When we first met it took you almost a month just to look at me when you were talking. I know I don't know all the details, but I know enough about you and I know enough about Jon to know that you're bigger than this. You mean more to him than just your ability to procreate. Besides' – a mischievous grin spread over her face – 'if that were the case, he'd have picked someone younger, no?' She laughed, trying to lighten the mood that was in danger of darkening the whole day for them both.

'Oi! How rude!' Anna laughed along with her, relieved that Kate had told her she was wrong but feeling a slight ache at the base truth of her joke. She was thirty-seven, he was forty-three; they didn't have a huge amount of time before their ages were against them. She didn't know if Jon felt the ticking clock, but she knew she did. She was running out of time to give him something she didn't know she could ever give. Something, that if she was being honest with herself, she didn't truly want. She wanted it for *him* but didn't know if she really wanted it for *herself*. She didn't think she wanted to find out. There were so many complications, so many threads all tied up and put away, that to untangle them all was too much. She smiled and threw her napkin at Kate, who caught it, laughed and handed it back.

'I'm allowed to joke that, cos I'm older than you. Honestly though, try not to stress. Jon loves you, you are enough for him, you deserve him and he deserves you. Your business is going from strength to strength and life is good, no? Why not focus on that?'

'I know. Things *are* good. We're busy but the business is still growing. The new website has really taken off, we're getting a whole new customer base which is great, but I'm so busy with the admin, I'm struggling to do the designing, which was the whole point. I'm absolutely shattered!' She winced, holding up the largest cup of coffee that the café sold. 'I'm living on caffeine, sugar and stress which can't be good for me. Jon keeps trying to suggest I switch to green tea but I need the coffee boost to keep at it.'

'Is there any end in sight? Any way you can take your foot off the pedal a bit? I mean, baby making or not, being shattered all the time isn't fun.'

Anna nodded. She knew they had to make some changes, but it felt like they didn't have enough time to put the changes in place without dropping balls to do it, which felt counterproductive. She was really proud of the business. She was using her finance brain and her design brain and felt in control of her career for the first time. She'd had so much of her life out of her control, it felt good to have this one bit sorted. She was her own boss; she was good at what she did and she knew it. Maybe *this* was what she was supposed to be doing with her life. Maybe *this* was her purpose. She just didn't think Jon would feel the same. She knew he didn't, and it was this aspect of the whole baby issue that was causing all the rows.

'I could but...'

'But what?'

'Well...' Anna paused as she tried to work out what she meant. 'Well, I'm not sure I want to. I like being in the thick of things, and it won't be forever, will it? I mean, this leap in sales. If it continues, then sure, we'd need to think about staff, but for now, I feel like we should just ride the wave and see where it goes?'

'Yeah, just don't let it drag you under, OK? You've got bags under your bags, love. Sorry but it's true. I'm not being mean, I'm just a bit worried. We rescheduled this lunch three times...'

'That was my supplier moving our meeting. Sorry. I'm here now though, aren't I?' she snapped, a little too defensively. Trying to be everything to everyone was difficult. How on earth would they ever cope if they did have a child?

'I know. I'm just looking out for you. That's all.'

Anna smiled. People cared about her. She was lucky. 'Sorry, I didn't mean to snap. Must be the caffeine rage.'

'Green tea?' Kate laughed and Anna joined in.

Things were good, or at least good enough. Did she really want to rock the boat? Couldn't things stay as they were? If everyone really was happy enough with things, why did they want to make changes? Change wasn't always a good thing; sometimes change was what brought things crashing down. Anna was only too aware of that.

2

The office was loud as Anna walked back through the door, carrying a green tea for herself and lunch for Jon. They couldn't both leave the office at the same time so on the days she met Kate, Anna brought food back for him. He was talking on one phone while the other line was ringing out. Another postal delivery had come while Anna had been away and her desk was hiding under a layer of parcels and letters. As she looked at the chaos and felt the tension in the room, the doorbell went and Jon's head snapped up, the stress clear on his face as he motioned with his head for Anna to get it. She nodded in acquiescence, put the lunch items down and headed to meet the courier.

Jon was just hanging up as Anna came back into the shared office space with a large heavy box. He leapt up to help her carry it.

'Let me.'

'It's fine, I'm OK.'

'I've got it,' he said as Anna felt the weight of the box lift off her arms.

'Oh, OK... Thanks.'

'You should have left it for me to come and carry. This weighs a ton.'

'It's just the ink samples. And it's starting to rain. I didn't want to leave them outside and the courier wouldn't bring the parcel in. Once I was carrying it, it seemed silly to just leave it by the door. But it got heavier as I held it, I swear!' Anna laughed, rubbing the parts of her arms reddened from carrying the box. Every time Jon offered to carry something heavy, she assumed it was because he thought she might be pregnant. She knew this was ridiculous. He was just being courteous.

'Shall we take a look while I have lunch? Thanks for that by the way. What did I get today?' Jon asked as his stomach rumbled, looking over at Anna's desk.

'Toasted BLT, is that OK?'

'Perfect – thanks.'

He grabbed his lunch and sat back down, ripping open the brown paper bag, sending a smell of hot bread and bacon wafting around the office. Anna was envious. She'd had a salad but the warm carby smell was making her mouth water. He took large ravenous bites of the sandwich, closing his eyes in appreciation. Anna watched him. He was so... solid. He was real. He was open. He just was himself. It was one of the many things that she loved about him. After years growing up with people never meaning what they said, or voicing what they were thinking, Jon's openness with the world, his ability to just *be* within it, was what drew her to him. There were no pretences, no hidden agendas. He was just solidly *him*. That did mean that any tensions they had usually came right out into the open. She preferred to push them away, but he wanted to deal with things. His way was healthier, she knew that, but a lifetime of conflict avoidance and people pleasing had left her at a disadvantage.

'Do I have something on my face?' He smiled at her, wiping

at his cheeks with the napkin that the café had packaged with the sandwich. 'Sorry, I was just so hungry. Breakfast was an age ago!'

Anna smiled, snapping out of her reverie. She wanted to say something nice. 'No, no, just looking at my husband and wondering how I got so lucky.'

He smiled back.

'Karma,' he replied.

'Obviously,' she said, winking at him, trying to keep the mood light.

Was he her karmic reward for overcoming adversity? When things were good, she felt maybe this was true. That she'd been through hell and kept on going, coming out the other side, and this, a loving husband, was her reward. Other times, when they did row, when they seemed so at odds with each other over what they wanted, she wondered if it was karma kicking her in the ass for all the bad choices she'd made. Giving her *almost* what she wanted, but not quite. Making things one step away from perfect, like the tantalising hanging fruit being just out of reach, water just beyond her lips. After all, karma went both ways, didn't it? That's what was so awfully delicious about it.

Anna walked to her desk to start sorting through the post. Their offices were in an industrial estate, but they'd tried to make them look as welcoming as they could. It was sort of an urban chic look – all granite floors and breeze block walls, iron girders and metal stairs – but Anna had added plants which hung from the ceiling and huge bushy ones in pots that broke up all the harsh greys and blacks with flashes of green. Jon had said it was a waste of money, but Anna had said that if they were going to spend so much time here, it had to be somewhere they wanted to be, without feeling like they were trapped in some B-movie prison set. And spend so much time there they did – they worked long hours, six, sometimes seven days a week. And still, the to-do list was overwhelming.

Anna couldn't hold her loud sigh in as she filtered through the post and the filing piles. There was so much to do and all this essential business stuff kept getting pushed and pushed aside as they fulfilled their orders. They nearly forgot to pay an essential invoice last month and it had been touch and go as to whether they would have had to stop working until it was sorted. All the utilities were on direct debit but the invoices in and out took up so much time. Time the two of them didn't have.

'Yes. I agree,' Jon said out of the blue.

'To what?' Anna was confused. Was he referring back to her comment on karma? Or something else? Had he been talking and she'd been so engrossed trying to work out where to start that she'd missed something?

'We need help,' he said, gesturing to the piles of paperwork that Anna was grimacing at. 'You and I need to free up admin time to get on with the other things. We need an assistant or a book-keeper or something. We live in this place and as nice as you've made it, I'd quite like to see our house from time to time too.'

Anna winced. It was true. But she felt wrong bringing someone else in. This was their own little bubble, just the two of them. Someone else would change the atmosphere, wouldn't they? They might judge the decisions that Jon and she made. Would they think they were ridiculous for their little printing empire dreams? She was confident they could really make something of this – they were still growing – and yet her lack of self-esteem sometimes told her she was being stupid, she didn't have what it took to run her own business, and she didn't know if someone else being here would make that voice louder than it already was. And as it was, there were already days when it screamed at her.

'I know. I know. Just...'

'What? You want to spend your evenings doing invoices?' Jon said, a little strained. 'Is my conversation at home that bad?'

Anna felt the double question in Jon's tone. They used to spend their evenings talking about everything and nothing, sharing their thoughts. Lately, their conversations had dwindled. It wasn't that they were strained as such. Just that they'd spent more time in different rooms, doing different things. More room mates than partners.

'Just, I don't know who I'd want here. Other than us. We work. We know how things go, we don't have to explain or manage, or ask, or sometimes even have half of the start of the conversation!'

'If we're going to make this work, expansion was always on the cards. You know that. We can't do this with just us forever. It was our wonderful little cocoon at first, I get that. But now? We're making good enough money. We can hire someone part time. I actually have someone in mind. Someone I've worked with on some of the church events, you know, the baby unit fundraising thing.'

'Oh. Really? Who?' Anna was shocked. This was the first time they'd discussed it, but clearly Jon was ahead of her. That wasn't usual; they normally talked everything through. Everything business-related anyway. She had not joined him on the church fundraising committee for the baby unit. It was too much, too painful. A lot of it was to do with the NICU and she couldn't bring herself to go there, to the office where some of the meetings were held. She'd insisted she needed that alone time for design work.

'So did I mention Grace before? She's on the committee. She's Patricia's niece. You know, Patricia, from church, whose dog sleeps under the pews during service?'

Anna smiled. Patricia was a stalwart of the community. She

had about a million children at any one time, biological and foster, and whoever else she had brought under her wing. She was the original earth mother and one of the kindest people Anna knew.

'Yes. Of course. Pat and Poppy, the dog. But no. You've not mentioned Grace before.'

Anna scanned her memory for any mention of a Grace. She felt abashed when she realised she'd not really been listening to Jon when he'd been talking about the project. It was difficult to hear him talking about how the work they were doing was saving sick babies, keeping families together. God's work. The cynic in her had managed not to ask why God was letting the babies get sick and die in the first place; her faith had been severely shaken by her life experiences, but she kept those dark questions hidden from Jon. Another part of herself she had not been able to share with him for fear of what he might think of her. In keeping that shut away, she'd been blocking out a part of his life too.

'Haven't I?' he said breezily. 'I'm sure I have done. She's a core part of the team. Anyway, she's smart, compassionate, keen and hard working. She'd be an asset to any team, I am sure. So I asked her if she would join us next week.'

Anna practically spat out her green tea. 'What?'

Jon went slightly pink. Anna could see it rising up his face.

'Well. She was saying how she was looking for some work, a bit of experience as she's fresh out of university. Graphic design.'

'And what? You thought you'd hire her without an interview, without references, without even so much as running it past me?'

'We don't need references. I *know* her.'

Jon wouldn't look at Anna. If he had done, he'd have seen the fury mixing with hurt on her face.

'But *I* don't. And this is *our* business. We have no idea how she might fit in, what her professional work is like. Where did she study? What were her grades?'

'We've not hired her as a graphic designer. I thought we could use another pair of hands here. She could do some admin, filing, sending and chasing invoices, that sort of thing. I could teach her some accounting and you could work with her on designs. She'd be sort of a paid intern, three days a week.'

Anna's eyebrows rose. 'You've thought all this through.'

'I have.' Jon looked pleased with himself.

'Without so much as mentioning it to me.' Anna's mouth settled into a hard line.

'No... Well... I just thought,' Jon muttered. 'We need help, I got us help. I don't know why you're being so...'

'Being so what?'

'Defensive. Look, I've suggested a trial period. If you don't like how it's working out then we can rethink things.'

'Oh, so *now* it's our decision.'

'Don't be like this, Anna.'

Anna swallowed. She was being awful, she could hear it in the tone of her voice. Jon was right. They did need help. They were drowning in unfinished tasks and sooner or later it was going to cause problems with the business. No matter what she'd said to Kate about going with the flow, the flow was going to flood soon enough.

'You're right. I'm sorry. We do need someone.'

'Good.' The relief in his voice was clear. 'She's great, she really is. She's interesting, funny, clever. She reminds me of you actually.' He smiled. He looked about ten years younger suddenly. Anna did not find this reassuring. She tried to make herself see the positives, but she couldn't stop the feeling in her stomach telling her that this was a mistake. She pushed it away. This Grace was from a good family, she was at least known to Jon so not a complete stranger and, like he said, if it didn't work out, they could call it quits. A trial period.

'Let's see how it goes then,' Jon said, looking pleased with himself once again.

Anna swallowed her discomfort. How bad could it be?

3

Anna's knees were jumping underneath the table as her feet tapped on the ground. Her fingertips tapped on her crossed arms, Her whole body seemed to need to be in a constant state of motion. She tried to tell herself that it was the extra shot of coffee that she had ordered for some reason when she'd called into the café on the way to the office. A sort of first-thing-in-the-morning version of Dutch courage? She knew she was nervous – even calling into the café was a delaying tactic; she was self-aware enough to know that. The coffee had been so strong when she'd tasted it that she'd added sugar which she never normally did and now her whole body was buzzing. Anna hoped that the inevitable caffeine and sugar crash wouldn't be too bad.

Grace was starting today and Anna didn't know how to be. Jon's mood had lightened considerably since they'd agreed to give this a go, and Anna tried to assume that it was due to his expectation of a lowered workload and more free time rather than his looking forward to Grace being here. How was Anna supposed to act? She'd never managed anyone before so she wasn't sure what sort of boss she would be. And how would Grace report to both her and Jon? The two of them had worked together elsewhere. Anna felt at a disadvantage already, like the new girl at school when the rest of the class all knew each other. But then again, wasn't Grace the new girl? Anna and Jon were married; you didn't get closer than that. Did you?

'Can you stop that please?' Jon asked through slightly gritted teeth.

'Sorry?'

'You're tapping the table.' He indicated to Anna's hands. She was knocking her pen against the edge of her desk without noticing, playing out the rhythm of her anxiety. It was a fast rhythm, matching the pounding of her heart. No wonder she felt lightheaded.

'Ah. Sorry. I'm absolutely wired!'

Jon nodded. 'Coffee was a bad idea then?' he said, smiling kindly, pausing before continuing. 'It'll be fine, you know.'

'What will?'

Jon looked exasperated.

'Grace. I know that's why you're nervous, but it'll be fine. She is the answer to all our problems.'

What problems? Anna thought, despite knowing what he meant. They were overworked and it had made them cranky with each other. Never enough time to just sit back and enjoy life.

'Will she stop you from grinding your teeth when you think?' Anna said. She had meant it to come out as a joke but when it came out of her mouth, it just sounded mean.

Jon sighed. 'Maybe she will.'

'Sorry – that came out wrong.'

'Doesn't matter,' he said, waving her away. 'I spoke with her on the phone yesterday. She's just coming in today for a chat. We can work things out from there. Very informal. Not all contracts and targets. We can sort out some paperwork for her when she's met us both and seen what we do here. Heck,' he laughed, 'she might not want to stay!'

Anna breathed out in relief. That sounded far less stressful, much more doable. She'd wound it up in her head as a *thing*, with Grace being some awful interloper into the bubble that she and Jon lived in. She was always doing that. Making big worries out of small things. It was connected with her need to control things, she knew that, and it was worse when she couldn't. And you could never control everything. Sometimes life just life-ed at you and you had to go with it, but Anna felt that never went well.

Just as Anna was managing to calm her nerves down, the office doorbell rang out, echoing around the silence of the office. Silence. That was one thing that Anna thought would need changing when Grace was here. She and Jon were perfectly happy to work in silence, just the sounds of each other's tasks as the background noise, Jon's teeth grinding included. But they were used to each other. Silence was fine for them, but it might be oppressive to someone new. She'd try to remember to bring in a radio or something. It didn't have to be loud or always on, but it might be useful if the atmosphere was off. She'd feel strange making phone calls knowing that the sound of her half of the conversation was the only noise in the room, like Grace would be listening. And why should she not be? The calls weren't private. But Anna already felt strange about it. Some background noise would be good.

Jon stood up.

'That'll be Grace. I'll go and get her.'

Anna stood up too. Then sat down. Then stood up again. Then she walked to the front of her desk and leant against it. She crossed and then uncrossed her arms. She nearly fell over. *Get yourself together! What on earth is wrong with you?* she admonished herself. She had just untangled herself and was standing by her desk, finally looking a little more relaxed, as Jon came into the office space, followed by a striking-looking young woman.

Grace was taller than Anna had imagined her to be, with dark hair in a pixie cut and dark eyes. She was dressed in an outfit that looked as though someone else had chosen it for her – her mother possibly – her hair, shoes and make-up being fashionable against her very conservative outfit. She looked like a doll that someone had dressed up.

She was absolutely beautiful.

Anna was mesmerised at first and she couldn't think what to say.

Grace was looking at her in silence too, intently. Too intently, Anna felt under immediate scrutiny. She had to work very hard to maintain eye contact and smile.

'Grace, this is Anna. Anna, Grace,' Jon said, sounding nervous himself for the first time, Anna noted. He nodded with his eyes towards her, a sort of *say hello* expression. When initially Anna still said nothing, he added, 'I'd hardly recognise you, Grace. You look very... chic.'

Anna tried not to laugh. Chic? No. Grace's outfit was frumpy, but it somehow managed only to emphasise how good-looking she was in contrast to it.

'I look ridiculous,' Grace said, smiling at Jon before stepping forward, her hand held out towards Anna. 'Nice to meet you, Anna. I've heard so much about you.'

Anna suddenly felt about a million years old. Something about Grace made her feel like an insignificant little old lady. She forced a smile onto her face and told herself she was being silly.

'Hi, hello. Lovely to meet you too, Grace,' Anna said, stepping forward, holding her hand out to shake.

Grace smiled, trying to hide nerves that now Anna was

looking more deeply, she could see in the tension around her eyes.

She waited for the conversation to continue. It didn't.

There was a slightly too long silence where no one quite knew what to do or say. Jon wasn't helping. He just stood there, looking at the scene with a satisfied expression on his face.

Anna cracked first.

'So. Um. You've been working with Jon? At the church?' Anna sounded unsure. Like she was asking rather than telling.

Grace's face broke out into a wide smile. It brought about a complete change to her face. It drew you in to her.

'Yes! Jon and I have been working really well together on the NICU project. We're such a good team that when he persuaded me to give here a try, I thought, why not?' She beamed.

Jon persuaded her? I thought he said she'd asked about work opportunities? Actually... no. What did he say? Anna wasn't sure, she realised. It had spiralled into the start of a row before Anna had got the details on how the conversation came about.

'The dream team, that's what Patricia called us when we hit the first target.' Grace nodded towards Jon and then back at Anna. 'I mean, here, that's clearly *you* and Jon,' she added deferentially, looking at Jon for assurance. He tried to hide his nod, but Anna caught it. They were talking about her, in front of her, without words. She felt a spark of rage catch within, but her reason dampened it down. It was going to take time to find the dynamic here. She had to be a grown up about this. Sulking helped no one.

'Yes, it's wonderful working with Jon. Being married and running our business is great. We get to bounce ideas off each other all day. It's a really collaborative way of working but I'm sure we can fit you into that too.'

Jon laughed.

'What?' Anna said defensively.

'Sorry. No, it's just that you make us sound like some breakfast TV team. Grace,' he said, turning away from Anna to face her, 'don't worry, we'll get you all set up, sort out some tasks and just give it a try from here. OK?'

Grace nodded.

'Great. Is... is that OK with you, Anna?' she asked, as though there was anything Anna could add that wouldn't make her look obsolete, petty, or both.

Anna nodded mutely. This was going exactly as she'd feared it might, with her being the outsider in her own business. Fleeting memories of feeling an outsider in her own family rose to the surface before she did what she always did and pushed them away. That was in the past. This was now and she wasn't going to get that confused.

'Fine with me,' Anna said brightly. Grace was not an obstacle, nor a problem, just because she was young and pretty. Life had taught Anna a lot and she'd happily swap the dewy, unlined skin and wealth of possibility that Grace had on her side for the strength and resilience that Anna had found in her years. Being young was hard as well as brilliant.

'I'll pop the kettle on then and we can all get to know each other a bit better before getting on with the administrative things,' Jon said, walking to the corner of the room where the kitchen was. He went about the business of making tea as Anna sat down with Grace at the meeting table. Grace looked around the room, trying to get her bearings. It felt forensic to Anna. Like she was scanning the office for information, and when she turned back to Anna, the smile on her face was fake. She was not feeling as cheery as she was trying to be. What she was actually feeling, Anna couldn't fathom.

Jon appeared utterly unaware of how uneasy both women were as he returned to them with the drinks.

'So,' he said, setting the steaming mugs of tea onto the table. They were decorated with the company logo, branded mugs being one of the many products that the company printed. In the beginning, Anna had almost been embarrassed by the corporate gifts they made, alongside their beautiful bespoke designed items, but Jon had quite sensibly said they had the set up to do it so why not do both, at first at least? One was a solid income and there was nothing wrong with regular, repeat custom after all. He was right, but her artistic ego winced all the same even when she told it to stop.

'So...?' Grace said, taking a sip from her mug before placing it down in front of her, wrapping her hands around it.

'Why don't you tell Anna a bit about yourself,' Jon suggested.

'That's putting her a bit on the spot, don't you think?' Anna said, taken aback by how annoyed on Grace's behalf she was, protective almost. Was that how Jon felt about her too? He certainly liked her.

'No, it's fine. It's OK, I don't mind. I mean, after all, your husband has brought in a complete stranger to you, a new girl,' Grace said. Anna's hackles rose. Was... was Grace *teasing* her? No. Surely no. No, she was being deferential. Wasn't she?

'It was a joint decision,' Anna insisted. Jon *had* asked, even if he had already asked Grace. If Anna had refused then he wouldn't have forced this on her, she was sure of that. 'Do tell me about you. I'd like to know.'

'OK. Um, great,' Grace said. 'Well, I've just finished uni in London. I studied Graphic Design with a speciality in advertising.'

'Is that what you want to do? Ads?' Anna asked, failing to keep a tone of disdain out of her voice. She hated ads. 'Monetised manipulation if you ask me.'

'Anna!' Jon hissed at her.

'Maybe,' Grace said, either not noticing or caring about Anna's comment. 'I like how by using art you can convince people to do something or think something they had not intended to. You know? It's like, mind control!' She laughed. 'I just think it's a really interesting aspect that mixes psychology with design.'

'Grace studied psychology also, didn't you?' Jon added, almost proudly.

'Yeah, only at A level though. It's really interesting. And, you know, ads are everywhere now, with the internet and apps. It's not just TV ads any more,' she said, looking at Anna as though she was about a million years old.

'I know about apps, yes,' Anna said, gritting her teeth slightly. Did Grace think she was completely clueless just because she was over thirty? She must have thought Jon was a dinosaur!

'Well, we need someone who's a bit more clued up on modern tech and what's hot.'

'Do we?' Anna said, looking bemusedly at her husband as though he'd put a backwards baseball cap on. What was he doing? Trying to be cool? Their business was not about apps, it was about beautiful bespoke design work. What was going on with him?

'Yes,' Jon insisted.

'OK,' Anna said, not pressing the matter. 'So, Grace, design and ads. We don't really do advertising here but we do print some corporate products so I guess that's along the same sort of lines.'

'Not really, I—'

'Right then,' Anna said, cutting her off. 'I'm not sure how much you already know so forgive me if I'm repeating anything. So what we do here is design and print in a nutshell. Jon has laid out on the table our look book for the sort of things we print and the designs we've done for some previous clients. How about you take a look at that and get a feel for the sort of thing we've done in the past? We're open to new clients, new designs, all the time but in order to do that, what we need help with, what we'd need you to do, is the administrative tasks that eat into the time that could be used for design work, finding clients or account management. So it's emails, filing, some minor payroll work, though we have an accountant who works one day a week paying invoices, but it'd be invoice creation and chasing...'

'Chasing?' Grace looked genuinely terrified.

'Don't worry, we won't set you on that first and it's not very often,' Jon assured her.

'But occasionally it's necessary, a polite reminder that the deadline has passed. We can set you up with a script of sorts, don't worry.'

Grace took a deep breath.

'OK.' She nodded.

Anna looked at Grace, trying to work her out. She looked confident, *seemed* confident. A little pushy even. Though that could have just been how she was with Anna. People took time to warm to her, she knew that. She wasn't immediately welcoming, and it took a lot to get through the armour she knew she wore. They'd get along soon enough, she was sure. Grace was only twenty-two and although she was officially an adult, a lot of life situations were new to her, especially if she came from a close and cosseting family. Anna felt a little twinge of envy; it must be good to grow up with the bad of the world held at arm's length by those who loved you. A safe space to be.

'Sorry. Yes. I can be a bit shy sometimes. But I'll get there, I'm sure,' Grace said, brightening up.

'That's my girl. I'm sure you will!' Jon said, jumping up from his seat. 'Come on, bring your tea, I'll give you the tour! Anna, could you remember to call back that client? The one interested in a range of postcards? They've a query and they've left a couple of messages already,' he said breezily as he took Grace into the printing area, leaving Anna by herself.

Now it was Anna's turn to feel insecure. She didn't like how she suddenly felt like an employee rather than an employer. It was odd, she couldn't place it, but she had a niggle that Jon was already behaving oddly, talking to her as if she was his subordinate rather than his equal, making himself look or feel like the alpha male.

No. No, he wasn't like that. She was being paranoid.

Wasn't she?

4

Anna was in the kitchen, staring out of the window as she waited for the kettle to boil. She'd come in to work early to get started without the hubbub of other people. Jon had taken up running again in an attempt to keep his 'middle-aged paunch' at bay, and Anna had decided that once she was awake, after Jon had failed to get up anywhere near quietly, she might as well get up and on with the day. Something she was regretting slightly now that the first buzz of morning energy had abated and the deep fatigue she'd been struggling with lately had settled over her. She was hoping a cup of tea might perk her up a bit.

She was miles away, mulling over a particularly tricky issue, and so she didn't notice Grace until she was standing right next to her. It was only when Anna turned slightly back towards the office that she noticed her and she physically jumped in response.

'Jesus!'

'Oh. Sorry. Sorry, I didn't mean to surprise you. I said hello but you... didn't... hear...' Grace tailed off and gestured at the now loudly boiling kettle, then held her hands up in front of her in an apologetic gesture.

'You just... Don't sneak up on me!' Anna said, a little more snippily than she had meant to.

'I wasn't, I didn't mean... Sorry.' Grace's brow wrinkled at the unfairness of the situation.

'No. No, I didn't mean to snap. I'm just struggling to get going this morning. That's all,' Anna said as her heart rate calmed after the shock. She'd nearly had a heart attack. She'd locked the door behind her as a security measure, being alone on the premises, so how on earth did Grace get in?

'The door – did I not lock it? I'm sure I did. I always do when it's just me here. Can't be too careful.'

'You did. Jon said because you or he aren't always here, we might need to check diaries for when I come in but I said it'd probably be easier if I had a key too? Like you said, I might be here alone as well sometimes and you can't be too careful. Sad but true, right?'

Jon had given her a key? Already? Anna could see it made practical sense but Jon had always been so funny about things like that. When they'd briefly had a cleaner, when they were at home enough to make mess but never home long enough to clean up, he'd resisted giving *them* a key. They barely knew them, he said. Anna supposed it was just *her* who barely knew Grace. But still, he'd not mentioned it.

'Hmm? Yes. Yes, we can't be too careful who we let into the office.'

Grace looked offended.

'No, sorry. No, I didn't mean you.'

She did.

Anna gestured to the kettle.

'Would you like a cup?'

'Sure – thanks.'

'How do you take it?'

'Just like my mum does – strong, no sugar. She's very particular about how she takes her tea. Said it's from years of looking after lots of kids. She needs a strong drink but not a *strong* drink, if you know what I mean.'

Anna nodded.

'How about you? How do you take yours?' Grace asked.

Anna thought this was an odd question as it was her making the drinks, but she supposed that maybe Grace was just getting ahead for when it was her turn or something. Maybe there would be perks to having an assistant about the place. Though Anna didn't want to exploit anyone, she wouldn't be asking Grace to do anything that she'd not be willing to do herself.

'Um. Similar, I guess. I don't like sugar in mine either. Though...'

'Yes?'

The way Grace was looking at Anna made her feel as though she had a mental pen and notepad at the ready. Profiling her or something, over tea. Anna was being ridiculous, but she couldn't stop herself from thinking it.

'Nothing. Just, my gran used to have the sweetest tea,' Anna said, smiling at the memory. 'Five teaspoons in an old-fashioned cup and saucer, not even a mug-sized cup. It was like tea syrup!'

Grace laughed and Anna relaxed. She was being overly sensitive, unused to other people. Grace was just trying to fit it.

'I can imagine! Why did she have it like that?'

'Oh, she used to say it calmed her nerves. Everything was always about her *nerves.* It was like having tea with a Jane Austen character. All "who had married who" and her nerves.'

'Oh,' Grace said, looking suddenly very serious. 'Did she... have a nervous condition? I guess you'd call it a... mental health issue now?'

Anna looked at her, confused. What an odd question – definitely overstepping the mark.

'No. No, not as far as I'm aware. She just liked the attention it gave her when she needed it. She was a solid ox of a woman. Took no prisoners.'

'Ah… OK…' It was Grace's turn to look confused. 'So was that your mum's mum? What was your mum like? Was she strict? Or was she the gentle one? You know how you get one strict parent and one you can always persuade if you try hard enough?' Grace laughed. 'I know I do! Which was she? Which do you think you'd be if…' Grace stopped suddenly. 'Sorry, I'm interrogating you. I—'

'Yes. You are a bit.'

'Sorry. I'm a bit nervous.' Grace raised her shoulders in a childish shrug.

Anna winched her lips upwards. More of a grimace than a smile. She couldn't make herself smile. She didn't want to talk about her parents and certainly not with the new intern, yet somehow, she still found herself answering. Maybe she ought to smooth things over. She was in the position of power, wasn't she?

'I'm not sure I got a gentle parent. I think I got two strict ones.'

'Really?'

'Yes.'

'So, were they both, like, old-fashioned then? A different generation and that?'

Anna gritted her teeth and hoped that frankly, Grace would see her jaw line tighten and let this conversation go.

'I guess…'

'What were they like?'

Grace wasn't letting go. She was like a dog when it gets its teeth into you and doesn't want to release you. She'd got Anna talking and now Anna didn't know how to make it stop.

'Um... Well, my father was strict, and my mother did what he said. Maybe... she could have been gentler if he had let her. But...'

'He didn't?'

'No.'

'OK,' Grace said, nodding, as though this information made sense. Anna got the feeling that they had been having slightly different conversations, though how, she couldn't tell. Enough. She didn't want to do this any more and she didn't have to.

With that realisation, Anna turned back to the tea and started to remove the teabags. The conversation had put her own mother into her mind, and she could practically hear her admonishing her for not using a teapot for when she had guests. Teabags were not acceptable for company. That was how she was with every-thing – her way was the only way and anyone else's way was wrong. Anna was always wrong.

'Right...' she said, hoping that it would bring the chatter to a close and she could go back to her desk and get started on her list. It was how she started every day – taking yesterday's to do list which she wrote before leaving the office every evening and then checking any emails that had come in overnight, from overseas or those clients working later than her, though these were rare, and threading them into her list of tasks for the day.

'My dad is the strict one,' Grace said, picking up the thread again, 'but my mum always said I was a gift to be treated gently so she's always been a bit more lenient. I'm the oldest but sometimes I feel like the baby of the group. What about you? Do you have any siblings? Or Jon? Is it just you two? No kids yet...?'

Anna took a deep breath. What was with all the questions? There's getting to know your colleagues and then there's this. She'd have to instruct Grace in professional distance.

'Oh, is that the phone? I'd best get it,' Anna said as she walked past Grace, gripping on to her mug and hoping that

Grace wouldn't say anything about the fact that no phone was ringing.

Grace looked confused but let Anna pass.

Anna sat down at her desk and picked the phone up. There was no one there as she knew there wouldn't be. She knew that, Grace knew that. Why had she done something so odd? Was it so awful for Grace to want to know more about her? Maybe she'd been told to ask questions, so as to seem interested. Anna would happily answer questions about the business, about printing, about art, design, whatever, for hours if Grace would ask those sorts of questions. Her family was not a topic up for discussion. They weren't part of her life now, and she didn't want to talk about them. In order for her to feel OK they had to be an irrelevance, edited out of her life for everyone's sakes.

But Anna had been rude. And she didn't want to be. She sipped at her tea leisurely, letting the warmth of it settle into her bloodstream as she worked out what to do. She watched as Grace walked slowly, awkwardly, almost defeatedly, back to her own desk and sat down. She looked up at Anna, opened her mouth as if to speak and then her face flushed with embarrassment and she looked down, took up a pen, and began to make notes on the pad in front of her. Anna felt shame flood her. She'd made things unnecessarily uncomfortable.

Where was Jon? He was the social smoother in the business and in their relationship, always able to make people feel welcomed, comfortable. He could make you feel that you were the only person in the room when you had his attention. It was one reason all the negotiations tended to be done by him. He charmed suppliers into their best rates, and he did it almost unknowingly. He didn't want to rip people off, that wasn't his style. He always said a good negotiation wasn't one in which one party had been battered down to the lowest price they would accept, feeling underappreciated and taken advantage of, but one where both parties could find a mutually acceptable middle ground, where both felt they had won. In her conversation with Grace, no one was the winner.

The silence was pricking at Anna. She had to fix this. She was the grown up here, the boss. It was her job.

'I must be losing it!' she said jovially across the office.

Grace looked up and Anna tried to ignore the hard look in her eyes. It wasn't that bad, surely? Anna hadn't been *that* mean. If anything, Grace had been impertinent, asking such personal questions. They didn't know each other.

'What do you mean?' Grace asked, a faux lightness in her voice. They both knew she was faking. They both knew Anna was bluffing.

Anna gestured to her desk.

'The phone, I could have sworn it was ringing but there was no one there. I was expecting a call this morning. Do... do you ever do that? Imagine the phone's ringing when it isn't?'

'Um. No, not really,' Grace said, looking at Anna, with what? Pity? Concern? 'Do you imagine things often then? I don't but... I could see how you could.'

How I could? Me particularly or you in general? What was Grace insinuating? Anna shook her head. She should start over.

'Maybe I'm getting old. Look... Did you want to come and sit here with me while I go through this new order? You can see how we do things.'

'Yeah! Yes, I'd love to. Thanks.'

'Great. Um, bring over a chair and I'll make some room for you.'

Grace looked excited as she gathered up her things to join Anna.

Anna didn't get Grace. Maybe she was too old, Grace too

young. A generational gap that meant they wouldn't understand each other. Then again, she wasn't that much older than Grace.

Grace pulled up her chair.

'What's your favourite band?' Anna blurted out and immediately regretted it. She sounded about a million years old.

Did Grace just roll her eyes at her? No. No, she was smiling.

'Really? You want to know?'

'Uh...'

Is it such a terrible question? Is Grace being petulant or protective? Or neither?

'Sure.'

'Well, OK. I'm a bit retro to be honest. My favourite musician is David Bowie. I've always loved listening to my dad's records and he's just the best.'

'Me too! Love him. No one else sounds like him. He's so unique and he does his own thing. And he's just... who he is. Unashamedly. I respect that.' She envied that.

'Exactly! As soon as you hear that voice, you know it's Bowie.'

'Yes! Shall we put some on?'

'Can we?'

'Of course! If the phone actually rings, we'll have to turn it down, but absolutely. I actually find music helps me concentrate.'

'Oh, me too. Especially if it's something I know well enough that it sort of flows over me. Sort of like a—'

'Comfort blanket,' they both said together.

Grace laughed, a genuine, honest laugh, and Anna found herself warming to her. She'd knew she'd been awful this morning. Grace's questioning had put her back up. She had a wall around her, she knew that. Even Jon hadn't wholly knocked it down, even now, but Grace hadn't been nosy, she was just trying to work out how to settle in. Anna would have to let her.

'What's all this?' Jon said as he walked in the door to find

Anna and Grace both singing their hearts out to 'Life on Mars?'.
'An impromptu work concert?' He hung his coat up on the hooks
by the door and walked to his desk.

Anna turned the volume down a bit and turned to him, a little
breathless.

'Just finding some common ground through the brilliance of
Bowie. Isn't that right, Grace?'

'For sure!'

Jon smiled.

'My two favourite ladies having a sing-along.'

Anna's stomach dropped. His what? That was too familiar,
surely. He'd be making Grace feel uncomfortable. She'd have to
mention that to him, otherwise he'd leave himself open to all sorts
of potential accusations. She looked at Grace to see how she had
taken that, expecting to see discomfort or concern on her face. But
Grace was glowing. She looked happy.

Anna looked at the floor as she knew her face would betray
her, her concern etched into her expression. Grace was just happy
at being included, that was it. Jon was just being kind, that was all.
Wasn't it?

She looked up again.

'Am I going to have to fight for the top spot?' she said before
she'd realised it.

Grace blushed. Hard.

Jon looked horrified.

Anna felt like she'd absolutely got it wrong, and yet, there
was... *something*. She just didn't know what.

'I think we're getting off track here,' Jon said, adjusting his tie.
'My meeting overran so I'm behind on things. Grace, might you be
able to help me with some printing and envelop stuffing for some
clients?'

Grace nodded, still looking embarrassed.

Anna could feel Jon's anger towards her radiating across the room. They would no doubt have to talk about this later when they were alone. She would have to work out how to explain herself, but what would she say? She couldn't even explain it to herself. Just that she had been worried that bringing someone else in might be a mistake. That it being someone that only one of them knew might knock things off balance. That the dynamic of the office might be pushed out of kilter by it. And that she had been right.

She just had no idea what she was actually dealing with. She would find out.

5

It was still dark as Anna whirled around the kitchen back at home, the sky at the horizon only just starting to show flickers of red and gold as the sun rose for the day, the odd streak of morning sun hitting the countertops as she wiped them down. She hadn't been able to sleep, her insomnia rearing its ugly head for the first time in as long as she could remember. Years ago, she spent so long awake in the small hours, battling her darkest thoughts, but she had overcome it, or it had released her once she felt that she had found her path. Since she and Jon had been together, she had slept soundly, peacefully. Safe. Though if he was ever away, bedtime had a dusting of anxiety to it. She had to dress it up at a 'treat' to have the bed all to herself. She would watch a film he would hate, eat food he did not like, run a hot bubble bath and sit in it, reading, until her skin wrinkled and her book was curling at the edges. She would wear her fanciest nightwear and get into freshly clean sheets, spreading out like a starfish even though she knew that she slept in the foetal position. Even she knew she was trying to convince herself. It did the trick well enough if not wholly. But tonight? She had lain, staring at the ceiling, feeling the reassuring presence of Jon next to her, yet unable to rest, her mind whirring through the recent days. She knew that the insomnia's return meant that something was unsettling her, but she couldn't quite pinpoint what.

The kitchen gleamed as she sat and took a sip of freshly brewed coffee. The room was filled with the scent of baking, the loaf of bread she had made from scratch that morning finally in the oven and rising. The meditative routine of making the dough, kneading, proving then doing the same again, helping her to clear her mind. She knew that stress wouldn't help their situation. She wasn't sure anything would, if she was honest with herself.

As she sat, still in her pyjamas, she looked at the gentle curve of her stomach and gently placed her hand where a baby would be. It was hard to feel it empty, and yet, she was terrified of the alternative. She'd never told Jon this, about her deep-set fear. She knew that he'd most likely just tell her about the miracle of life, the miracle of birth, how it's all part of God's great plan and sometimes we have to experience the hardships in order to receive the joys. It's easy to consider it a miracle when it's not you doing the ground work. When the nausea, the cramps, the stretched skin and repositioned organs aren't yours. When the pushing, the tearing and the pain is done for you by someone else. Pain. They say you can't remember pain, but she could. She did. The physical and the emotional. She shuddered. Nothing about it seemed joyous to her. Jon wanted so desperately to be a father that it scared her. She didn't know if she could ever give him that, even if she wanted to.

So, in the absence of the one thing keeping them apart, everything else had to be perfect. The past few days had showed her the cracks that had crept into their solidity. She needed to smooth them over.

She looked at the spotless kitchen, which backed onto a spotless living room, their modern home all open plan and airy. She'd have vacuumed but she didn't want to wake Jon so she'd swept instead, thinking of all those generations of women who'd cleaned their houses on their hands and knees, who'd scrubbed and brushed and buffed until their skin reddened and split. Things had come a long way and yet she still felt the pull of jobs she thought of as *hers* if she was to be a good wife. The perfect wife. Jon wasn't hugely conservative that way; he'd lived alone and insisted he was wholly capable and perfectly happy to handle housework – after all, they both worked the same hours at the print works, so why would he expect her to do more than her share at home? And yet, she still felt a glow of accomplishment when she'd ticked some housewife box, as if she was assuring herself that she was a good wife, even in the face of their current fertility issues. She was struggling with the feminist implications of that when the buzzer for the timer went off. She leapt to switch it off, not wanting to wake Jon before his alarm.

She was turning out the hot loaf, its warm, comforting aroma filling the room, when Jon came shuffling into the kitchen, sleep rumpled and wrapped in his 'old man dressing gown', as he called it. Her heart flipped. She really did love him. She really did want to make him happy, to give him what he wanted, what he needed. She knew they'd have to come back together otherwise they would crack apart. But in the immediate absence of a magic trick to solve all their issues, freshly made bread and freshly ground coffee would have to do. A flicker of *who do you think you are? Martha Stewart?* came to her, but she ignored it. Making bread and coffee wasn't getting above herself. It was just breakfast.

'Morning.' He yawned as he ruffled his bed hair. He looked around the room, taking in the picture-perfect scene. 'What's all this?'

'Breakfast?' Anna said in reply as she reached into the fridge for butter and jam and the chopped fruit she'd prepared while the coffee brewed.

Jon smiled but then his brow wrinkled.

'How long have you been awake? This would have taken hours and it's only half past six. Did you not sleep well? It's still the middle of the night almost.'

'Too early? I'm sorry. I wasn't planning on waking you yet, but I needed to time the baking.' Anna waved her hand over the scene, trying to be breezy, not actually answering his question and hoping he'd not notice. She'd struggled to get to sleep and then woken from a nightmare that she couldn't recall, only the horror clinging to the edges of her mind, dread of an unspecified type sitting in her stomach. Then she had started to think, then spiral about all that had happened in the last week. How on earth were they going to make this Grace thing work when Anna was so uncomfortable with it? She had no real argument as she had no specific reason that she could raise. Especially when Jon was so keen on the idea. And why was he so keen? Was it just business?

'Are you OK?' Jon looked concerned. Anna knew she was being manic.

'Something woke me. Not sure what. A fox or a cat fight maybe. But then I couldn't get back to sleep. I was thinking through new projects and then I got excited about them and got up to make some sketches. You know what I'm like!' She laughed, hoping Jon would believe her.

Somehow, she couldn't share this niggle with him. It felt like questioning his decisions without a tangible reason, and she didn't want to do that. She didn't want to undermine him, make him feel that she didn't trust him. She knew the anxiety was hers, and most likely unfounded. She had nothing to hang her fears on but fear itself.

Jon smiled.

'Wonderful. That's what you're like!' He leaned and kissed the top of her head and she breathed him in. He smelled like himself first thing, before showers and cologne sanitised him. She thought he always smelled good. Apparently, that's a strong sign of biological compatibility, liking your partner's smell. She reminded herself of that whenever she felt insecure about things. Their very molecules thought they should be together. And who was she to argue with that? All their recent tensions were secondary to their solid compatibility.

'Shall I cut the loaf? Is it cool enough yet? It smells amazing!'

'Probably not, but we could tear it if not? I won't tell anyone.' She smiled as she poured them both coffee. She'd be buzzing before the day had even started but she was going to need the energy from somewhere. She already felt like she needed a nap.

'Let's. I'm too impatient to wait and the smell is making me ravenous!' Jon said as he carefully tore at the bread, letting the steam from the inside escape a bit before tearing some more, moving his hands round to avoid getting burnt.

Anna laughed.

'Careful! You look like one of those cartoons. You know, "hot hot hot" as you're throwing the bread about!'

'I am "hot hot hot" – as are you!' Jon laughed as he placed hunks of bread back onto the bread board and pulled out a chair to sit down. 'This all looks amazing. I am a lucky man!' he said as he spread butter, which melted as soon as it touched the bread, and heaped a spoon of jam onto it, before cramming it happily into his mouth.

'You are.'

They sat in companiable quiet, starting the day as Anna hoped it would go on, both of them feeling the gratitude of having the other by their side in all things. They were a team, unbreakable. All her anxieties were just the devil on her shoulder, an echo from her past where she could never do anything right, trying to tell her she was worthless. Jon could see that that wasn't true and he helped her see it too.

Anna took a deep breath and felt the contentment. This was how it was meant to be, and nothing – not work nor colleagues nor an inability to sleep – was going to spoil it.

She wouldn't let it.

6

The early spring air was drifting in from the French doors that led from the living room into the garden. The smell of the narcissi from the large terracotta pot by the door was powerful as it settled into the room and Anna was curled up on the sofa, trying to read a book but mostly dozing. In a move quite unlike her, she had told Jon that she wasn't well and had stayed home from work. She was tired from poor sleep but other than that, she was fine. She just could not find the energy she needed for another day in the office with Grace. And Grace and Jon. She knew it had only been a couple of weeks; things were new and would take time to settle, but she hated the atmosphere there now. It was tense with Grace and weird with Grace and Jon, and Anna kept finding herself on the outside of jokes and anecdotes. On the outside of a business that was *her* idea.

The resentment this caused made Anna snippy, which of course made things worse. A break, she thought, would be a chance to reset. To re-evaluate things and to work out how she could move forward, productively, positively. She tried to sell it to herself as her being the bigger person, being sensible and taking a step back in order to see things clearly, rather than merely reacting to things. In reality, she was just hiding.

Anna had already decided that if she was not going to push Jon away any further than she unwittingly had already, then she was going to have to compromise on this, no matter how much that went against her instinct and fed into her anxiety. It was getting so hard to tell the difference between anxiety and true danger these days. Her mind felt them all the same. With Jon, she knew she had to keep herself open, even if that ran the risk of her getting hurt. And Jon was convinced that Grace was good for the business, which would in turn be good for them. Anna had decided to be OK with it. But today that had felt like too much. Today she had allowed herself to pop back into her protective shell and rest.

She had just closed her eyes and admitted that she was going to nap, pulling the green and grey blanket from the back of the sofa over herself, when there was the briefest of knocks at the door. Feeling slightly drowsy, it took her a little while to get up and out into the hallway. By the time she got to the front door and opened it, whoever had knocked was gone. She stepped out onto the doorstep and looked each way down their street but there was no one there. Maybe she imagined it? Perhaps she had already fallen asleep and had dreamed it. She stepped back inside but as she closed the door, she stepped on something on the mat. It was an envelope with *ANNA* written in capitals on the front.

Confused, she picked it up, opened the unsealed leaf and took out the photographic paper that was inside.

It was a baby scan.

A black and white photo with a grainy image, a little like a peanut in shape, but human all the same. A new life curled up in the widening expanse of a womb. You could see the profile of the baby's face, the outline of a growing brain inside the skull. A person.

A baby.

Anna felt like she'd been slapped in the face, the black and white outline bringing both the trauma of her first baby and the lack of one with Jon right to the forefront of her mind, assaulting her as she stood on her own doorstep.

Why would someone post a baby scan to their house?

She felt sick as she thought about it. *She* wasn't pregnant. Despite all the changes that Jon and she had put in place – more rest, healthier diet, reduced caffeine and alcohol – Anna wasn't pregnant. There had been no scans for her. The only scan she'd ever had, back then, had been a frightening experience that ultimately led to only more loss. There was an acidic taste in her mouth now as she stood in the hallway but it wasn't the metallic taste that pregnancy hormones give. It was guilt.

There would have been no need for Anna to have a scan now. She was on birth control and had been for years. She didn't want to be pregnant. She couldn't do it again. Not even for Jon.

There had been a very brief period just after they were married when she had decided that she could risk it now, that perhaps as her situation was different, the outcome would also be different. She had stopped taking the pill, but the sheer and absolute terror that she'd felt when there had been a pregnancy scare meant that as soon as she was able, Anna had returned to her doctor to resume birth control. She had been taking the pill ever since, all through her marriage, each month her period a construct, each pregnancy test taken a piece of theatre to keep the peace.

Jon didn't know the truth. Anna hadn't ever been able to tell him, month after month, year after year. There was never the right time. He had always been so keen to have a baby, to start a family, that Anna never felt there was space to discuss it, to discuss an alternative. And she had wanted so badly to be the wife that Jon wanted, the wife that he deserved, to be the person she saw reflected in his eyes when he looked at her, that she just went along with it. She ought to have learned by now. Her passivity always came back to bite her. Always.

Did he know? Had he... had he sent this baby picture, of some random child, to make a point?

Her breath caught in her throat as she held the scan in her shaking hands. Is that why he'd taken a step back from her, like she felt he had done? Did he know that she was lying to him? Figured out all the tiny, miniscule, not-a-big-deal lies that added up to one really big one? Had he worked it out?

At first it was difficult, painful, to lie to him about it. To pretend that she shared his monthly disappointment at their lack of baby success. To make sure he believed her that she had no idea what they might be doing wrong. She had gone along willingly with his suggestions to help, only pushing back when he wanted her to step back from work and even now, with Grace installed in the office, she had sort of acquiesced to that. She would do anything to make him happy. Almost anything. Just not that. She couldn't. And she couldn't tell him why. It would ruin everything.

Surely if he'd found her out, he would just talk to her about it. Difficult or not. Subterfuge was not his style. Was it an encouragement from him? To show what they *could* have?

Eventually, he had got used to the disappointment, his enthusiasm waning as he found it harder and harder to believe, despite his faith. It was only his faith that kept him holding on to this idea of his soon-to-be family, and Anna could see how he had adjusted his mindset accordingly. She did the same. She convinced herself that she also had no idea what was causing things not to go to plan. She swerved discussions of doctors and IVF because it was not 'God's way', not the grand plan that their maker had for them. He seemed to accept this, hard as it was. Another challenge that the Lord had laid for him to bear. It had felt wrong but also necessary. A lie to protect the bigger picture. A lie to keep from all the other secrets that she held.

Anna walked, breathless and light-headed, back to the living room where she sat down heavily on the sofa and placed the scan in front of her on the coffee table. *Be rational*, she told herself. *This is clearly a mistake. Posted to the wrong house.* And yet, the envelope had been addressed to her.

Wracking her brains to try to decipher the message, Anna picked up the envelope again to look at the handwriting. It was no one's she recognised. Nothing particularly special other than the uppercase letters seeming like whoever it was didn't want their script recognised. But even that was a guess.

Putting the envelope down, she picked up the scan again. She noticed this time that the details that usually sit at the top of the scan, with dates, ages, hospital details and most crucially, mother's name, had been cut off. Why? If this was connected to her then surely that made no sense? Whoever sent it didn't want her to know who the mother was. Was it a specific baby, or just meant to be any baby? Anna's mind was reeling. She sat back and closed her eyes. She was too tired for someone to be messing about with her. She wanted to sleep.

The scan was definitely not hers. So why had someone posted it through her door?

She sat back up and threw the photo onto the coffee table again. If someone was messing with her, it wasn't funny. This was nothing. She would just ignore it.

But as the scan fluttered to rest on the table in front of her, it flipped over in the air and settled face down. There was writing on the back.

She sat forward to read it and as she did so, her throat tightened.

In beautiful sweeping handwriting, it said:

God's benevolence on the undeserving

Her eyes caught on a single word: underserving. Anna's whole body started shaking.

Someone *knew*.

They must do. They must know why she and Jon were not being blessed with a child. Because Anna was *underserving*.

Memories, cruel and harsh, from her upbringing flooded back at her. All the times, and there were many, when she had been punished for being undeserving of God's love, unworthy of his forgiveness, unfit to receive his grace. Growing up, it didn't seem to matter what she did, nor how innocent of the world she was, she was never good enough.

She had gone to hell for it, she had experienced His anger and what it could do. What He could take from you if you failed to live up to His standards. The God of her childhood was vengeful and angry. But she had escaped. She had survived, been forgiven and forgiven herself, setting her enveloping guilt aside and moving forward. Leaving her family and her church community behind, no doubt clocking up another moral failing in their eyes.

Had they found her? Had they even been looking? Anna had assumed that they had cut her from their lives as she had cut them from them hers. Before she had left, her mother had said that she 'had no daughter', that Anna was 'dead' to her. Anna had been dead inside, the baby she had lost leaving a space that would never heal. And yet, it had started to heal. She had met Jon. And with the hole that he carried within himself, he allowed her to heal.

But now? Someone was picking at their scars, making them bleed again. Someone had decided that Anna had not paid enough and that perhaps she had not quite given the pound of flesh required. She had thought that her new church, her new family, believed fully in God's forgiveness no matter the situation, but there were others, ones that Anna had known before, some she knew now, who were more fire and brimstone about it all. More believers in the requirement for confession, for repentance, penitence. Without these, you could not and would not know God's love. You were *undeserving* of it.

Someone *must* know that she was lying to her husband about something so significant, so integral to a husband and wife. The whole point of marriage in the eyes of the church was the bearing of children. Anna was deliberately, callously, but worst of all, covertly, denying this to Jon. Worst still, denying this to someone who had already lost so much. She was wicked. She must be. She had been told that enough in her lifetime. Bad. Sinful.

Evil.

Did someone think that of her now?

But who? Anna stood up, a little wobbly still, and put the scan back into the envelope. She moved to the bookshelf, searching it for what she needed. A book that Jon would never notice, something that he would be unlikely to casually open and flick through. Her eyes landed on a book about the history of lino cut design. She laughed at herself. It was the first craft that she had taken up to try to still her tortured mind. Something that she could use to block out all else and it had not gone unnoticed that to create the picture, you have to remove parts of the block with a knife. To cut away pieces, to show the new image. Just like her.

She slipped the envelope between the thick heavy pages of the book and slid it back into place. Hidden.

Just like her. Or at least, like she had been.

A bone-deep tiredness suddenly overwhelmed her and she could only think of retreating to her bed. She climbed the stairs, kicked her shoes off and fell onto the mattress, lying on one side of the duvet and flicking the other side over her, like a parcel, until she was cocooned in its weight and warmth, keeping her safe. Just like the baby in that image, kept safe from the world by its mother, before it was ejected into this world.

Maybe telling Jon the truth and being done with it was for the best. He would know, he would finally see her for herself, and if he rejected her based on that? Well, then maybe he wasn't the kind man that she thought he was. Maybe he was as bad as the rest of them. She couldn't bear to be beholden to someone else like that again.

When the time was right, she would tell him everything.

Whoever was blackmailing her – though, they hadn't actually *demanded* anything – would have the rug pulled out from under them. Anna smiled as she imagined the cruel smirk being wiped off their face when Jon would say, 'I know.'

She would enjoy watching their smile fade as they had expected hers to do. Whoever it was, she would outwit them. She just had to find them first.

7

Anna stood in the hallway as Kate closed the front door and led her into the living room, where Kate had laid out drinks and snacks for their evening in. The room was lowly lit by the lamps that were dotted about and the atmosphere was like walking into an underground bar. Chic but without trying too hard. That was how Anna felt about Kate. Kate worked for various international charities helping with education and healthcare for communities in need of those things. She was a staunch feminist who had decided not to have children herself but to help those already born and in need of support. Anna admired her more than she had ever voiced.

But now, Anna was questioning everything, everyone, including Kate, and it felt awful. She had worked hard to allow herself to trust anyone and now it felt like that had come back to bite her. She should trust no one.

She forced a smile onto her face.

'It looks lovely in here as always – thanks for the invite,' she said, sitting down and making herself comfy in the plush dark green chair that Kate used for reading. It was one of those snuggle chairs, cosy for two but luxuriously comfy for one. She took the glass of wine that Kate proffered to her and sat back. She had slept badly since the scan had been delivered a few days ago and she wanted nothing more than to relax and chat things over with Kate. But she couldn't. Whoever had sent the scan had taken her peace of mind away with them.

'Well, it's been ages since we've done this,' Kate said, breaking Anna's internal thoughts. 'You've always been difficult to tie down, busy busy, working. But lately it's been ridiculous. You've not returned calls, answered messages. I'd half thought you'd disappeared! What's going on with you?'

Anna had spent all hours since the scan had been delivered trying to decipher the message, trying to work out who had delivered it and why. She had let everything slide while she tried to work out what was going on, who might be watching her. She didn't want to think it was Kate, but she also couldn't shake the thought that it might be. Anna had decided to confront her. And if it wasn't Kate then she would at least have someone on her side who could help work out who it was. Except that now she was here, Anna was tangled with nerves. If she outright accused her and was wrong, would she lose her closest friend?

'Oh, nothing, you know. Just life.'

How could she start? Where would she even begin?

'Pssht. I know you, Anna, and you have not been yourself lately. Jon looks strained. Is there something going on?'

Why is she asking like that? What does she already know?

Anna took a mouthful from the glass of red wine she was holding and let the feeling of it wash over her tongue. She focused on the tingly sensation that the acidity of it created, making her taste buds buzz.

'No. No, everything's fine.'

She shook her head breezily, as if dismissing even the idea.

Kate said nothing, only raising her eyebrows disbelievingly. She waited.

Anna took another gulp of wine. It burned at the back of her throat, the tension knotting in her body. She had to talk. She had to ask her. Maybe she should not accuse Kate outright. Maybe she'd just show her the scan and watch for her reaction. She had to tell someone. This was driving her insane.

She took another gulp for courage, put the glass down and picked up her handbag.

'OK. You're right. You always are. Things have been really weird lately. Especially this last week.' She stopped, waiting to see if there was some recognition in Kate's eyes as to what she was referring to. There was none.

'Did something happen?'

'Well. Yeah.'

Here goes nothing.

Anna reached into her bag and pulled out her book. She had decided that the safest place for the scan and note was with her, rather than hidden in the bookshelf at home. Knowing where it was made her feel less anxious about it. She placed her bag back down on the floor, took a deep breath and handed the envelope to Kate.

She watched and waited as Kate looked confused, then opened it, took out the contents and took them in. Kate looked at the scan, then up at Anna, an expression of wonder on her face. She put her hand to her mouth as her eyes started to fill with tears. She took her hand away and Anna could see that she was smiling.

'Oh my goodness. You're... are you? Is this...? Congratulations! Oh my goodness! How far along are you?' she exclaimed, getting up to give Anna a celebratory hug. She stopped as she saw Anna's face, first confused, then grim. 'What? Are you not? What is...?

OK, OK, I'm confused. What am I looking at if you're not? Or were you and now...?'

'Kate...' Anna cut her off. She didn't want to be curt, but Kate was staggering around in all the wrong directions and she needed her to stop. She should have given some explanation. Maybe she should have asked Kate outright, though now she was pleased that she had not. Kate very clearly had not seen the scan before. Anna had been watching for a flicker, for a second of recognition before a fake reaction. There wasn't one. Kate was not the one who posted it. Anna knew her well enough to know a genuine reaction when she saw it. She was relieved but still confused as ever.

It should have occurred to her that Kate would assume that a baby scan would be of Anna's pregnancy. She clearly did not know of the impossibility of that. If Kate didn't know about the scan, then she didn't know about the pill either, and her assumption that this was good news was understandable.

'No. It's not mine. I'm not pregnant. I wasn't. I'm not.'

Kate shook her head, her lips pursed as she tried to recalibrate the information. 'So... whose is it? Why are you showing me? Why do you have it? I... I don't understand.'

Anna had to check. To be 100 per cent sure. 'So, you didn't post it to me?'

'No. Why on earth would I do that?'

'To make a point?'

'What point?'

'Look... Look at the back.'

Kate turned the scan over, to the back with the quote on it. She read it, her face screwing up as she became further confused. 'Benevolence. Unworthy. I... No. I don't know what you want me to say.'

'That *I* am unworthy. Of Jon. Of a child with Jon.' Anna picked up her wine glass again. Not drinking from it, just something to keep her shaking hands busy.

Kate's face darkened, just a touch. 'You think... You think that I posted this to *berate* you for not being good enough for Jon?' She looked appalled. 'Is... Is that what you think of me?'

She looked close to tears. Anna could see her processing the information, trying to work out what to do with it. A lesser person would have thrown Anna out. Luckily for Anna, Kate was not that.

'Oh, darling,' she said finally, her face softening with love. 'Look. How long have I known you?'

Anna swallowed down the tears that were threatening to spill down her face. 'Seven years.'

Kate nodded. 'Seven years. And in all that time, have I ever made *your* personal business my business, without your specific invitation to do so? Have I ever judged you for choices that I may perhaps not agree with?'

Anna thought and then shook her head. 'No.'

'No. So what on earth makes you think I'd start now? And like *this*? Underhand, sneaky.'

'I don't know... I'm sorry, I...'

Anna started to cry.

'Come here.' Kate wrapped her in a hug. 'What's going on? What the hell is this scan? Are things difficult with Jon right now? I've known him a long time, you too, and things seem a little... well... strained. I mean, I know no one ever knows what it's really like on the inside of a relationship, but...'

Anna released herself from the hug and faced Kate.

'You're right. It has been. I keep telling myself that it's because we're so overworked and busy, that growing a business together is bound to cause issues with our relationship, even without taking the baby issue into account.'

'It is a lot, that's true.'

'But we have Grace now, and the workload isn't so much...'

'What are you not saying?' Kate looked at Anna.

Should she tell her everything? About the pill? About how she couldn't bear to have another baby after what happened to her first? About why she was so concerned about this scan and what it meant? 'It's just... since Grace joined the office. It's stupid but—'

'But what? Nothing is stupid if it's what you feel.'

'I feel left out.'

'Left out? By your husband?'

'Yeah. They get on really well and I'm, well, you know I'm not a social person and it takes me time to get to know someone. But they've worked together already, and they have these in-jokes and I... I just feel like I'm back at school and I'm being picked last for the team or... You know.'

'Ah, I'm sure it's just teething troubles, and he's just helping her settle in and...'

Kate stopped as something had occurred to her. Anna could see her face change as the thought came, then her mind seemed to register it and what it meant. She picked up the scan photo again and stared intently at it. She looked up at Anna, an expression of shock on her face.

'Kate? What? What is it?' Anna asked, suddenly terrified, beyond inpatient to find out what Kate was thinking. 'What? You've gone pale. What is it?'

Kate took her own glass of wine and took a big gulp of it, looking down again at the scan, flipping it over and back again. Looking at the scan, then the quote, then the scan.

'Kate, what? What do you think?'

Kate looked up at Anna, anguish in her eyes. Anna felt her stomach turn.

'Grace.'

Now it was Anna's turn to be confused. 'What? What's she got to do with it?'

'I don't know exactly. It's just... This "God's benevolence" quote. It's *grace,* it means grace. It's what the quote is about.'

Anna blinked hard. She hadn't made that connection; she had been so focused on the word *undeserving* that she had not considered the quote as a whole. Her mind was swirling. Was it a connection? What did it mean?

'Surely that's just a coincidence? Isn't it?' Anna asked, her mind reeling, trying to put together the missing pieces and coming up short.

'Is it? I mean, she... Is *Grace* pregnant?' Kate asked, jumping to one potential conclusion. 'Is this *her* scan?'

'No!' Anna snapped, but then... 'No, no I don't think so. She's... No, I don't. I don't know? If she is, she'd not have to tell us yet anyway. As her employers, I mean. This is a twelve-week scan. I googled cos the details at the top have been removed so I didn't know for sure.'

'But why would she post her baby scan to you even if she was? And with this note? I mean, if she is pregnant, what has that got to do with—' Kate stopped herself, as though she had clamped her own lips shut to stop herself from talking.

'What?'

'Nothing.' Kate looked guilty. She looked at the floor. She looked anywhere but at Anna.

'No, not nothing. What are you thinking now?'

'What are *you* thinking?'

'Well,' said Anna, trying to be rational. 'She's young. Her family are religious. Maybe she doesn't know who to talk to, who to turn to. Maybe she thinks I might be more understanding? But we're not close. And why would she not just talk to me? I'm not that intimidating, am I?'

Kate looked at Anna, a 'come on, catch up' expression on her face.

Anna looked back at her, still nonplussed.

'No, you're going to have to fill me in here, Kate. I don't know what you're getting at,' she said, exasperated by Kate's charades in place of words.

Kate pursed her lips.

'Jon.'

'What do you mean, Jon? She meant to send it to Jon? I mean, they are closer than she and I are but I don't think she'd do that. Yes, he's very pro-baby, we all know that, but still. No, I don't think so. The envelope had my name on it.'

'No, Anna. I mean *Jon*.'

'You already said that,' Anna said, irritated. Kate was annoying her now. She wasn't helping. Anna tried to remind herself that Kate only had half the information – she didn't know about her being on the pill, and yet she was still being ridiculous. This was a dig at her for lying to Jon. But a dig by who? 'What do you mean, Jon? What about him?'

'Grace. Grace and Jon. A baby.'

Anna's heart jumped into her mouth. 'What? What are you saying?'

'If the baby scan is Grace's, then Grace is pregnant. Yes?'

'Yes... I suppose so, but that's a big if.'

'So why would she be posting it to you? Because...? Jon. And she can't think of another way to tell you. Maybe he was supposed to have told you, but he won't. Or not yet, maybe waiting to see if it all goes away? Maybe she wants to tell you but she can't do it to your face? Because, well, because... Jon.'

Kate sat back in her chair, sipped her wine and looked somewhat too triumphant for Anna's liking. This was not some mystery TV show that needed solving, this was her *life*.

'You're saying that Grace is pregnant? You're saying that Jon is the father? Of Grace's baby? That my husband and our intern have been... having... relations?'

'You just said they were close. You said it annoyed you how much so, how you felt pushed out. They've worked together for how long? A year? Less than a year? But you were never around, always at the office...'

'Well... yes, but... he wouldn't.' Anna looked up at Kate, appalled, shocked. Urging Kate to take it back, so that she could un-think it, make it stop. This was supposed to be about someone knowing about her lying to Jon, someone who felt she ought to stop. This was not supposed to be about the truth in her marriage, the trust in it turning into a crumpled heap on the floor.

He just wouldn't... Would he? Anna hadn't given him what he most wanted. A child. Grace was younger, obviously attractive. To be three months pregnant, well, something would have needed to have started before she joined the office. Is that why he hired her? Because they were already an item? Did he get some sick satisfaction of having his mistress in the office right under Anna's nose?

'No. He wouldn't. I know him. That's not how he works. I don't think there *is* an actual baby. I think this is just meant to taunt me about there not being one.'

'That's a bit extreme, don't you think? Why would someone go to all the trouble of getting a scan – and this is an actual hospital scan, isn't it? – just to niggle you about not being pregnant? I mean, lots of people don't get pregnant for lots of reasons; but people don't go around posting nasty letters about it, do they?'

Anna thought back to her childhood and her church. To the mean and judgemental people that she once knew there. This was exactly the sort of thing they would do. From their position of believing themselves to be chosen. And especially if they knew that Anna was lying to Jon, taking medicine to go against God's chosen way for women – motherhood. Actively turning down that choice and deceiving her husband about it. Maybe it was them. Maybe Grace had nothing to do with it.

She was about to tell Kate everything. Explain about taking the pill and why she felt she had to so that her own theory made sense to her, when Kate started talking again.

'I know it seems off, like it's not the sort of thing Jon would do. It's just, before you met Jon, while he was with his first wife, there was a rumour. That's all. Nothing ever came of it, nothing ever substantiated. Probably just someone who wanted to cause trouble. That's all.'

'And what was the rumour?' Anna felt like the world had slowed. None of this had occurred to her and suddenly the one part of her life that she felt was solid was starting to shift under her feet.

Kate fixed her mouth in a hard line. She was obviously wishing she'd never said anything. 'I thought it was all just clouds of nothing. But now, with this...' She fluttered the scan in her hands.

Anna felt sick. 'Yes...' she pushed.

'There was once a rumour that Jon and one of his younger female colleagues were closer than was appropriate. But no one ever said *who* or *how* or *what*. His wife never said anything. I don't even know where it came from, but it was never anything more than that. Like I said, probably based on nothing more than spite, or boredom, like most gossip. I shouldn't have even said anything. I just want... I just want to protect you.'

Anna took a breath. Then another. Allowing time to let what Kate had said sink in.

It didn't fit. He wouldn't do that. But...

Do we ever really reveal our whole selves? Didn't everyone withhold something of themselves from the world, keep their deepest darkness locked away and hidden? She knew she did. She was lying to Jon every day. She knew she was never 100 per cent open with anyone, not fully. It was too risky. Maybe Jon was the same.

Maybe she didn't really know her husband at all.

Anna felt dizzy. She couldn't believe it. She didn't want to believe it. That would mean that everyone, *everyone* in her life had betrayed her at some point. Apart from maybe Kate, though if she knew about this rumour about Jon and his previous colleague, why had she waited until long after they were married to even mention it? Did everyone think that she and Jon would get married, have babies and that would miraculously fix everything? Suddenly Anna felt the need to protect herself from everyone, even from her best friend.

'I know we've not been blessed with a baby. I know it's been hard. I know Jon has felt abandoned at times, but this? For him to turn away from me, from his values? No, I think you've got the wrong end of the stick here.'

'Maybe he thought the issue was with him? Maybe he thought it wouldn't happen? Or maybe he needed to prove that it could? That he could. Who knows? Men are weird about virility and stuff like that, aren't they?'

Anna held on to the locket at her throat. It had been a wedding anniversary gift from Jon the first year that they had been married. It was supposed to have been a gift, ready to carry a photo of their children in. It remained empty. It felt tight around her neck.

She had been lying to him. She knew that. She knew her reasons for that, and she could justify them, at least to herself. But was he lying too?

'I don't know. I don't know if I don't believe it or if I just don't *want* to believe it. I... I understand what you mean. The scan, the quote, their... friendship. But something doesn't fit right.'

'What do you think then? What did you think before today? I mean, I could be wrong. It is a jump, I know, but like you said, it sort of makes sense.' Kate shook her head.

'Well, I thought someone was either weirdly encouraging us to keep trying, maybe someone from the church... or maybe someone...' *From my past.* She couldn't say it out loud. '...someone trying to blackmail me, or...'

Kate wrinkled her face.

'That doesn't make any sense though. What would they be blackmailing you *with*? There's no threat or demands here, are there?' She turned the paper and the scan over, checking to see if she'd missed something. Then she looked up at Anna. Stared at her, into her. She tilted her head to the side and said disapprovingly, 'What are you not telling me?'

Anna wrung her hands together. She couldn't.

'Anna...' Kate said in a stern tone. She was not impressed. 'What aren't you saying? You said they're blackmailing you, but what for? Why would someone be threatening you? This...' She gestured at the scan. '...is not a threat. So, what makes you think it is? Are you in danger?' She suddenly turned from reproachful to concerned. 'Has Jon ever—'

'No. No!' Anna shouted before stopping. Now Kate was taking the wrong of the stick and running away with it. 'No. Never. It's... Don't judge me for this. Please? I have my reasons for thinking I'm being blackmailed but... I can't share them. I don't know if I'll ever be ready to, but you have to trust me that they are good reasons, solid reasons for this. OK?'

Kate exhaled slowly. 'OK... We're friends. I won't judge you. You know I won't. But I feel like I've only got half the information in an increasingly complex situation here. So I can't promise you I won't get it wrong. But I will try. I will do my best for you.'

Kate was right. She did only have half the information, and perhaps with all of it, or at least more of it, she might back down on this idea that Jon was cheating on her with Grace. Anna was terrified but perhaps it was a risk she had to take. Even if she would be diminished in Kate's eyes.

She closed her eyes and spoke. It felt less real that way. 'Jon and I have not conceived in all these years for a reason. I know why. And I've never told him. Or anyone.'

'You're infertile?' Kate interjected.

'No...' Anna opened her eyes.

'Sorry, I just—'

'Can you stop talking please?' Anna couldn't do this if she had to keep stopping. 'I need to just get this out before I can't. OK?'

Kate nodded and mimed zipping her lips shut.

'We haven't got pregnant because I don't want to be. I've never wanted to be. I was taking the pill when I met him and I didn't ever stop. I can't. I just can't have a baby. I can't. The idea terrifies me. It's just... You know about the baby I lost. I can't risk that again. I can't.' She shuddered. 'So I wondered if someone, anyone, though who I don't know, has found out and is telling me that I'm undeserving. Of him. Of Jon. And using such an emotive thing as a baby scan to do it. You know, how anti-abortion factions use photos for impact?'

Kate nodded again, mute, taking this all in. Her face was ashen.

'I know I shouldn't have lied to him. *Be* lying to him. I just... I couldn't tell him. I couldn't. He's such a good man. I didn't want him to look at me like... like I'm nothing.'

'You've been taking the pill this whole time and pretending to try to have a baby?' Kate paused, perhaps to check that she had understood correctly. When it was clear that she had, she continued. 'Wow. That's... not what I was expecting you to say. That's a whole can of worms right there. Random baby scan aside.'

'Do you hate me for it?' Anna asked, terrified that Kate would tell Jon or reject her as a friend. Or both.

'Hate you? No. I'm not sure I *understand* it, but as you said, there's more that you can't share right now and I'm assuming it would make more sense to me if you could?'

Anna nodded. She wasn't able to share any more. She felt exposed, vulnerable, alone.

Kate paused, nodding, her eyes to the floor as she digested all the information and worked out how she wanted to react. Anna loved Kate for this – considered, always. Thoughtful. Never quick to assume. Which was why her instinct about Jon and Grace concerned Anna. What if she was right?

'So not now,' Kate agreed. 'I do think things might be way less complicated if you just told me everything, but maybe I'm being naïve. Maybe my life isn't dramatic enough and my truth isn't as complicated as yours.'

'Thank you.' Anna stood up and went to hug her. Maybe one day she could tell Kate everything but right now there was just too much else to deal with. 'What am I going to do?'

Kate looked at the scan and the quote again, inspecting it as though more information could be found if she just looked harder.

'So what I can see is that we know this: there may or may not be a baby. If there is a baby then somehow this baby is connected to you. And someone wants you to know about it and perhaps to know that *they* know. And lastly... it may or may not have something to do with Grace.'

'So we don't actually *know* a lot, do we?' Anna laughed bitterly, though relieved at the plural in that sentence. She was not alone in this mess. 'You think it's definitely Grace the person, not grace the state of being?'

'I don't know anything for sure. Neither do you. So we assume both? Until we rule one out or rule one in?'

'How?' Anna was so wound up inside that she couldn't see a route out, only the darkness of betrayal, or blackmail. Neither was good.

'I guess you follow both routes? Find out if Grace is pregnant? Or if someone knows about your lies.' Kate blushed. 'Sorry, but that is the other option we're looking at, isn't it? That someone knows about your deceiving Jon and is trying to, what, to guilt you out of it? To reprimand you? Just... that option doesn't make sense to me.'

'Grace and Jon doesn't make sense to *me*. And the people I have in mind, well, you're lucky enough not to know them.'

'I'm sorry you do.'

Anna chewed her lip. 'Me too.'

'Maybe start with Grace then? Or maybe you could just ask Jon outright. Wouldn't that be simplest?'

'No. I can't. I can't take this to him. He's either lying to me and cheating, or he's wholly innocent and yet I'm still lying to him. I can't risk accusing him without at least some more information from somewhere. If there *is* a baby, then I need proof. If there isn't, he'll wonder why someone is targeting me. And I can't tell him that, not yet.'

Kate sighed. 'I guess. It's all very tangled.'

'I know, I'm sorry. I don't mean to tie you up in all my mess. I just, I didn't know what I should do or where I should go.'

'So you thought you'd start with me?' Kate said, a tone of upset to her voice.

'Not like that as such – more, if I could rule you out, then I knew I could rely on you to help me.' Anna smiled apologetically, hoping it would be enough to smooth over the insult of suspecting her.

'Fair point. Forgiven.' Kate smiled back.

What Anna needed to find out now was if she could rely on her husband.

8

It should have been a normal day in the office. Jon had woken up in a good mood and had made Anna breakfast while she'd got ready and they'd sat together over eggs and coffee and talked through the day's plans for the business. He wanted to enter some local business awards, but Anna wasn't convinced.

'I just think we're not ready to put ourselves forward for an award. It feels like putting our heads above the parapet before getting our armour ready.' Anna was feeling far too exposed to consider actively seeking scrutiny in any other area of her life.

'We're not going to war, my love. It's a local business thing!' he'd said, ruffling her hair affectionately as he walked past back to the kitchen to tidy up. She should have felt loved but in her vulnerable state, she felt patronised, unheard. He wasn't listening to her.

They'd travelled into the office in pretty much silence after that. That in itself wasn't unusual – Anna often used the commute time to think, to map out possible ways of doing things for the day's tasks ahead. But this felt oppressive because she was on hyper alert. She felt like she was both being betrayed and taking part in a betrayal. She felt a chasm widening between her and Jon, who had once been the only person she felt truly knew her. Now, she had a splinter of doubt over his fidelity and it felt like it was pushing its way deeper into her skin, trying to see if it could make her bleed.

'Here we are!' Jon had chirped as they pulled into the office car park. She was tired, tense and stressed, and she didn't know what was best to do or who to believe. Everything was in freefall. She had thought that part of her life was over, that she was safe, secure and stable now, but she recognised those flickers of terror from before. The waves that crashed over you, telling you they were going to drag you down. She tried to ignore them as best she could.

Sitting at her desk, Anna tried to focus on her emails but found that she couldn't read more than a sentence or two at a time, nor find the enthusiasm to take in what they said. She kept raising her eyes over the top of her laptop to stare at Grace, who had her head down and was slowly working her way through the pile of notes that needed turning into invoices to be sent out. Anna hoped that Grace was more focused than she was. For the sake of the baby, she didn't want the father to be bankrupt.

Anna caught herself. There *was* no baby.

Was there?

'How are you feeling this morning?' Anna called over to Grace, trying to sound light-hearted.

'Oh, I'm fine thanks,' Grace called back, before going back to her work.

'You sure? You look a bit peaky if I'm being honest.'

Did she? Or was she glowing? Or did she just look like she always looked? Anna couldn't work out if she was seeing the truth or what her mind had constructed. She couldn't trust her own eyes. She was painting over reality with her fears.

'Yeah, thank you for asking though.' Grace got up and walked over towards Anna, who took the opportunity to look at her stomach to see if she was showing any signs of a bump. 'I got to bed late. I was having a bit of a row with my mum.'

She perched on the side of Anna's desk. This forced Anna into looking up at her, and she immediately felt small and uncomfortable, like the power was in the wrong place.

'Oh?'

'Yeah,' Grace said, picking at her nails. Anna could see this was a habit of hers; they were red round the cuticle. 'There's... something that is important to me but she thinks I shouldn't be doing it. Like, it's my life, right? I'm an adult. It's up to me, isn't it? The choice is mine?' Grace looked at Anna, as though she was asking her advice.

'Oh. Well. It's hard to know really, without the specifics.'

Was Grace trying to tell her? Was there a baby, and was she regretting it?

A crazy thought suddenly entered Anna's head – about surrogacy, and her and Jon bringing up the baby, once Grace had given birth. Would that fix all these potential problems? Or would it cause more? Then Anna reminded herself that she didn't know if there *was* a baby, and would she even want to bring up the result of Jon cheating on her anyway?

'Yeah. I get that. I... I can't say. Not yet anyway. I...' She looked at the floor. 'My mum thinks... Well, we disagree...' She trailed off.

'Are you sure you're OK?' Anna asked. 'You're all flushed. Are you feeling sick?'

She was genuinely concerned now. Grace really did look flustered and upset. If the scan *was* hers then she was in an awful situation. And so young. It wouldn't really be Grace's fault as such. Young people don't always have enough life experience to make the best decisions. Some good luck is just that: luck, rather than good sense. When Anna considered her own younger years, she could see how many situations could have gone the other way than they did, even taking into account the ones that went so badly wrong.

'I am feeling a bit light-headed...' Grace put her hands to her forehead. Not her stomach, Anna noted.

'Jon?' Anna called out. She wanted to see his reaction. Did he even know, if there was anything to know?

'Yes?' he called out as he came over. 'Oh, is everything OK?'

'Grace is feeling sick.'

'Just dizzy suddenly. I'm OK. Really.'

'As you're the office first aider, I thought you could help.'

Jon pulled up a chair. 'Well, if you think you're going to faint, we should sit you on the floor and raise your legs.'

'No, really, I'm fine.'

'We wouldn't want you to hit your head if you fell though.'

'It's OK, honestly.' Grace started to get flustered with him.

Anna looked from one to the other, trying to see if there was more there than on the surface. Was Grace flustered by Jon's attention in front of Anna? Was Jon being more cautious because he knew of the girl's potential condition? Or because he felt more for her than just friendship?

Anna looked so hard, and yet she couldn't see it. But she knew that her instinct had been so misused in her past that she often didn't trust where she should, or trusted where that trust was misplaced. But even knowing that, she just couldn't tie up what Kate had suggested with what was in front of her face. Grace was odd, withholding something of herself at times, oversharing at others. She and Jon got on well, that was true, but was that flirting, or just friendship?

'Maybe you'd best go home,' Anna suggested.

'No. Honestly. I'm fine. I think I just stood up too fast. If I go home, Mum will just give me a lecture about responsibilities and behaviour at work and I've had enough of that already today. I'll maybe take five minutes outside for some fresh air and then I'll be fine. I'm sure. Thank you though Anna, thanks Jon,' she said, taking time to look one then the other in the eye.

As she left, Anna shook her head. This idea of Kate's was ridiculous. There was nothing going on. She was a young girl, learning the ways of work. She and Jon were just friends, in an appropriate way. The scan wasn't Grace's. There was no baby.

No, the scan was something else. There was the other suggestion, that it was a blackmail of sorts.

Anna waited until Grace was out of the office and Jon had gone to make everyone a cup of tea, and then she got out her notebook that she used for random doodles, jotting down of ideas or just freeform writing. She wrote *WHO* in large capital letters and underlined it twice. It shouted at her from the page, as if the loudness of the very word would force an answer from her subconscious.

Anna thought and then wrote out a list.

Jon. He knew her better than anyone. He knew their struggle to conceive. He knew more about her past than anyone in her life. They spent more than twenty of every twenty-four hours of each day together. Had he worked it out? Had he found her pills and put two and two together?

Kate. Her closest friend but also Jon's friend first. Had all her 'there's a baby' guesses been a ploy to throw her off the scent? Maybe she'd always had a thing for Jon and seen her opportunity to drive a wedge between them? Had Anna unwittingly given her more information with which to do that?

Grace. She had to go on the list. Things had been odd since she arrived at the office and the scan arrived after her starting at the business. Grace was connected to her and Jon via her family and the church. The note on the back of the scan could have been a reference to her name or that could be a coincidence. Even if there was no baby, Grace needed to be on the list as the last person to join their circle.

Was there a connection with Anna's GP? Or the pharmacy from where she got her birth control pills? Anna couldn't think who might want to hurt her in this way, but she would research and find out. Maybe someone from the church. At church everyone knew everyone else's business, which was both a wonderful, supportive thing – people there for you in hard times, there to celebrate the good times with you and live out the daily normality of life with you – but sometimes it stepped over the mark. No privacy, everyone knowing about your foibles, your rows, your worries. If you needed to keep a secret, the community made that difficult.

A client? Did someone want to extort money from her? This one seemed so ridiculous that Anna felt insane for even putting it down, but she wanted to consider all possibilities. Perhaps the plan was to unsettle her with the scan – which had worked; she was all over the place – and then come back in with demands. It wasn't a secret that she and Jon were trying for a family. Throwing such an emotive question mark into the mix would work for stage one of a potential blackmail. If this was the answer, then the blackmailer was in for a shock. Their business was doing OK but financially, it was still in its infancy.

But despite all these potentials, with their possible but implausible reasons, there was one person Anna suspected the most. One person she did not want to even think about but one whose face kept popping into Anna's mind, unbidden. One person who once controlled every element of her life, pushing her to rebel, to fight against her and push back so hard that the bond was eventually broken.

The sheer judgement of it. The not saying what you *really* mean. The use of bible quotes to make a point. The use of overly emotive elements to push home a point. These were all the modus operandi of one person Anna knew.

Her mother.

9

Anna hadn't seen or spoken to her mother in nearly two decades, but she knew exactly where she would find her on a Sunday morning. At the Church of Our Lady of Lourdes, at 9 a.m. Every week, without fail, Anna's mother, Marie, would be at her church, on her knees, declaring her sinfulness to her Lord, despite believing herself to be godly. Anna hadn't moved that far away from where she grew up, just far enough to be outside the small world that her parents lived in. They focused all their joys on getting into the next life rather than making the most of this one, and so they didn't travel, didn't expand their horizons. Pleasure-seeking was sinful; visiting new places was a sign you were disrespectful towards the home you'd been given.

As she pulled up outside the church, Anna felt sick to her core. That morning she'd still been in two minds as to whether to go or not. She had been making tea for her and Jon and it was the smallest thing that convinced her. When she had left home all those years ago, the only memento that she had taken was the small ceramic dish that her mother used to put teabags on. It was a slight but significant thing because it was a small rebellion, the only rebellion, that her mother made against her father. He believed that tea should only be made in a pot. With leaves. But her mother once said that he would say that because it was not him who made the tea nor him who washed the pot, and when it was just her at home during the day, who had time for all that faff for a single cup of tea? And so, during the daytime she used teabags, put them on the dish to dry out and then would surreptitiously add them to her compost pile. Her father never knew. It was the one thing that made Anna think that perhaps her mother might have a mind of her own, separate to her father's iron will. But with all that happened that caused her to leave, Anna took the dish to remind her that when it mattered to her mother, she would defy her husband. And so it was clear that it was *both* of them who'd made the decisions they did, *both* of them who'd decided their faith mattered more to them than Anna did and *both* of them who'd decided cruelty was more godly than kindness. The ceramic dish was the reminder that Anna had got away and that she should stay away. But now, Anna knew that she had to speak to her mother, just one more time.

Anna parked the car in line of sight to the church doors, which were flung wide open to welcome parishioners to the service. The deacon was stood in the doorway, welcoming people, and just the sight of the vestments he wore brought back a rush of feelings. Feelings of what it was like in *that* particular church, never feeling good enough or that you could ever *be* good enough. Humanity was lacking and always would be. Anna never wanted to feel that way again – small, worthless.

Shaking her shoulders to feel braver, she reminded herself that this was now. She was not the Anna of then and she would never be again. She was stronger, more resilient. She had survived and she had thrived and she was here to make it clear to her mother, if indeed the scan had been sent by her, that she had no control over her daughter any more, that whatever she thought of her daughter, Anna gave it no credence. She had no power over her or her life. Anna had moved on.

She watched as groups of worshippers arrived and filed into the church. Some she recognised, despite it being so many years since she'd last seen them. Then she saw *her* and Anna gasped. She knew that her mother would have aged, obviously. But it was only then that Anna realised that in her mind's eye, her mother still looked the same as that night when Anna had packed a handful of things into a bag and walked out of the door, not stopping to say goodbye or even announce her departure. She had wondered what her mother had felt when she realised that her daughter was gone. For a time, Anna checked the local newspaper, and the church website, in case there had been any appeal for information, pleas for news about her, for her family to want to know that she was safe. There had been none. Her family knew why she'd left, and Anna suspected that they knew she would not be back.

Now, Anna's mother looked frail. She was in her early eighties, had a stick to help her walk and Anna suspected she had arthritis. Her grandmother suffered badly with it and her mother often assumed out loud that she would be the same. She looked older than her years and beaten down and for a second, Anna's heart went out to her. Then it hardened when Anna remembered what her mother had done to her.

The plan had been to approach her going into church, so that all her fellow parishioners could hear, but now, heart racing, hand gripped on the door frame, with her knuckles going white, she couldn't do it. Seeing her had been a shock. Anna needed a little time. So she decided that she would approach her coming out. That would give her time to recover and to plan what she intended to say.

The forty-five minutes passed slowly.

Anna got out of the car when she heard the rousing chords of the organ strike up for the closing hymn. With so much time spent in church as a child, she could still tell which sort of hymns opened Mass and which were closers. As the voices of the congregation rose to meet the heavens, the harmonious sounds echoing out into the morning air, Anna sat herself on the wall opposite the main doors and tried not to let her fast-beating heart make her feel too dizzy. Her mouth was dry and although she knew what she wanted to say, she also couldn't trust herself to remember when the time came.

Anna had convinced herself on the drive over that her mother was the culprit. That she had taken it upon herself to chastise Anna once again for all her perceived failures, without a trace of irony that many of those failures had been caused by herself as her mother. But seeing her walk alone, slowly and carefully into to the church, Anna wasn't sure. Also something else occurred to her that had not registered before. Her father had not been with her. Why? He was the more devout of the two. Perhaps he was already inside, undertaking some important task before the service.

Before she had time to think further, the music stopped, there was one final lower register of the priest closing the Mass and then people started to file out. Anna took a deep breath, got off the wall and waited. She was convinced that people were staring at her as they filed out of the church, stopping to chat with the priest, who was stood at the doors. Anna angled herself to be out of his line of sight. Even now, priests made her nervous.

Her breath caught in her throat as her mother left the church, leaning on the arm of a fellow parishioner who was helping her with the steps. Her eyes came towards Anna... and passed right over her. Her mother looked at her and yet did not see her. Anna laughed wryly. Her mother had never really seen her, why would she start now?

She took a breath and walked towards her, placing herself in her path, blocking her way.

'Excuse me, Miss,' her mother said as she tried to manoeuvre around her.

'You really don't recognise me, do you?' Anna shook her head slowly. She knew that the last time her mother had laid eyes on her, she had really still been a child, rather than the woman she was now. But she was still her mother. She should recognise her immediately.

She looked at Anna, confused. 'Should I? I'm sorry, my memory isn't what it was, and I was never one for faces I'm afraid. Have we met?'

A dark throaty chuckle erupted from Anna's lips. When would her mother ever lose her ability to cut her heart into pieces? After all these years, she thought she wouldn't care, but does a child ever really lose that desire for their parent to love them, despite, in Anna's case, all the evidence to the contrary? Does that need ever truly go away?

'You could say that, Mother,' Anna said, crossing her arms in front of her. She was aiming for strong; aggressive, even. But it looked defensive, as the line of her jaw vibrated at the emotions she was trying to keep in check.

'Pardon?' She looked at Anna again, this time with more scrutiny. And there it was – the moment when recognition hit, and she realised that she was looking at her estranged daughter. 'Anna? Anna, is that really you? It's been... Lord, I truly thought that you were dead. I...' Tears welled in her eyes as a smile crossed her face, lighting it up. Her prodigal daughter returned.

'No.'

'I'm sorry?'

'Yes. Yes, you are sorry. But in your case that is not an apology. It's far too late for that.' Anna was surprised by her own anger.

The fellow parishioner must have caught a hint of the tone as they stepped up next to Anna's mother, taking her elbow. 'Is everything alright here, Marie? Are you OK?' The gentleman turned to Anna with a look of distaste.

Marie fluttered his arm away light-heartedly but Anna could see the anxiety behind it.

'Absolutely, Matthew, yes. All fine, all fine, thank you. We're just catching up. It's been a while.'

'Well, if you're sure...' he said, leaving but checking over his shoulder.

Anna glared at him until he stopped looking. What did he think she was going to do, right in front of the church, right in front of the priest? Anna was only here for the truth, and it was only truth she brought with her.

'I *was* dead,' Anna spat at her. 'At least, dead to you, as you said when we last saw each other. Dead to you for making choices you disagreed with, for making mistakes, for daring to question anything, everything that you and this church told me.'

Marie looked confused. Then she looked angry.

'I said that you were *lost* to me. Lost. Not dead. I would never have said that. That would be to blaspheme. I would not do that. I would not have done that.'

Anna baulked. 'You said what you said.'

'No, child, you *heard* what you *heard*. We gave you everything. We brought you up to know right from wrong and then you did... that.' Her mouth settled into a hard line. Any kindness that had been present departed the second Anna's criticism landed on her.

'Everything? You gave me no support, no encouragement, no love. You gave me scripture, judgement and expectations that I could never meet. No one is perfect, but you expected me to be.'

'The Lord is perfect, don't forget that.'

'Is he?'

'Don't you question the will of the Lord, my child. If your father could hear you now...'

'I am not your child. I stopped being that years ago. And Dad? Where is he anyway?'

Marie's mouth quivered, whether with rage or sorrow, Anna couldn't tell. 'He's with the Lord now.'

Even though that possibility had occurred to Anna while she had waited in the car, it still took the wind out of her sails and the fight out of her mouth. 'I... I'm sorry. When?'

'Are you? You walked out without so much as a word. We'd no idea if you'd be back, where you'd gone. The distress was awful.'

'When?' Anna repeated.

'Last year now.'

Anna felt her stomach relax. She'd feared that her leaving had somehow caused it. That it would be another element of her past that she could punish herself with. But no. Her God-fearing, iron-rod ruling father had made it into his ninth decade.

'I am sorry. For you.'

Stuck now alone, to live with the consequences of letting him rule over our lives the way he did.

'Thank you.' Marie sniffed, pulling her shoulders back, replacing her spite with the genteel behaviour befitting a widow.

'Is that why you did it? Because he'd gone?'

Marie wrinkled her nose. 'Did what, child?'

'Stop calling me that.'

'You are though, my child, and you're behaving like one now. Turning up out of the blue, accusing me of... whatever. You've not been in touch these twenty years. What do you want with me now?'

'Me with *you*? What did *you* want with *me*?'

'Honest to God, I have no idea what you're on about.' Marie was starting to look nervous. The congregation was thinning out now, this conversation becoming more of a focal point than either she or Anna wanted. 'If you're not here to apologise then spit it out.'

'Apolog—' Anna spluttered incredulously. Her mother hadn't changed, not one iota, in all this time. Still the same, all high and mighty, bothered by what everyone thinks, rather than about what matters. Anna bit her lip. She had not come here to apologise, but she had also not come here for a row. That part of her life was done with, locked away where it belonged. She had only so much as opened the door to it in order to get some answers.

She reached into her bag to get out the scan but then thought better of it. She did not want to wave it about in such a public place. If her mother had had anything to do with it, she would know what Anna meant.

'The scan. I'm here because of the scan. The one you posted through my door with a fire and brimstone quote on the back.'

'Oh, for the Lord's sake, what nonsense are you going on about? Scan? Post? I didn't know you were alive, let alone where you live, Anna. I've more important things to do with the time the Lord has left for me than to go chasing after ungrateful daughters who have strayed from His path. If all you are here for is to accuse me of this claptrap, then I suggest you go on home now.'

Anna was suddenly ten years old again, the dismissive, cold tone of her mother defining things that were important to her, that mattered to her, as pointless. A waste of time. She should never have come. She should have known her mother had already accepted that Anna would never be willing to undergo the supposedly required penance in order to restore her mortal soul. She was a lost cause. No matter what Anna was doing now, whether that be lying to her husband or going against God's way by using birth control in the first place, these all paled in comparison to the sins her mother already believed she had accumulated. Anna would not have been worthy of her mother's time now. She had not been worthy of it then. The whole idea that her parents might have been behind the scan was based on the assumption that they still cared about her, if they ever did, and the woman standing in front of Anna now was making it quite clear that this was not the case.

Anna stepped back. 'Yes. Perhaps that is best.'

'Indeed.' Marie folded her arms in front of her, her stick dangling from the crook of her elbow. There was nothing on her face that suggested she was pleased to know Anna was alive, or that she was happy to see her long-lost daughter.

Anna had no parents. She had no child. And she was scared that she was about to have no husband either.

Whoever sent this scan would surely plan on telling Jon the truth, or insist that Anna did. Why else would they send it if they didn't intend on following through? She stood to lose everything. Again. That was why she needed to find them before they did anything rash.

She was wasting her time here. The past should be left in the past.

'Well.' Anna didn't know what to say.

Marie nodded.

'I guess, goodbye?'

'At least this time you're doing me the honour of actually saying it, rather than packing up in the middle of the night and leaving, not a word, not a note. I hope God forgives you.'

'I hope he forgives *you*.' Anna turned and walked away, leaving Marie looking as though Anna had slapped her. Despite knowing it would not have been as cathartic as it might have seemed, Anna sort of wished she had.

10

Bristling with tension, Anna could not see left from right, nor up from down. She sat back in her car, physically shaking. She waited, taking deep breaths until her eyesight stopped going fuzzy, then she started the car and drove. She didn't know where she was going, just, like the night she upped and left, that she had to be somewhere else. She needed to put distance between the lies, the guilt-tripping, the gaslighting that had been both her upbringing and her downfall.

After pulling the car over in some nondescript residential street, Anna turned off the engine and fell apart. She was fucked up, she knew that. She had accepted that. She'd had therapy to discuss why and how best to deal with it. She had thought that somehow she'd found a happy medium – not wholly healed – she doubted she ever would be; she had lost too much and some wounds never close over – but healed enough to move on. Forwards. And yet this scan, and the events since it had been posted to her, had dragged her backwards into a life of lies, secrets and of never really being able to trust anyone.

When you are made to question yourself, your beliefs, your worth as a human, it gets hard, sometimes impossible, to trust your own judgement. Anna had been absolutely 100 per cent sure that the scan had been the work of her mother, despite there being no contact with her for years. It made sense to her that perhaps her family had tracked her down and had just been keeping tabs on her. Maybe they were the stranger at the back of her wedding ceremony, the person behind her in the pharmacy queue when she collected her prescriptions, maybe that feeling you get that you're being watched, only to look up to find no one there. Maybe even a part of Anna *wanted* that to be true. It would at least be a sign that she did care, in her own controlling way. But no. Her mother did not care. She had not laid eyes on her for decades and apparently had given her up as a lost cause.

Grabbing hold of the steering wheel, feeling the grain of the faux leather against her hands, seeing her knuckles go white as she gripped harder and harder, she let out a howl. Of rage, of frustration and of sorrow. She yelled and yelled until her voice went hoarse. She had too much energy zipping through her body, and she needed to let it out.

Tap tap tap.

There was a knock on the window.

Anna blinked open her eyes. A woman, at a guess in her sixties, with a dog on a leash beside her, was looking in at her with concern.

Anna rolled down the window, the rush of chilled fresh air on her face a welcome balm. She took a deep breath.

'Yes?'

'Um, this is a stupid question, but are you OK?'

'Yes. No. Maybe, I don't really know.'

The lady nodded. 'I know that one. Either too many fucks to

give or not enough. Never any bloody middle ground in life.' She chuckled.

The shock of this sweet-looking lady swearing made Anna laugh along with her. Then tears welled up in her eyes again. This complete stranger had taken time from her day to check in on a crazy woman screaming in her car. The world had good people in it. Anna had to hold on hard to remember that. Even if she didn't feel that she was one of them. She could be. She could try to be. Every day she had to try hard to be.

'Yeah...' Anna nodded back.

'Do you have somewhere you can go to be looked after? You look like you need a cup of tea and a space to just be. Do you have that?'

Initially Anna thought not but then, she realised, she did. 'I do. Yes.'

'Good. Then go there. And let yourself be held up for a bit. Life is hard, we all know that. But we can keep each other upright through the shitty bits. That's what brings the joy. OK?'

'OK.' Anna nodded, tears threatening again.

'And besides, all those tears, you'll be dehydrated. Cup of tea. That's what you need.'

'OK. I will go get one. Thank you.'

The lady tipped her head, and then went on her way, the little dog trotting obediently beside her.

Anna knew that some of the worst people in her life had been religious. But she also realised, in that moment, when the lady asked her where she could go, that some of the best people in her life were religious too. She started the ignition and drove to the church where she had first met Kate and, through Kate, Jon.

Sitting in the car park, seeing the shadows and outlines of the congregation moving inside the building, past windows both clear and with the beautiful stained-glass at the front of the building,

Anna felt a dread spreading itself through her body. If this threat, this reminder of her unworthiness, this *gotcha* message about her lying to Jon had not come from her past religious family, there was a chance that it came from *this* one. That this group of kind, wonderful, supportive and non-judgemental people were in fact not that at all. Anna had gone to her mother's church to prove that it had been her who had sent the scan but now, as Anna stepped out of her car and walked towards the church hall, she wanted desperately to prove that it hadn't come from here. She knew she had to consider it but she didn't want it to be true.

Anna walked in to find Grace's aunt, Patricia, bustling around in the kitchen, making multiple cups of tea with the huge metal hot water urn that lived on the side of the counter. She would have come in here before the service to fill it up and turn it on so that it would be ready for thirsty parishioners who were not quite ready to go home – often the elderly of the parish who would be facing a lonely afternoon in their homes, rather than a crowded table for Sunday lunch. She and Jon would always come to this in order to chat and ask after them, so that they knew they mattered.

'Good morning,' Anna said as Patricia turned to face her, 'would you like a hand?'

'Oh, yes please, darlin', the morning rush is about to start!' Patricia smiled and gestured with her head to the opening doorway, where the first of many were walking through.

Anna nodded, headed round to the little serving hatch, lifted it and moved through into the kitchen. She smiled at Patricia as she put on the old school flowery apron that was probably older than she was and started handing out cups of tea, with a biscuit of choice balanced on the saucers.

'So, I noticed you weren't at service this morning?' Patricia said, her eyes forward towards those she was making tea for.

Did Anna imagine a hint of accusation in her voice? 'No. Not this morning, I had something I had to do.'

'More important than church?' Patricia side-eyed her.

There was definitely a *tone* there that Anna didn't appreciate. Suggesting that what Anna was doing was not more worthy than being at church. Anna's stomach clenched. *Unworthy...* No. Surely... surely it would not have been Patricia? She was the church matriarch. She would not stoop so low as to send blackmail. Would she?

'Yes. Something that clashed. Something that had to be done today.' Anna put stone in her voice as she replied.

'Hmm, OK,' Patricia said, lips pursed.

'Was it that obvious?' Anna asked. 'That I wasn't here?'

'No...' Patricia said in a way that meant yes. 'Only I looked out for Grace as she was here this morning too, rather than at her own church for some reason, and I saw her sat with Jon, which she doesn't usually do when she's here, and then I noticed you weren't here. I assumed you were sick, and I prayed for your swift recovery, but now? Well, you're here and in good health. Which, of course,' she added hastily, 'I am happy to see!'

Anna wasn't sure why the idea of Patricia praying for her recovery made her uncomfortable, but it did. Grace sitting with Jon made her uneasy too. Why would she choose to do that? They saw each other every day in the week; would Sunday be necessary too? Grace went to a different church, albeit a sister one. She supposed that *she* saw Jon every day but that was different. They were married.

'Well, thank you for your prayers.'

They continued their task, chatting with the others, and Anna started to relax again. She was being silly. This was her home now. She was not in the same judgemental space as she had been this morning. Whoever had sent the scan was not from here. Here, people noticed if you were absent and prayed for your good health. These were not hellfire people. They were forgiveness and love people. They were *her* people. Patricia was asking after her, not assuming of her.

After a while, when the rush had calmed down and the hall was filled with the sounds of gentle chatter and the clinking of teacups, Patricia spoke again. She was drying her hands on a blue striped tea towel and did not look at Anna as she said, 'Jon said you'd been sick a lot lately.'

Anna blanched. 'Did he?'

Jon was discussing her with Patricia? Or at church in general?

'Yes, he's been worried.'

Anna thought about the past couple of weeks. She had distanced herself from her husband, that much was true. What with worrying about who knew about her lies, and worrying if she was about to be outed as a terrible wife, she had not had the brain space to consider him much, which was ironic, as her fear was about losing him. She had feigned headaches and sicknesses but hadn't really considered how that'd looked when you added them all up. That morning, she'd said she wasn't feeling up to church and he'd been concerned, but she dismissed him, her mind else-where. No wonder he was wondering what was going on.

'You... you talk about me?'

'Oh, child.' Anna flinched initially at this use of the word last spoken to her by her mother, but the tone here, warm, loving, was so different to the cold, authoritarian use she had rejected this morning. 'I remember when you joined us, not so long ago. Jon had been part of our community for years, and we had supported him through the awful tragedy of his first wife, the accident and his losing both her and their unborn child. We held him up whilst he processed his grief. But you? You were what healed him. I still remember that day you walked in the door, all timid and quiet, hoping both not to be noticed but also seen so that we could welcome you. And Jon? His face lit up like sunshine the very first time he saw you. I remember even now, it was like God himself had opened up the clouds to let warmth back into Jon's heart. So that Jon would know you were a gift from heaven.'

A warmth spread across Patricia's face as she spoke. Anna searched for any splinter of anger or disapproval, but there was none. There really was none.

A sob caught in Anna's throat.

Patricia went to her.

'Oh, lovely. I know you healed him but he healed you too. I know of your own loss. You've spoken a little of it. So many of us women have lost a child at some stage, we know the gaping hole it can leave in our soul. I like to think that God gives that loss to those who can fill that space with love. I know you can. I know I try to.'

'You... you don't think I'm broken?' Anna said through her tears.

'Broken? No. No more than we all are. We are all the broken pieces of humanity, trying to use the love we have to put ourselves back together.'

Anna grasped at this chance to ask outright about the scan but the direct words failed her as she opened her mouth.

'You... you don't think I'm... unworthy of him? Of Jon? Unworthy of forgiveness?' She looked up at Patricia, not realising the desperation in her eyes.

Patricia held her even tighter, as though she could squeeze self-belief back into Anna on her behalf.

'No one is unworthy of love, child. No one. We are all sinners, we know that. But we are all worthy of love and redemption, of forgiveness and the right to start again. And I may not know you as well as I know Jon, but I can tell you that I know you and he are both deserving of the love you have found in each other. Hmm?' she said at the end, as though emphasising that there was to be no discussion on this; that her word was the truth.

Anna hugged Patricia back, tightly.

'And know that Jon chose you. He was the eligible bachelor; well, widower, I suppose. He could have had his pick of the ladies here. Your Kate was sweet on him for quite a while.'

'Really?'

Kate had hinted at it before but never admitted to it. Was Kate still harbouring some feelings for him?

'Yes, but that all changed when you arrived. He was so smitten with you it was clear he had eyes for no one else. And time heals all. That's all in the past now.'

'Thank you. I'm all over the place today. I—'

She was about to say more when Jon walked over, having spotted her from across the room.

'Is everything OK here?' he asked, concerned. 'I wasn't expecting you to come, Anna. You said you weren't feeling well.' He glanced back across the room. Anna followed his gaze. To Grace.

'You said you had something to do?' Patricia said, looking confused.

'Anna?' Jon said, looking hurt at this potential lie.

'I... Yes, I...' Anna blustered. Why couldn't she have told the same white lie to them both? Now, when she was trying to find the guilty party, the one who sent the scan, she was the one who looked guilty. And she was. Guilty of lying, of withholding the truth to her husband. 'Both. I wasn't feeling well and then when I'd missed the start, I didn't want to disturb so I did what needed doing and then came here to help.'

She hoped she'd fudged over the explanation enough.

'Ah... Well. Yes, I suppose that makes sense,' Patricia said, pouring herself a cup of tea. 'Well, I'll be off to do the rounds and chats. Anna, are you OK to stay? In case anyone wants a top up?'

'Of course. And thank you.' Anna nodded, grateful for an excuse not to have to do the rounds. She wasn't in the mood for chit chat.

'What was all that about?' Jon asked, looking after Patricia as she settled down on one of the comfy chairs.

'Oh, nothing. We... we just chatted about... life.'

'Very philosophical.'

'Don't belittle it please.'

'I'm not!' He held his hands up in defence, then walked towards the serving hatch and leaned over to give her a kiss. 'I'm not,' he said again, more gently this time. 'Are you feeling better?'

She was. In one morning, she had ruled out two potential avenues as to who sent the scan. It had not come from her past, her mother. And after talking with Patricia and looking at the community she was now part of, she was convinced that it had also not come from here.

'I am,' she said, taking off the pinny and coming round to the front to join him.

'Good,' he said, a spark lighting in his eyes. 'Cos Grace and I have been talking and she's had a great idea for the business. Come and listen to it?'

'It's Sunday, Jon. Supposed to be the day of rest, as you always remind me. And I promised Patricia I'd stay here.'

Jon sighed.

'You're right. OK. It can wait until tomorrow. I'll go and let her know.'

He walked off across the room, leaving Anna by herself.

As she watched her husband interact with Grace, she could

see why he enjoyed her company. He was relaxed, light-hearted. His laughter rang out across the room. She used to make him laugh like that. When was the last time she had done so? Patricia said she'd healed him, but for what? To then let him down month after month?

Maybe she *was* undeserving. Maybe the scan was right.

11

Sunday was a day to rest and recharge and Anna usually arrived home from church feeling at one with the world and her place in it, her spiritual battery recharged before the cynicism of the week started to creep in. She and Jon often spent the afternoons reading, or walking outside if the weather was good. Something calming. But when she got home, Anna couldn't sit still. Something Patricia had said would not leave her alone.

She couldn't shift the idea that Kate had once had feelings for Jon and whether or not she still did. Was Anna looking at her relationship with Jon and feeling it was a sham when perhaps the true sham relationship was hers with Kate? Before she came here, she hadn't really had any close friends. She wasn't comfortable enough with herself to let her guard down to make any. Any friends she had were very much surface level – the chatter never going any deeper than last weekend's must-watch TV show. People she would happily spend time with, but not reveal her soul to. She had thought that Kate was different. But now there was a question mark. She needed to see her.

She picked up her phone and selected Kate's number.

'Hey, Anna, how are you? Didn't see you at church this morning,' Kate chirped into Anna's ear, having picked up almost immediately.

'No, I had something I had to do.'

'Sounds ominous. You OK?'

'Not really. Look, are you free this afternoon?'

'Ah, no, sorry, I'm away today. Left straight after service.'

Anna's heart slumped. She didn't want to spend any more time feeling like this. 'When are you back? Tomorrow?'

'Yeah, well, back tonight but late. Why?'

'Don't suppose you fancy Monday morning pre-work coffee, do you?'

'Um, sure, I guess? Half eight? Text me where. Close to me if you can. I'd have to be quick but could do it. That OK? Are you OK? Has something happened? Have you...' she whispered. '... have you found out who sent it?'

Did Kate sound worried? For whose sake?

'No. Not yet. No, there's something I wanted to run past you, that's all.'

'Oh, OK. Sure. Look, I have to go...' She sounded distracted.

What was she up to?

'Fine. Sure. See you tomorrow.'

'OK, lots of love. See you then. Bye.'

And she hung up.

Anna tried her best to relax. She had a plan. She would see Kate tomorrow, find out if she did have any feelings for Jon. If there was something there that she'd never seen before. Being her only bridesmaid didn't mean she was incapable of betrayal. People carried on with their husband's best man, or their wife's sister, didn't they? Sinners. Like her.

* * *

Kate was already waiting for her when Anna walked into the café. She'd not been there before but it was close to Kate's work. It had a converted warehouse aesthetic, all stone and metal, but lovingly draped in hanging greenery and large potted plants. Almost as though nature had come to reclaim the industrialised space. She realised that it felt like her office. At least she felt at home. Kate waved her over to a table by the window, which overlooked the just-off-the-main-street residential road, with the occasional passer-by with a dog or a toddler, though at this time of the day, it was mostly deserted.

'I already ordered for us, your usual, hope that's OK?' Kate said. She looked nervous. Why was she nervous? But Anna herself was nervous; maybe she was projecting.

'Thanks. I'm going to need a vat of coffee this morning, I barely slept.' Anna half-laughed.

'You do look wired. What's going on?'

'I could ask you the same question,' Anna said, more accusingly than she had meant to. Kate's eyes widened in shock.

'I beg your pardon?'

'Sorry. That came out wrong.'

'I hope so. What's this all about? You dropped off the radar, missed church and now you're here, absolutely jumping with what? Nerves, adrenaline, anger? I can't tell, other than you're not being yourself.'

Anna sighed. Kate did know her, and Kate was right; she was flinging herself from accusation to accusation. Her two places of safety – Jon and Kate – were both in question right now. It was like someone had placed a carpet on water and asked her to walk on it as though it was on land. Everything looked as it should from one angle and yet keeping her footing was impossible as the ground moved beneath her feet.

'I went to see my mother.'

Kate looked shocked.

'Wow. I... I know you've not told me everything about that period of your life, but I know enough to appreciate that doing that would be difficult for you. Why? Is that why you missed church yesterday?'

'Yes. I know nothing about her any more, but I knew where she would be. Where she always was on Sunday mornings. And I was right. Nothing had changed. There she was. And nothing else had changed either. Well, other than my dad having—'

At just at that moment, the waitress arrived with their coffees. It was a welcome distraction. It was so early for such a heavy conversation and for a moment, Anna just wanted to close her eyes and sleep.

'Thank you,' they both said as she handed them their drinks before walking back to the serving station.

Kate sat forward and took a large sip. 'Oh, that's good. I'm shattered, I got back late last night.'

'Where did you go?'

'We were talking about you...'

'We *were*. But now we're talking about you!' Anna said, trying to force some levity into her voice. She didn't want to talk about her parents. She didn't have parents any more, if she ever had done. 'What's going on?'

Kate blushed. She was definitely hiding something. She wouldn't look at Anna. Could she not look her in the eye?

'Kate? What are you not telling me?' Anna was serious again.

Kate looked up to see the fear on her face and she nearly dropped her coffee. 'What? Oh, oh, Anna. No. I'm not hiding anything. Look, I know you're having a hard time, I know you're feeling all over the place, but please, this is *me*. I'm not the bad guy here.'

'I didn't say you were.'

'You didn't have to,' Kate said, her jaw line set hard.

'So just tell me,' Anna said, her voice coming out a high croaked pitch.

Kate sighed. 'Fine. Fine. I'll tell you if it'll stop you assuming the worst all the time. I'm seeing someone. It's new, but it's good. He's lovely but he doesn't live near here. We met online and I've been going to see him at his.'

'You're... seeing someone?'

'Yes. And I really like him!' Her shoulders raised up to her ears as she smiled widely, happiness radiating from her.

'How long? How long have you been seeing him?'

'A few weeks now.'

'Why didn't you tell me? This is good news, isn't it? Why didn't you say?'

Kate blushed again. 'It's hard. I didn't know how I felt about him when we first met. Then I realised I liked him but I needed time to know if he felt the same. And... Well... You and Jon are so damn perfect for each other, it's hard to open up about my car crash of a love life sometimes.' She chuckled.

'But we're friends. You can tell me anything.'

'Oh, I know, I know I can. Just then this scan thing happened, and I know you and Jon have been having rows and, well, it didn't feel right to just be so happy in front of you.'

'I *want* you to be happy!' Anna protested.

Especially if it's not with my husband.

'I know.' Kate reached over and squeezed her hand. 'And I appreciate that. But you're having a hard time. I didn't want to bother you with something that might not have gone anywhere.'

'Can I meet him?'

'Sure... When the time is right,' she said off-handedly, closing the conversation. 'So, what did you bring me here to talk about?'

Anna swallowed her coffee. It tasted burnt. How could she

accuse Kate of having feelings for Jon, just after she'd told her all about this new man? Assuming he actually existed and wasn't a smokescreen.

Stop it, Anna, you're being ridiculous!

'Have you found anything out? About Jon?' Kate was fiddling nervously with her teaspoon, making distracting clinking noises with the cup. It grated on Anna's nerves and she wanted to reach out and take it from her. She grabbed on to the cushion instead, squeezing hard.

'About his *affair*?' Anna said sarcastically.

Kate sighed. 'I'm not going to stay here if you're going to be like this. Did you bring me here just to shout at me? Honestly.' Kate pursed her lips. She took a breath, trying to calm herself. She looked furious. 'Do not shoot the messenger here. Again, I did not outright say Jon was having an affair, I merely suggested that it was one possibility amongst others. I know going to see your mother was hard and I'm going to assume it's put you off kilter and because of that, I'm going to let this go. But please, remember I'm on your side.'

'I won't deny it shook me going back...' Anna hesitated to say the word *home* because it wasn't. It never had been. 'But despite everything I'm feeling, I do know it wasn't her, my mother, who posted the scan. Which is something, I guess. You're right. It has got me all messed up. This whole thing has. I don't know who sent it, or why, or what they might be planning, or have planned. I don't know if someone is about to pull the rug out from under my life, and if they are, what for? Have I wronged someone? Haven't I been good enough?'

'It's OK. I understand. Just, don't come for me, OK? I'm Team Anna, whatever that means.'

'I went to church, got chatting with Patricia. I even wondered if *she'd* sent it.'

'OK, now you're really clasping at straws. Firstly, she'd never emotionally torture anyone; secondly, she doesn't have a judgemental bone in her body, and thirdly, if she had a problem with you, she'd tell you outright. Probably whilst making you eat food that she'd made!' Kate's eyes crinkled with affection. 'But I guess she *is* Grace's aunt...'

Anna nodded. 'Exactly. Well, Patricia and I were talking and...'

'Yes...'

'She did say... that you... that you once had feelings. You know, for Jon.' Anna spoke fast, as though she had to spit it out or never say it at all.

'Ah. And you decided that, what? I'd still got the hots for him? Was just being friendly to you in order to get closer to him? That I'd put a wedge between you by making you question him? Honestly, if I didn't know your state of mind and your tendency to take a flicker of an idea and blow the whole thing out of proportion, I'd be a lot more offended than I actually am.'

'So... you don't? You didn't?'

'I absolutely had the hots for him about a decade ago, yes. He was young and tragic – don't judge me – and yes, I was attracted to him. But then I introduced him to you and I could see the two of you were meant for each other. But Anna...' Kate paused, her face switching from open to pinched and worried. 'I would be careful. I really would look at him and Grace. I'm not saying anything for sure, but they were whispering together in church yesterday morning, looking all animated. Why was she so keen to come and work for you at a small printing press? No offence meant. Shouldn't she be out, travelling the world or something? I truly think that the idea of the scan not being an actual baby is just, well, it's just too random. Who would do that? What would they be trying to say?'

'That they know about my lies—'

'Then why not go with that? Why not something more direct? All the quotes and mystery doesn't make sense. If they're trying to say something, they're not making it very clear!'

Anna felt herself get clammy as nausea started to roll in. 'You really think he's cheating on me?'

'I don't want to think so. But, yes, I think it's possible. He has always wanted a baby. You and he haven't been able to have one for... well... reasons. You've said yourself that you and he have felt like hard work lately. Like you've run out of things to say to each other.'

'I never said that.'

'OK, not in so many words, but you've said when you talk these days it often turns into a row.'

'We've had a few fights. Doesn't every couple?'

'Maybe. I don't know. But just consider it as an option. Take a closer look at Grace. Something's not right there. You said that she behaves weirdly. Why? What's really going on with her? She and Jon clearly get on well, so why is she weird with you? What has Jon omitted to tell you about why she's there? Just ask the questions, OK? And if it turns out that it's all squeaky clean, then great. I'll be as happy as you. I don't want this to be the answer, I truly don't. But sometimes when it looks like a duck, quacks like a duck and swims like a duck, it's a duck, you know?'

Anna felt cold. Even the heat from the coffee cup she was holding didn't seem to register. Either her husband was cheating on her, had committed the ultimate betrayal, or she was sitting in front of her only real friend, who had a 'mystery' boyfriend she didn't want Anna to meet, who admitted that she had once had feelings for Jon and still loved him, allegedly platonically, pushing the idea, the ridiculous idea, that Grace was *pregnant* and by Jon, for goodness' sake. What was Kate up to? Anna believed her when she said she didn't send the scan. And yet, she couldn't make what she was saying now fit. None of this made sense. She had wanted to meet with Kate, to do what she had done with her mother and rule her out.

And yet, she found she couldn't entirely do so.

If they were going to old sayings, then one occurred to Anna immediately. Keep your friends close but your enemies closer. If she really did think that Kate might be behind all this, then she had to make sure she didn't make her suspicion known. She would go along with looking at Grace and she would not let it out that she didn't wholly trust Kate; she would keep her on side and see if she slipped up.

Anna refused to have her life turned upside down by someone who wasn't even brave enough to do it to her face. She refused to let all she had worked for be taken from her by someone who was pretending to be something they were not. She was done with being lied to. Done with being stabbed in the back. Sure, she was a liar herself, but didn't it make the whole situation easier? It takes one to know one, after all. And she would find out who it was and she would find out what they wanted from her.

There was a lot that Anna didn't know. But she knew this: whoever it was, if they wanted something she was not prepared to give, then they were in for a fight.

12

Anna really wasn't in the mood for work, which was so unusual for her as to make her feel even worse. Whenever things were difficult before, she had thrown herself into the business and now it was Monday morning and all she wanted to do was to go back to bed, pull the duvet over her head and stay there. There was no escape from this – at home, at work, at church. She realised her world was actually pretty small and it was at risk from imploding, just like her old life had. She didn't know if she could walk away from her life again. She didn't want to; she wanted to fight.

She had decided to take the day off. Being in the office was too hard. Kate's words were echoing in her head and she felt that she needed a day to get her head together and calibrate her thoughts. She was only going to pop in, check the post and go home again. Emails and voicemails she could pick up remotely. She hated being out of the loop, as though she was out of control of her own business, even if only for a day.

Feeling on edge, Anna was quiet as she let herself in to the building. The atmosphere felt different, as though she was trespassing, and Anna wondered if this was how the office felt every time she wasn't there. It was as though the air was thickened with something. Everything felt strange. Her brain was telling her to be cautious, like when you come home and find a door unlocked, and you have to determine whether it was an oversight on your part or if an intruder is there at that very moment.

She usually hung up her coat in the small vestibule just beyond the main door but she felt cold for whatever reason, so she kept it on. Slowly she walked into the main office space and she heard the rustling of papers. Something stopped her from calling to Grace. The girl always looked right at her, with such intensity that Anna couldn't meet her stare. She'd not had the chance to properly watch her without feeling she was about to get caught. So now, she stood deliberately behind one of the large potted plants, one taller than her, so she could observe her from a distance.

Grace was at Anna's desk. She looked harried. She kept running her hands through her hair and her face was strained. What was the matter? She opened the top drawer and went through the contents. Was she looking for a stapler or a hole punch? A working pen maybe? Entirely innocent. But something was telling Anna that this wasn't normal. This wasn't right. And she held back to see what Grace was doing. To catch her in the act – but of what?

Anna watched as Grace opened the next drawer down, flicked through documents, as though looking for something in particular. She stopped at one, reading its details, before sighing and putting everything back, being careful, it seemed, to make the documents look untouched. Anna felt sick. What was she looking for?

Grace went through every drawer in the desk, seemingly increasingly dissatisfied with what she was finding. There was nothing bar stationery, a few draft documents, some sketches for designs, some notebooks, perhaps a printout of a business plan, a budget or two and some files with invoices and tax returns. Business. Just business. But what if Grace wasn't trying to find business information?

Suddenly incensed by this invasion of privacy, though Grace had not been told *not* to go through the desks, Anna stepped suddenly into the centre of the room, revealing her presence.

'What are you doing?' she asked, trying not to sound accusing but aware from the tone of her voice that she had failed.

'Oh! Oh. Gosh, you scared me! I thought I was alone. Oof.' Grace had gone pale and she put her hand to her chest as though to stop her heart racing.

She looked... How did she look? Guilty? Ashamed? Or just shocked? Anna couldn't tell. She was bad at judging people, either assuming the worst or, in the past, giving far more credit than someone was owed.

'You were. I just popped in to check on things.'

'Jon said you had an early meeting. Like he has.'

'What were you doing?' Anna repeated. She felt like stone. She wanted an answer.

'...Pardon? What? Me...? What was I doing? I...' Grace stuttered, looking flustered. 'I was just looking for something.'

She stood up tall and then smiled. It was an odd smile, like when a face is supposed to be doing one thing, being kind, but somehow it looks the opposite, like an attack.

'Clearly. What?' Anna said coldly, before realising she was being unfair. Grace had only been with them a few weeks. She didn't know where everything was kept, and she was here by herself. There had been no one to ask and so obviously she'd have needed to just look for whatever it was she needed. Anna wasn't being rational. She had nothing but the niggle in the back of her mind, based on pretty much nothing, to determine how she was feeling. She wasn't being fair.

'There's no need to get all wound up,' Grace said.

'Who said I was?'

'I'm saying it. I know you're...'

'What? I'm what?'

'Look,' Grace said, holding her hands up. 'I think we're getting all messed up here... I am not trying to start an argument.'

Anna bit her tongue. She *was* wound up. She was the one trying to start an argument, but for what? She was lashing out at everyone. She reminded herself about keeping enemies closer, about catching more flies with honey.

She pasted a smile on her face.

'Can I help? With whatever you're looking for?' She stepped closer towards her desk, shrugging her coat off and putting down her bag. 'I can show you if you need?' she said kindly. She needed to be nice. Even if it looked like she was flip flopping all over the place emotionally.

She thought that Grace looked relieved, like a grateful puppy who had thought it was about to be reprimanded for something it wasn't aware it wasn't supposed to be doing.

'I... Well, thank you! I was looking for...' She paused. She looked at her hands.

'Yes?' Anna asked, trying to keep the amusement from her voice. Grace was floundering.

'That, um, that supplier invoice. From the supplier of the gold leaf?' she blurted out as though it had just occurred to her. 'I was paying their new invoice and the payment details, they looked, well, I remember it being different, so I just wanted to cross reference to check if we needed to add a new supplier or if I'd misremembered or if this was some sort of scam. I was trying to help.

I could have just paid it, no questions asked, but I didn't think you'd like that.' She looked put out.

'No, no. Always ask questions.'

Right now, I'm questioning everything and everyone. Including you.

'Exactly. You never know who you're dealing with, do you?'

'Oh, absolutely.'

The two of them stood looking at the other accusatorily. Anna wasn't sure what Grace had to accuse *her* of. She seemed angry. Maybe she was standing in the way of Grace getting what she wanted: Jon. No, no, that was ridiculous. Anna had to calm things down. They were getting all het up over nothing. Air and whispers.

'No, I'm sorry,' Anna said. 'I've come in here, all guns blazing. I didn't expect you to be here by yourself, that's all. You scared me.'

'Do you scare easily?'

Anna baulked. It sounded like a threat. Surely not?

Anna stood firm; she was not going to be intimidated. 'No, it takes a lot to spook me actually. I've been through worse things than most people can imagine.'

'I've got a good imagination. Jon commented on it.' Grace tipped her head to the side, looking pleased with herself.

'What do you mean by that?'

'Nothing!' she said, suddenly breezy. Had Anna imagined the tone in her voice before? Was Grace saying one thing but Anna hearing something different? Was she so freaked out by everything that she was seeing and hearing things that weren't really there?

Grace's stance softened suddenly. 'I really wasn't snooping, you know? I just didn't know where to look and as you'd previously looked after the invoices, I thought maybe it was in your things. Don't worry – I won't tell Jon about this.'

'No need to keep it from him. We don't have secrets.'

Grace's eyebrows went up in surprise. 'Really? I thought every married couple did. It's how to keep the peace, isn't it? Little white lies? Sure, he doesn't need to know everything.'

Now it was Grace's turn to look abashed. Did she not want Jon to know she'd been snooping? *Invoice, my arse*. What was she looking for?

'He doesn't need to know that you accused me of... of, well, what? Stealing?'

'I didn't accuse you of anything!'

Anna could feel her cheeks heat up and she knew she was going red. She hadn't accused Grace of anything really, had she? Yes, she had been a little harsh in her tone. Oh god, Jon was going to be annoyed. She couldn't tell him about this now. Then Grace would tell her version and it would be her word against Grace's. It sickened Anna that she wasn't sure Jon would take his wife's side.

'It felt like you did,' Grace said.

'It felt like you were snooping.'

The accusation slipped out of her mouth before she could stop it. She was in a hole; she had to stop digging.

'Anna?'

'Yes?'

'Shall we do a start over?' Grace said, sickeningly sweet.

'A what now?'

'A do over. Start afresh. We're getting all kinds of dumb here. Let's not. We have to work together.'

No, we don't. I own this business. I could fire you now. If Jon was going to be furious, he might as well be furious for a reason.

Anna seriously considered saying this before the realisation that Grace was waiting for an answer hit. Grace was right. There was no proof of anything. Anna would look hysterical. Grace would come out on top. If there was something going on, then Anna needed to catch her at it. Or *them* at it. The idea made her retch. She clutched at her stomach, putting a hand on her desk to steady her.

Grace suddenly looked concerned.

'Are you OK? Look, shall I make us some tea?'

'That'd be lovely, thank you.'

It would get Grace away from her for a moment. She could think straight.

Once Grace had popped to the kitchen, she breathed deeply. She could hear the sounds of the kettle boiling and cups being brought out of the small cupboard there. Anna reached into her bag for her bottle of water and took big gulps, finishing all of it, hoping to flush the fuzzy-headed feeling away. She was all over the place. Work had always been her refuge from other people, from feeling she was not getting things right. Had they spoiled that by hiring Grace?

Grace returned with two cups of tea, and they sat at the little table to the side which did for meetings, for drawing space and for lunch breaks. She took a sip and briefly closed her eyes. The room span, so she opened them again. She'd not be doing any work today; she was too stressed. She would have this cup of tea, check through the post but not do anything with it and then go home for that nap. Maybe a bath. A proper day off. She needed time to think through and figure out what she thought for herself. So she could see through any lies or bullshit. So she could see what was in front of her eyes. Or not.

Right now, she was spiralling, reading things at least two ways and tying herself up in knots. But right now, Grace was winding her up, either coincidentally or on purpose.

The pair sat in silence for a while. Grace blew on her tea as it steamed.

'So,' Anna said.

'Yes?'

'Tell me a bit about yourself. I don't think I know anything. Jon doesn't talk about you at home.' Anna wanted Grace to know that in the pecking order with Jon, she was at the top.

Grace shrugged.

'Well, um, OK.'

Anna waited. Grace looked at her hands.

'No? How about I start instead?'

Grace's head snapped up.

'That'd be great actually.'

'OK, well, I moved here about ten or fifteen years ago now...'

'From where?' Grace almost demanded.

'Oh, not too far, a few towns away. I just wanted to be somewhere new.'

'How come?'

'Um, well, I wanted to be more independent, so I moved away from my family home.'

Ha! Family...

'Yeah, I suppose I get that.'

'Do you? You're living at home at the moment, aren't you?'

'Yes.' Grace nodded, her face taut. 'Don't get me wrong, I love my family. My... my mum and dad are wonderful. They're just very protective and it can be...'

'A bit much?'

'Yeah,' Grace said, nodding. 'Makes me want to do something crazy! Something they'd disapprove of, just to show that I can. But I know they're just looking out for me. I'm grateful. They're good people.'

Was Grace a good person too?

Was Anna?

'That's a nice thought. Someone looking after you.' A knot tightened in Anna's stomach. You learnt how to parent from your parents, didn't you? She would have no chance of knowing

how to do it. What would Jon be like? She didn't know his
parents well and when they did meet, she felt very much that
she did not live up to his first wife. She felt that they constantly
compared the two of them and that she came up short every
time.

'Yes, but it makes it hard to...' She stopped. 'Never mind.'

Grace shook her head, her hair falling over her face in that
way that Anna remembered doing herself when she wanted to
hide away from the world.

'They sound lovely. You're lucky.'

'I guess.' She looked petulant. 'You know you are too, don't
you? With Jon, and this.' She gestured around her. 'You've your
own little empire. Don't you want to start a family at some point?'
she asked, immediately looking away, clearly aware she'd over-
stepped the mark.

Anna took in a gasp of air. She was shocked at the stab that the
question posed, cutting down to the core of her. She wished
people knew not to ask. It hurt too much.

'Is that too personal? Sorry. Just something Jon said.'

'What did he say?'

Anna's harsh tone was back with a vengeance. He was talking
about their private life with *her*? He'd stopped talking about it
with Anna. How could he talk about it with someone they barely
knew? Or did he know Grace better than Anna had assumed?

'Oh, nothing, nothing. Just something about building a business, a legacy. And I sort of assumed he meant for a future family.
That's all. He didn't say anything specific.'

'It's just, it's a little private. Family, you know.'

'Yes, sorry. Mum said I should look into journalism; I ask too
many questions. I didn't mean to upset you. I just wanted to know
more about you.' She suddenly looked contrite. How she
managed to swap from needling, to intrusive, to kind, in barely a

moment – it made Anna feel dizzy. She didn't know where she stood with her.

'Let's forget it. It's nothing,' she said. 'I should be getting home. I'll leave you.'

She got up and cleared her things away. She noted as she did how Grace's face darkened, how something like anger flitted across her expression as she also stood up.

'Are you OK?' Anna asked, confused as to why Grace suddenly looked so angry.

'Fine. Fine,' Grace said. Anna could see Grace was trying to be breezy but it wasn't working.

'You sure? You don't need anything from me?'

'It's fine, I'll work it out.'

Anna arched her eyebrows. Work *what* out?

'If you're sure then...'

'OK. Leave. I'll be OK,' Grace snapped.

'Great then,' Anna said as she walked to the door. She was going to take Grace at her word. Tone could be misinterpreted, after all.

She felt wobbly as she put her coat back on. She would go home, sleep, rest and forget about this whole weird, uncomfortable morning. She had got nowhere. She had more questions than she had answers. She couldn't trust Kate, not wholly, but she also couldn't dismiss Kate's suggestion to look more closely at Grace and Jon. Grace had definitely been weird but not in a way that Anna could definitely say why. Maybe she was just *odd*; some people were, weren't they? It didn't mean they were all having an affair with your husband. Anna laughed out loud at the idea of going home to find the world and his wife crammed into her bedroom, with Jon looking overwhelmed by the situation. Yes, it was that ridiculous that he would cheat on her.

Wasn't it?

13

'Anna? Anna, are you home?'

Jon's voice drifted into her brain, but she was half asleep and she couldn't quite process it. Her thoughts were muggy. She felt like she was trying to wake up from under a thick layer of mud. She'd never been this tired before. It was like her whole being wanted to melt into nothing.

'Anna?' Jon said again, peeking his head around their bedroom door, the room darkened by the curtains, closed against the red sunshine of the evening. 'Anna, are you OK?'

Gingerly, she opened her eyes and pushed herself up. She had fallen asleep in her clothes and the seams and buttons had dug painfully into her body while she slept. It felt like everything hurt. Her mouth was acrid and there was a funny taste on her tongue. What had she had? Just the coffee and the tea that Grace had made. Nothing out of the ordinary, surely?

'Hi,' she croaked in response. She blinked heavily to try to shake off the drowsiness from being woken from such a deep sleep. She felt atrocious.

'This isn't like you, sleeping in the middle of the day. Are you

OK?' Jon asked, a hint of annoyance in his voice. Anna caught it. She felt reprimanded, despite him always saying she should rest more.

She was annoyed in response. She'd taken a day off; she was allowed to do with it whatever she chose. Besides, it felt like a sick day. She really didn't feel good.

'I'm fine. Just resting. You told me to rest so that's what I'm doing,' she snapped. His eyebrows rose as he noted her tone, coming further into the room and sitting on the end of the bed. He'd been in meetings all day, was still dressed in his suit and tie and for a second, a memory flashed into her brain. Her own father, dressed from his day at work, sitting on the end of her childhood bed, and her, feeling awful, sitting up at the top. His expression one of disappointment, of judgement. Her feeling small. Feeling like she'd let him down. The memory sat in her stomach, souring her from the inside.

'I can see,' he said, perhaps attempting levity, but failing to keep a hint of snideness from coming out alongside it. 'Are you feeling rested?'

'No. I feel awful. I think maybe something I ate disagreed with me.'

'Something you ate then? Not guilt?' He raised his eyebrows disapprovingly.

'What do I have to feel guilty for? I'm sorry, are you trying to say something?'

Anna wasn't in the mood for this. She wanted a large glass of water. Maybe a piece of toast. Or maybe to just go back to sleep and stay that way until she'd slept off whatever this was. She was not in the mood for Jon to not say what he actually meant. She always hated people doing that. Just say what you *mean* and be done with it. Then she stopped.

Guilt.

She *did* have something to feel guilty for, didn't she? Did he know?

'Yes. Yes, I am actually,' he said. 'I went back to the office after my meetings, to tidy up and sort things out ready for tomorrow, and I found Grace...'

'Found her what? Doing what? What was she up to?' Anna sat up, suddenly alert. Had Jon found her rummaging through things too? Had her assumption been correct after all?

'Up to? She was working, Anna. Like we pay her to. I found her fairly upset, actually,' he said, with too much accusation in his voice for Anna's liking.

'Upset? Why? What on earth has upset her?' They'd left on good enough terms, hadn't they? She'd said she'd be OK.

'You! You upset her!'

'What? How?'

'You turned up, out of the blue after saying you'd be off work for the day, and accused her of going through your things. That's how. Honestly, Anna, what were you playing at? You made her feel so unwelcome.'

'Well, she was going through my things!'

'Yes, Anna, trying to check an invoice. You know, doing her job. Unlike you. You've taken the day off to do what? Sleep? We're all tired, we'd all like to do it, but we don't run a business like that.'

'You *told* me to rest! The whole point of getting Grace in was to lighten our workload, wasn't it? Or did you have another reason for wanting her?' The accusation slipped out before she could stop it.

There was a pause, just a millisecond of a pause.

'Like what, Anna?' Jon stood up, standing over her. For the first time, she didn't feel safe. He was angry with her.

She stood up, trying to lessen the difference in their heights. It didn't work.

'Like what?' he repeated. 'If you think I need reproaching, please do go ahead.' He waved his hand in invitation.

Now it was her turn to pause. She wanted to think, not to react. If he was trying to hide something, getting defensive was the way to do it. Turn the situation around onto Anna. Or was he genuinely insulted at what Anna had suggested?

'Nothing,' she said eventually. 'I just... She was looking through my things.' She could hear how childish she sounded but it was all she had.

'You're going to have to apologise. You were aggressive and accusatory. Grace wouldn't be rummaging in things she's not supposed to. She's trustworthy.'

Anna felt like she'd been punched, as if all the air had been knocked out of her. He was taking Grace's side of things. What had Grace said to him? Was she covering her tracks? Getting her side of the story in first?

'That's not true! And "out of the blue"... I *work* there. We *own* it. I can turn up whenever I like! I was not aggressive; I was making my point known.'

Jon snorted derisively. It wasn't something Anna was used to hearing from him, and she was shocked.

'Not aggressive? Yet I found Grace quiet and tearful. I had to send her home.'

'I did not upset her! I came into the office, quietly, and found her going through my desk, going through my things actually. Rifling through my desk drawers! I just asked what she was doing!'

'You asked her what she was up to. "Up to" is accusatory. What on earth were you accusing her of? Honestly, she's our new employee, she's been great so far. The first time we leave her by herself in the office and you sneak in and accuse her of... Well, I'm not sure, to be honest. She didn't want to say much. She was too upset.'

Jon shook his head in disappointment.

'No. No, I asked her what she was doing. She was going through all our paperwork. Looking for something. I wanted to know what.'

'She was looking for the invoice information. She told you that. But for some reason, you don't believe her.'

'No. Yes. Look, I don't know.' Anna's heart was pounding, and she couldn't think straight. She and Jon never argued. Yes, they'd bickered more than usual lately, but never like this. She didn't know what she thought. Did she believe Grace, that she wasn't snooping? The girl seemed to have told a different version of the truth to Jon. For what? To gain sympathy? Divide and conquer? Conquer what? Or who? How well did they really know her, after all?

'You were harsh and accusatory, and she said she's not sure she ought to come back tomorrow. I assured her that you were out of sorts, and we're not accusing her of anything, and she should absolutely come in as usual. I had to calm her down, make her feel better.'

Make her feel better. What did he do?

'Honestly, Anna. I know you weren't sure about us getting another person in but you have to admit, it's working. She's good, efficient. My workload – your workload – has got more manageable. You got to have a day off and things haven't fallen apart. When could we last say that?' His tone softened as he tried to talk her round. Tried to make out all was OK.

Anna put up her defences. She wasn't in the wrong. She didn't need convincing of anything. Grace was putting a wedge between them. She knew it. Why, she didn't know. Grace was half Jon's age.

Whatever Grace was up to, Anna would work it out. She had to.

'You're right. I know, you're right.' Anna acquiesced, if only to bring this spat to a close. She didn't think he was right, but she couldn't have this rift between them. She loved him. She loved their life and she was prepared to fight for it. Maybe she needed to try harder to give him what she hadn't been able to do so far: a child. Maybe that's why he'd taken to Grace; maybe he saw her like a daughter. She was young enough to be that to him. Maybe his protective tendencies were kicking in, in the absence of a child of his own to care for. If his first family was still here, his child wouldn't be that much younger than Grace was now. Did he look at her and see his never-was daughter?

She would remind Jon of what they had, what they could have, together.

She smiled at him.

'Come here,' she said as seductively as possible, ignoring the swirling in her stomach. She'd power through.

She took a deep breath and pushed the tide of sickness back. She knew she probably looked more ruffled than sexy, but she could pull this off.

A questioning smile raised itself on his lips.

'Now? You sure?' He didn't look convinced.

'With you? Always...' She flipped the duvet back next to her and patted it invitingly.

Jon hesitated until Anna repeated the gesture and then, smiling, he took off his tie and moved next to her.

'You... don't... have... to...' he said as he kissed her neck.

'I want to. I hate it when we argue. So... let's make up.' She slid her hands round his neck and pulled him to her, pushing her hips forward to meet his, running her hands over his back.

She'd make him forget all about Grace.

14

'What about this one?' Anna held up a dress to show Kate.

'Hmm. Nice but maybe a bit fussy? I'm not a huge fan of all the ruffles and lace that seem to be on everything this season. I'm not sure I'm going to find anything I like,' Kate said, wrinkling her nose.

Anna sighed. They'd been walking around all afternoon trying to find an outfit for Kate to wear to a work conference. She wanted to feel 'professional, confident, stand-out' but so far had rejected anything bright, too structured, too tight, too long, too anything. Anna thought she probably had an idea in her head of a dress that didn't actually exist and that they were traipsing about town, getting increasingly hot and bothered looking for something they would never find. They'd even gone into shops that Kate wouldn't normally shop at, places that were very high-end which went against her ethos of not spending too much on frivolous things. For Kate, clothes were practical things. But apparently this outfit had to be right.

'Well, it would help if you started saying what you *do* want rather than what you don't?' Anna said bluntly. She wasn't sure she wanted to be on this trip; she still wasn't wholly sure that Kate didn't have something to do with the scan, despite her assurances that she didn't. Anna had only agreed to today on the basis that spending a longer time with Kate might make her drop her guard long enough to let something slip. If there was anything to let slip, that was. Anna's stomach was cramping and she felt like being anywhere but here.

'Oh, I'm being a pain, I know. I'm sorry. It's just, well there's a promotion coming up and I think I could do it and I *want* to do it, but all that "dress for the job you want not the one you have"? Well, all the predecessors have been men, so I have no idea really what that looks like!' She threw her hands up in the air.

'You're not a pain.' Anna let her words hang just long enough for it to be unclear whether she meant them or not. 'Let's take a break though and work out what you actually want rather than traipsing about aimlessly?'

'Ha! You're right. Let's go and get a coffee and maybe scroll some websites and then target the shops that way. It's my fault, I've left it far too late and then I tried the outfit I thought I was going to wear, and it just feels... wrong.'

Anna knew plenty about things just feeling wrong, despite there being nothing obvious out of kilter. She felt miles away from Kate at the moment and that was weird enough in itself.

They got coffees at the shopping centre's food court and sat overlooking the main thoroughfare of the shops. It was a great people-watching place and Anna often sat here, not for the coffee, which was distinctly chain-café mediocre, but for the opportunity to watch people without it being weird or off-putting. It was difficult to stare at people going about their day without them noticing, but Anna liked to do it. She often wondered at some people's effortlessness, trying to work out if they were that way naturally or if they'd worked at seeming that way to others. Did people always put on a front, or did some people just go through life being unreservedly themselves? The idea both terrified and appealed to Anna.

'Penny for them?' Kate said, nudging the shared piece of cake they'd chosen to refuel with towards her.

'Sorry, miles away. Thinking about a work project.'

Which was mostly true; she was thinking about Grace.

'You don't need to specify; you're always thinking about work.'

'True. That whole saying about do something you love and you'll never work another day in your life?'

'Yeah?'

'It's rubbish!' Anna laughed and Kate joined in. 'Do something you love, and you'll get up early to work, work late into the night and find that on a Saturday, you'll *just* check your email, or in Sunday service you'll realise you've missed half the sermon cos your mind has wandered and you're thinking which shade of green to use for a particular client. Endless.'

'I guess it's who you are, not just what you do?'

'Yeah. That's not healthy though, is it?' Anna said. She knew her mind needed constant distraction otherwise she'd think too much. Too much about the past. Was that why she lied to Jon? Is that why he'd... become distant? Or was something, or *someone*, on his mind instead? Jon was a talker, a sharer – he'd have been great at confession, Anna often thought. Sitting in a box and opening your mind to God. It was almost a shame he wasn't Catholic, like she had once been.

'No. So I guess you've got to spend part of your Sunday afternoon helping your good friend find this elusive outfit!' Kate laughed then took a sip of her coffee. 'I do appreciate it, you know that, right?' she said, suddenly serious.

Anna had to try not to flinch. She pushed it down. She had to believe Kate. What else could she do? Never trust anyone ever again? Even the idea of it made her feel achingly lonely.

'Of course! And I wouldn't want to be anywhere else. So, what are we looking for here?'

Kate sighed. 'OK – so it has to be professional, conservative but not look like I'm trying to be one of the boys. Not too feminine, hence no ruffles, but also I don't want to look like Margaret Thatcher.'

'So, a trouser suit? More Hillary Clinton? With absolutely no handbag in sight?'

'Hmm, see... I don't know. I think that perhaps a skirt would be better but I do tend to look like an air hostess in them. Now there's nothing wrong with being an air hostess, that's a hard job that I don't think I could do, but it's not quite the right look.'

'Well, then, that leaves us with dress and jacket? Might that work?'

'Yes. I think that's what I need.'

'Right then. I know where we should... What? What are you looking at?' Anna said, suddenly confused by Kate's attention switching off.

'Isn't that Grace?' she said, indicating with her head towards a younger woman with an older one, possibly her mother.

Anna stiffened. It was. She hadn't spent more than half an hour with her since that day she'd found her rooting about her stuff in the office. She'd apologised since – stiltedly, to Jon's satisfaction – but things were still odd and uncomfortable, and Anna couldn't work out what do to.

'Grace!' Kate called out, ushering her over when Grace caught her eye.

'What are you *doing*?' Anna hissed.

Kate plastered a smile over her face.

'Catching her off-guard. See what she's like when she wasn't expecting to see you.' She waved and beckoned the pair over.

'Stop it!' Anna hissed again, but it was too late. Grace was coming over to their table looking as uncomfortable about it as Anna was.

'Hi,' Grace said, a strained smile on her face.

Anna felt bad but then reminded herself that Grace had stepped over a line and Anna shouldn't have to feel guilty about pointing that out.

'Hi. I thought it was you,' Kate said, tipping her head to one side. 'I'm Kate. We've met before. I go to the same church as your aunt. You were there last weekend, weren't you?'

Grace nodded tensely but said nothing.

There was an uncomfortable silence as no one quite knew who ought to be leading the conversation. Anna as the link between everyone, Kate as the one who called them over, or Grace as the one who had yet to introduce the woman with her. As usual, Kate broke first.

'And who is this lovely lady with you?' she asked, throwing a huge smile towards the small, meek-looking woman.

'Oh, this is Liane, my... um, my—'

'I'm her mother,' Liane said. 'She's embarrassed to have been caught hanging out with her mum on a Sunday afternoon after church when I'm sure there are much cooler places to be.' She chuckled.

Grace's brow wrinkled. 'I'm not embarrassed by you, Mum. It's just...' She left her sentence unfinished.

Kate nudged Anna in the ribs. Not wholly subtly either.

'Oh! Ahem. Yes, and I'm Anna. Grace's... Well, I guess, boss?' she said, somehow feeling embarrassed to be pulling rank out of the office set-up.

Was Anna imagining it or did Grace go pale?

'Oh, I must have got myself mixed up,' Liane said, looking confused. 'Grace said her boss was a man. Jon? From Patricia's church?'

'Yes, I suppose I'm her co-boss really. Jon is my husband. We run the business together.'

'Mum, it doesn't matter. You don't need to know everything about everything! I can be my own person. I... I'm sure I told you about Anna.' Grace smiled nervously at Kate, clearly wishing that the ground would open up and swallow her. What was making her so uncomfortable?

'It does matter, love. I was worried about you working alone in an office with a man, however nice Patricia said he was. Now I know he's married, well, then that changes things.' Liane smiled. 'She'll always be my baby.'

'I can imagine – I'd have to, no kids myself,' Kate said. 'But I understand – pretty, young girl; older, experienced man. We all know how that can go... So, Grace,' she said, turning her full attention onto her. It must have felt intimidating; Anna nearly felt sorry for Grace. 'How *are* you finding working with Jon? And Anna, of course.'

Grace looked at the floor, before looking up defiantly at Kate. 'It's fine. I'm learning a lot.'

'Just fine?' Anna added. Kate was pretty much accusing Grace right in front of her mum and if there was any way this got back to Jon, well, he would be absolutely livid. There would be no way to persuade him to calm down again like she had done last time. Kate was so clearly convinced that something was going on, but there would have to be proof. 'I thought we were all getting on well!'

That wasn't true. The atmosphere was horrible.

'I'm sorry,' Liane said, 'Anna. You said your name was Anna? And how long have you been married to Jon?'

It was an odd question, but it broke the tension, which Anna was grateful for.

'About seven years now.'

'Hoping to avoid the seven-year itch!' Kate said.

Liane's face dropped like a stone. She turned to face Grace who could barely look at her mother. The two of them stared at each other for what felt like an eternity, having a silent conversation of sorts between them. Liane had clearly put two and two together and was obviously horrified at whatever equation she had solved. Grace had turned pink and looked as though she knew she was in a lot of trouble. Liane looked away, her jaw clenching as she tried keep her cool in this now too public a place.

'We ought to be going,' Liane said, turning to smile warmly at Anna and Grace. 'Lovely to meet you... Anna.'

She took Anna's hand into both of hers and looked directly at her. It made her feel awkward under intense scrutiny, but somehow, also seen, and held by it.

'You too, Kate,' Liane said less warmly. If she had picked up on what Kate was inferring, it seemed that she was not impressed by it.

Anna's stomach dropped. What had Liane worked out? What did she know that Anna didn't? Was Kate right and something *was* going on? She felt that she was on the outside of an understanding, and she didn't like it. She had thought her days of being on the outside looking in were over. Clearly not.

'Um, OK. Bye,' Grace mumbled, keeping her head down.

'Nice to meet you too, Liane.' Anna waved as they walked away.

'Me too!' Kate added, before turning to Anna and saying, 'Well, that was weird. No? Why on earth had Grace not mentioned you to her mum? Why did she not want her mum to know that Jon was married?'

'I know what you're trying to say,' Anna said, her voice hard. She didn't want to admit it. Kate might be right. She felt dizzy, she needed to be somewhere quiet, not in the middle of a busy shopping mall. Her marriage might be on the line, and this was not the place to realise that. She needed to go home. She needed to see Jon and know that this was all just a mistake, a misunderstanding. That her Jon was still hers. She had to get out of here.

'I'm not saying anything. Just that we were all obviously having slightly different conversations at the same time. Did you see how her mum's face dropped? She looked utterly furious. A real "wait till I get you home" face. I would kill to be a fly on the wall on their drive home.'

'Stop it! Just stop it! This is not some gossipy drama. Some soap opera. Some reality TV show where betrayals and lies are part of the entertainment. This is *my life!* And it's falling apart, and I don't know what to do.'

Kate looked shocked. Then she composed herself. 'I'm not enjoying this. And you're wrong about that.'

'What do you mean?'

'You *do* know what to do.' Kate crossed her arms.

She was right. Anna did know.

She had to go home and make Jon tell her the truth.

She just didn't know if she was ready to hear it.

15

Jon wasn't home when Anna got back. At first, she paced angrily about their home, unable to settle. Then she went back into the kitchen, flung open the fridge door and got all manner of ingredients out. Ever since she was a teenager, she had found the act of chopping vegetables almost meditative. Somehow the focused and repetitive action had a calming effect on her and so she spread out items in front of her and started to prepare a meal. She chuckled to herself about how it might not be wise to start the conversation that needed to be had whilst she was holding a large kitchen knife. It should have worried her that she found that funny, and yet her emotions were so complicated that she didn't know, if Jon admitted to an affair, if she would fall apart or succumb to unbearable rage.

As it was, Jon was so long in returning that by the time he did, Anna was standing at the stove, stirring over and over. She loved risotto but there was always a point, right about now, when she was hungry and tired, hot and flustered by standing so close to the heat of the hob, wishing that she'd decided to cook something, anything but this. She had hoped to be cool and collected when

Jon came home but right now her blood was pulsing and she felt frenetic.

'Smells good!' Jon said as he came into the kitchen. He opened the fridge door wide and pulled out a bottle of white wine. He looked at it. 'You opened it already? Drinking without me? Not drowning your sorrows, I hope?' he teased.

'I needed a glass for this!' Anna snapped back.

She was making his dinner; he'd been out goodness knows where – had he been to see *her*? – while she made their food, and now he was cracking jokes at her expense?

'Best keep going then,' he said sheepishly, aware his joke had fallen flat. He handed her a glass of the chilled wine, which she gratefully sipped on and then took a large gulp of. As the coolness of the liquid and the chill of the glass brought her temperature down a bit, she reminded herself that the point of this evening was to get some answers. Provoking a pointless fight would not achieve that. She'd been thinking all through the process, considering how she would broach the subject. Would she just accuse him outright and see what he said? A surprise attack, not giving him any time to come up with a story? Or should she be subtle, try to catch him out but make him tie himself in knots? She could just show him the scan and see what his face betrayed. Or not. There was a chance that he was cheating but that he didn't know about a baby.

The baby. God, if there was an actual baby then some innocent little life was about to get caught up in a grown-up mess...

'Ouch!'

'Are you OK?' Jon asked, coming over to where Anna was, staring at her fingers.

'Sorry, yes.' She winced. 'I just touched the pan. What an idiot. I was miles away.'

'Get your hand under the cold water, now,' Jon instructed as he turned off the heat under the pot. He was one of the first aiders at church and went into authoritative mode whenever his skills were needed. Anna liked it. It suited him.

He moved her to the sink and stood behind her as he reached to turn on the tap and place her reddening fingers under the cooling water.

'How is that? You OK?' he asked, whispering.

The sensation of his breath on the delicate skin of her neck, combined with the heat of him so close behind her, had an immediate effect. It always did. There was something about him that just connected for her. Anna closed her eyes, ignoring the stinging in her fingers as the heat from the pan fought with the icy cold of the running water, ignoring her mind telling her that she was supposed to be demanding answers from him, not enjoying his close presence. She focused on the feel of his chest pressed against her back, the solidity of his hands around her lower arm. Whether he was aware of it or not, he was gently circling the inner part of her wrist with his thumb, and it was sending waves of warmth through her. Instinctively, she pushed back against him, and she felt him react.

'Hello,' he said, sounding pleasantly surprised. He took his free hand and swiped Anna's hair away from her neck and peppered it with little kisses. She felt her knees weaken and heat flood her body. She gently swayed her hips from side to side, pushing against him, and she heard him emit a sort of *growl*.

This is what it used to be like, she thought. Feeling with your body rather than thinking with your brain. Spontaneous. Fun. Your senses rather than your mind leading the way. Her thoughts were on hold, her mind so tired from all the what ifs that it had simply decided to let her body take over for a while.

The two of them stood there, facing out of the kitchen window, Anna's hand under the tap, Jon caressing her, her caressing him until she thought she couldn't take it any more. She genuinely considered lifting up her dress, but the sink was hard and cold and she wasn't really tall enough. So she reached out and closed the tap, turned and put her arms around Jon, keeping the closeness between them.

'Hello, you,' she said, smiling as she stood on her tip toes to kiss him. Whatever was going on, she really did love him.

'Fingers feeling OK? They've not been under the water long enough really,' he said, serious for a moment. His concern for her was genuine.

'Fine,' she whispered, noting and appreciating his care for her but trying to keep the moment going, unbroken. She wanted this. They *needed* this. They'd been apart. They needed to reconnect. Maybe whatever was going on could be fixed.

'So...' he said, stroking her shoulders, leaning back to face her but keeping them connected from the chest down.

'So...?'

Jon glanced at the hob. 'What about the risotto?' he said, a teasing look on his face.

'Fuck the risotto.'

They laughed and Anna led Jon upstairs to their bedroom.

The light in the room was perfect, an early evening soft sheen of sunset-pink and gold. As Anna lay down diagonally along the bed, she felt like she was a pre-Raphaelite painting, her hair spilling out across the duvet, fanning around her head. The wine from earlier was coursing through her bloodstream, making her feel light and relaxed. She hadn't felt this relaxed in... Well, she couldn't remember. Maybe Grace being at work *was* helping. She shook her head, her face screwing up. No, this was not the time to be thinking about her. This wasn't the time to think at all. Anna didn't want to think, she wanted to feel.

Jon followed her into the room and leaned over her, putting

his hands either side of her shoulders and bending down to kiss her. Anna put her arms around him, feeling his muscles working as he held himself upright. They were hard and taut, and she ran her hands over them, enjoying the sensation. She wanted to feel his skin, so she reached to the front and unbuttoned his shirt, peeling it off his shoulders and dropping it to the floor. He let her and then started to work on her clothes as well. Soon they were naked and tangled in each other.

'We're falling off the bed!' Jon laughed suddenly. They'd shifted from the centre and were at risk of collapsing on the floor in a heap. Jon stood up, the rays of dusk catching on his skin as he scooped Anna up into his arms. She was always surprised at how easily he did this, and the feminist in her was always a little appalled when she got a frisson of excitement when he did. She felt safe. He kissed her and then gently threw her back onto the bed, climbing on all fours to join her and pressing his weight down on her as he did so. She shifted to allow him to enter her and they moved together. Anna closed her eyes and enjoyed the sensations running though her body until she climaxed. Jon became more frenetic in his movements until he came too, then sank onto her, breathless and sweaty. She held on to him, holding him close, wanting to keep the moment a bit longer. He was her husband; she loved him. Everything would be OK. Whatever 'everything' was.

Jon rolled off her and then snuggled in from behind. For a while, neither said anything, both of them just basking in the afterglow of each other. Goosebumps started to form on her skin as she cooled down, and Jon kissed them before reaching for the bit of the duvet they weren't resting on, wrapping it around them to make a cocoon. He didn't want to let go either.

'I've missed this,' he said sleepily.

'Me too.'

Anna thought how nice it would be to just go to sleep like this, wrapped in each other, no worries, no cares, no responsibilities. You couldn't do that if you had children, could you? There were advantages to not having a family. She could make Jon see that.

'You're wonderful, do you know that?' he said, nuzzling on her neck, the endorphins buzzing around his brain.

'I do,' Anna teased.

'It was almost like that time.'

Anna stiffened. 'What time?'

Jon hadn't registered the change in atmosphere. If he had, he might have stopped there.

'You know, the time it worked. Or nearly did. I wonder if it will this time. It would be so wonderful, don't you think? To know exactly when it happened. When our child was conceived.'

Anna didn't reply. That time he was referring to had terrified her. She had thought she was pregnant. She had all the symptoms, and she was late. But it had turned out to be her hormones playing tricks; her period arrived with a vengeance a few days later and she had never been 100 per cent convinced that she hadn't been pregnant despite being on the pill. How would she have coped if she was? It was what he wanted. What they wanted in a way.

Jon hadn't noticed her lack of reply.

'I was thinking, you know, the other day in the office, with Grace, about how nice it was having someone to lead, to inspire.'

Anna clenched her teeth. They were alone, naked and post coital and he was thinking about *her*? OK, so Grace had briefly entered her mind earlier, but that was different. That was about Anna having more time, not about how good it was to have someone else in the office. Surely if Jon were having an affair, he'd want to *hide* it, not bring her into the conversation? Or was it a double bluff?

'Hmm?' was all Anna managed to say.

'I just thought, it was good to have someone to pass knowledge on to. And then I thought that's what it'd be like to have children and I let myself dream a bit, you know?'

'Uh-huh.'

'Whether we'd have a boy or a girl, and whether they'd be like Mum or Dad. If they'd be a total surprise, like if some far-back gene would jump out in them, like red hair can do.' He stroked her hair. 'You've always had a red tint in yours – did your grand-parents or parents have red hair maybe?'

Anna flinched. She didn't want to talk about her family. She wasn't like them, and she didn't want to be like them. She certainly wouldn't want any child of hers to be like them.

Jon wasn't picking up on her body language – how she'd shifted away from him; they were no longer skin to skin; how her teeth were on edge, grinding together as she tried to metaphori-cally bite her tongue.

Was he thinking about a baby because there was one?

The wine in her stomach rose up to the back of her throat, burning. She was going to be sick. She sat up, pulling the duvet towards her. She hadn't really accepted the fact that Jon might have cheated, not really. She had been trying to find a solution, any solution that wasn't that, but things kept bringing her back to that answer. She'd not been able to think of anyone who might have sent the scan. Kate was utterly convinced of her theory and meeting Grace this afternoon had done nothing to dispel the idea.

Anna felt cold. She started to shake.

'Hey, hey, are you OK?' Jon asked, concerned.

'Fine. I'm fine.'

'Here,' he said, getting up to pass her a dressing gown for her to wrap up in. He went to close the curtain on the way back to the bed. 'The evening's got a chill in it now,' he said, staring out towards the darkening sky.

Anna looked at him, followed his gaze to the street outside. How could it be that the world was going along as it always did, people on their usual way home, Jon mindlessly chatting about the weather, while in the meantime inside her was a tornado, a storm waiting to tear her life apart and her with it. She had weathered a storm before, but it had damaged her. She didn't know if she could weather one again.

Jon turned back to her.

'Are you sure you're OK? You've gone awfully pale. Are you feeling unwell? You've been... not yourself lately.'

'No. No, I'm not OK.' Anna's voice hardened. She needed to ask. She just needed to ask him outright. She wrapped the dressing gown more tightly around her. She felt more vulnerable than she had ever done before. She could feel her strength seeping out of her by the second. She was cold, she was tired, it had been a long day. She didn't think she had it in her to know the truth right now. Or if she had the strength to endure the row that a denial on his part would undoubtedly cause.

She couldn't do it.

'What's up?' Jon asked, shifting towards her on the bed.

She looked up at him and felt her heart break. If she asked him now, either way she would lose him. She didn't want to lose him. Not tonight. It could wait until tomorrow and then she would find the strength she needed.

'I'm hungry,' she said. 'Shall we go and see how second-rate the risotto is?'

'You're selling it well!' Jon said jovially.

Sometimes second-best was the best thing on offer.

Anna knew that too well.

16

The world was too loud, too bright and too much. Anna screwed her eyes up against the harsh morning light as Jon pulled back the curtains in one swoop, and it hit her face like a sledgehammer. Everything hurt.

'Wake up, sleepyhead.'

He was always far perkier than her in the mornings as it was, but it was obvious from their respective states that it had been her who had finished more of the empty bottles of wine that she remembered would be strewn over the kitchen counter when she stumbled downstairs. Resting her pounding head back on her pillow, she took several deep breaths to calm the churning in her stomach. She tried to recall the events of last night after they had gone back downstairs to eat. She couldn't remember a great deal, other than she knew she had drunk more than was wise in order to quiet her mind. She knew she should have confronted Jon and she had planned to do it today. She couldn't work out if she was feeling quite so awful due to the wine or the fear that things were about to come crumbling down around her. Whatever the cause, she felt sick to her core.

Jon went downstairs and Anna could hear the sounds of him clearing up last night's washing up and getting ready for the day. It should have been a normal, everyday sort of morning. Simple domesticity. Predictable in the best way. Tears escaped Anna's eyes as she closed them against the strident sunlight. Was she being ridiculous? In the very cold light of day, weren't all the 'clues' that she had just circumstantial? If she were to talk to someone else, would they laugh at her? Anna didn't know any more. She was just so tired. It felt like her bones were tired. Her soul was tired.

Refusing to get up just yet, she pulled the duvet cover up to her shoulders and rolled over towards her bedside table. It was organised as usual. A lamp with a shade that matched the green curtains. The book that she was trying to find time to read propped on top of a pile of other books that she believed she would get to. Her phone, charging. She really ought to swap it for an alarm clock. Didn't they say it was bad for you to have your phone so close to you while you slept? There was also a coaster made out of glass from the trip to the sea they'd taken last spring, A water bottle that she kept there to remind her to... Anna's heart dropped. To remind her to take her pill. It was easy to forget once the hustle of the day got started and usually, in the morning, Jon would get up first and bring her back a cup of tea in bed. It was the perfect time to take it quickly, discreetly. She had a spare packet in the office in case for whatever reason she forgot to take it first thing. Both packets well hidden, though she wasn't sure that Jon would really know what he was looking at, even if he did find them.

Anna suddenly felt clammy and hot, and she threw the duvet back off her as she sat bolt upright. She couldn't remember last taking her pill. Her mind was racing as she tried to picture it. It was such a regular thing; had her brain just edited the memory out as not of use? Or in all the panic of the recent weeks had it slipped her mind? They'd not been having sex much lately anyway. It hadn't mattered so much, but last night... She reached for the pile of books, one of which was fake, one of those security books where you hide your passport or cash and valuables, the book merging into many others like trees in a wood. Except this was where Anna hid secrets from her husband. It was where she kept her pills.

Trying to keep the shake out of her hands, from the hangover or from stress, she opened it up and checked the packet. Today was... It was Monday again, wasn't it? She took a moment to be clear about that, her mind muggy. The problem with working all the time was that days merged. Working for yourself, weekends were only distinct if you made them so. The usual hooks that you can hang things like days of the week on weren't always there, or in the right order. She checked her phone. Yes. Monday. She looked back at the packet. Thursday, Friday – empty. Saturday, Sunday – still there, blinking up at her like little dots that floated around her vision. Shit. Shit!

'Anna?' Jon called from upstairs.

Anna took a deep breath. 'Yes?' she replied, trying to keep panic out of her voice.

'We're out of teabags. Coffee OK?'

'Um, sure. I'll come down.'

'OK.'

'...Thanks.'

That bought her more time, more thinking time. Had she forgotten but remembered in the office? She'd gone into work on Saturday, hadn't she? But not yesterday, Not Sunday? Or had she just forgotten altogether? Two days missed, sex last night. She would need the morning after pill, and fast. How did it work?

She picked up her phone, selected an incognito window and entered the search terms. Racing through the information that appeared on her screen, she tried to take it all in. OK. Pharmacy, quick chat, pill, done. She could do that. She could swing by somewhere on the way to work, fabricate an early meeting or something to avoid going in with Jon. Then she could check at the office and take it if needed. Or just take it anyway; doubling up didn't seem to be a problem. Better safe than sorry, after all. The absolute carnage that adding an unplanned pregnancy into the mix right now would bring. No. She would sort this out. And then go back to figuring out what the hell was going on with her marriage and her business.

After popping today's pill and carefully placing the rest back into the book, Anna stood up and threw her dressing gown on. She felt absolutely horrendous. She'd not been this hungover in forever. She would have to be beyond careful not to be sick today. She walked downstairs slowly, holding on to the banister. Her hands were pale and clammy; was the rest of her the same?

'Oh, you don't look well,' Jon said as she walked gingerly into the kitchen.

'Thanks,' she said, her voice hoarse. She started to get offended; after all, he'd drunk as much as she had, hadn't he? He had no high horse to get on to. Then, it occurred to her that a pharmacy trip wouldn't be odd if she *was* under the weather, so she decided to go with it.

'Actually, I don't feel well. I think I might be coming down with something.'

'So not these then?' He clinked the empty wine bottles together, a little too loudly for Anna's liking. Was that really necessary?

'Funny. No, it doesn't feel like a hangover, though I don't doubt that I am also hungover. Why did we drink so much?'

Jon's smile dropped from his face, and he turned away before replying.

'Things have been... strained. You know they have before you start denying it.' He still wouldn't look at her. 'So, I don't know. Maybe it loosened us up a bit. Stopped us overthinking or something.'

So Jon felt it too, their being disconnected. He'd never said as much before, though Anna thought he couldn't possibly not have noticed how they'd drifted apart. How the much longed-for baby had started pushing a gap between them. It just hurt to hear it out loud.

'Maybe. Maybe we should stop thinking so much,' Anna said, wishing that if she could stop going over all the ways this marriage could go wrong or might already have, that all would be ok. One of those moments where you wished it were possible to hit pause, to get off the merry-go-round that it sometimes felt like you were on, and just breathe for a moment. To ignore everything and have it get no worse.

'My brain isn't up to it this morning. Thinking, that is. I drank too much as well,' Jon said with affection in his voice. He poured Anna a cup of coffee from the cafetière, put it down in front of her and kissed the top of her head. He did still love her, she knew that.

Whether he loved Grace as well, that was another question. She pushed the thought from her mind as she sipped on the hot coffee, hoping somehow it would settle her stomach, knowing that it probably wouldn't.

'I'll pop by a pharmacy on the way in, see about some first defence medication or something. Can't afford to get sick right now; there's too much work to do.'

'Good idea. I'll go straight in.'

Spend some alone time with Grace.

'OK,' Anna said flatly, pushing the coffee away. 'I need a shower.'

She got up and went back upstairs to the ensuite bathroom.

She spent a while staring at herself in the mirror, which, despite having flattering lighting, showed Anna the effect of the strain she was under. Her eyes were shadowed, her skin was dry. She looked drawn. Not the most kind comparison to a perky twenty-something, that was for sure. In the shower, she could tell from the drop in water pressure that Jon was in the other bathroom. By the time she got out, feeling a fraction better for being clean, he was dressed and heading out of the door.

'See you later!' he called as he shut it behind him.

Anna sat down on the edge of her bed, wrapped in a large fluffy white gown. For the first time in a long time, she felt utterly alone.

There was already a queue when Anna pushed open the door to the pharmacy. She sighed. She had hoped that the slowness with which she had got herself ready would have meant that she had missed the early morning rush, with most people already at work for the day. But there were at least five people ahead of her, including a mother with a small, fractious baby in a pram. Though her heart went out to the stressed-looking mother, it was exactly what she did not need to see on this of all mornings.

'It's too much, ain't it?' the elderly man in front of her in the queue said to her.

'Hmm?' She hadn't really been listening.

'I said it's too much. All this waiting around. I just need my repeat prescription. I'll only be two minutes and yet I got to wait for all this lot,' he waved around the hand not holding his walking stick dismissively, 'to tell their whole damn life stories first. I'm old. I haven't got all day.'

Anna was not in the mood to placate a cantankerous old man, so she just said 'hmm' again.

'Not feeling chatty then?' he snapped as though she owed him conversation.

'Not feeling too well; that's why I'm here in the first place.'

'No need to be sarky,' he snapped again.

'I'm not.' She smiled, hoping it would be enough.

'Well.' He sniffed. 'Youngsters think they ought to go first, cos they've got busy lives. I think I ought to go first, cos I got less of m'life left. Can't be wasting it on queuing.'

And with that he turned his back on her.

Anna could feel her nerves starting to fray. Maybe she should just take double the pill and hope all would be OK.

No, she insisted to herself, that's how mistakes happen. She'd made enough of those already. The queue moved very slowly, with everyone apparently needing a long discussion with the available pharmacist who was looking harried and stressed already, it not yet being even ten in the morning. Anna hoped the woman would be gentle with her. She didn't need someone who would judge her for being a thirty-something married woman in need of emergency contraception.

Anna took out her phone and scrolled through work emails, mentally putting together a to-do list for when she got into the office. She realised that she'd have to get some sort of cold and flu medication, or something that settled the stomach, in order for her story of being here to play out. She thought how lies are all interconnected. One lie – in her case, one big lie – led to so many other small lies, layer upon layer until she was wrapped up in a web of them so tightly that she couldn't see a way out. She was just there, stuck, until a spider came to eat her.

'I said, can I help you?' the pharmacist repeated.

Anna looked up, unaware that she had been slowly working

her way to the front of the queue and the pharmacist was now talking to her.

'Oh! Oh, sorry. Yes. I, um...' She looked around her. The grumpy old man was on his way out and no one else was paying any attention. She turned back and said as quietly as possible, 'I need the morning after pill, please.'

She looked directly at the pharmacist, almost challenging her to question the request. She didn't need to. The pharmacist looked her up and down briefly, making whatever assumptions she was going to, and then quietly ushered her into the consulting room. There was an audible sigh from someone in the queue, annoyed that Anna was going to be a while.

In the room, more like a cupboard, there was a desk and two chairs, a sharps bin, a small fridge and very little else. Anna sat down, smoothing her hands over her dress. She realised that she was subconsciously trying to show the pharmacist her wedding ring. Her Catholic roots went deep – sure, she was taking contraception, which the church disagreed with, but she was at least married.

'So you would like the morning after pill?' the pharmacist said kindly. 'Can you tell me a little about your situation?' She tipped her head to one side. There was a question that she was not asking.

'Um, well, it's really straightforward really,' Anna stammered. Why was she nervous? 'I take the contraceptive pill.'

'Which brand?'

Anna told her. She made a note.

'Go on.'

'And I realised today that I've missed the last two doses.' She omitted that she wasn't 100 per cent sure about this. She could in theory wait, check at the office and then come back, but the pill was a sooner rather than later thing, and frankly, Anna was a fan of sooner.

'OK. And have you had sex in the past seventy-two hours?'

Anna felt herself blush.

'Yes, yesterday.'

The pharmacist nodded.

'And you think you might be at risk of pregnancy?'

'Yes, and I can't have that, I just... I can't.'

'Please don't worry, I am absolutely pro-choice. It's what gave women their freedom in this country. I am a supporter of it,' she said, smiling, clearly aware of Anna's embarrassment.

'Thank you.'

'No problem. Right, let me just get a script sorted and you can be on your way. You'll need to take the pill as soon as you can. It's more effective the earlier after unprotected sex you take it. I can see from looking that the dose and your weight will be fine. It can make some people feel sick but it's important that if you actually do vomit, you come back for another dose. That's important, OK?'

She suddenly looked very serious. Anna noted her glance at her wedding ring, followed by a quick scan over her. She realised that the pharmacist was looking for signs of abuse. At first Anna wanted to voice how that wasn't necessary, how Jon wouldn't, but then she thought better of it. It was reassuring that a complete stranger was looking out for her, looking out for all women. It briefly made her feel part of a community that she had not been aware she was in. The sisterhood. It was comforting.

She smiled and nodded. 'Noted.'

'OK. Here's a leaflet about the medicine.' She opened a drawer and pulled out a flyer. 'Pop back out and wait. I won't be too long.'

'Thanks.'

Anna let the pharmacist leave and then she took a moment alone to compose herself before heading back out into the busy shop. She had been so nervous, but it had been easy. By taking the pill, she'd be taking one thing to worry about off her mind. She picked up the leaflet, opened the door and came face to face with Grace.

Grace looked shocked.

'Oh! Hi!'

Then she looked down at Anna's hand. At the leaflet. Then back up at Anna. Her face drained of all colour. Anna's mouth went dry and she parted her lips to speak, but nothing came out. She swallowed. Her brain wasn't working fast enough. It was too flooded with panic.

'Here you are,' the pharmacist said, handing a sealed medicine bag to Anna, who took it wordlessly.

'Oh, come on! We haven't got all day!' another impatient person in the queue shouted out.

Flustered, the pharmacist replied, 'I'm with a patient, I'll be right with you, sir,' before turning to Anna and continuing, 'I forgot to say that it doesn't react with the pill, so you're fine to keep on taking that.' Her face flickered as she realised this was sensitive information which she should not have revealed to whoever the shell-shocked-looking girl next to Anna was. She blinked rapidly before smiling tightly and returning to deal with the growing queue. 'Who's next?'

Initially frozen to the spot, Anna suddenly turned and fled the shop. She waited to hear the door close behind her but instead she heard footsteps following her. Anna stopped and closed her eyes. She was about to have to have a conversation that she absolutely did not want to have.

She turned around to face Grace. She looked, what? Shocked? Angry?

'What's going on? Jon said you weren't feeling well. A stomach upset, he said?'

Anna laughed mockingly. Well, he was sort of right.

'I don't really think it's appropriate to—'

Grace cut her off.

'You're taking the morning-after pill? And you're taking the pill anyway? I thought you were trying for a family? Are you... Are you cheating on him?' A flicker of something crossed her face. Anger? Confusion?

It was hard watching Grace try to put together the pieces of who had been lying to whom. Anna didn't know whether it was best to try to style it out, throw out another lie or whether, within reason, come clean and beg her to stay silent.

'Don't be ridiculous.' It came out of her mouth before she could think. It *was* ridiculous. She would never do that. But she was in a way, cheating him out of a family. Cheating him out of the truth. She felt ashamed. But then her defences rose and she snapped back.

'What are *you* doing here? Shouldn't you be at the office?'

Anna had deliberately chosen a pharmacy a way out of her route to avoid precisely this possibility, of being caught by someone she knew. What was Grace doing all the way out here?

'I... My auntie, not Patricia, a different one, lives out this way and I get her prescription for her as it's easier for me to do it on the way to work than it is for her. I called Jon to ask if it was OK if I was little late this morning, and that's when he said you were going to a pharmacy too. What are *you* doing all the way out here?' she accused, before the realisation dawned. 'Jon doesn't know...' she said slowly.

Anna wondered if she was working out what to do with this information.

'No. He—'

'He'll be over the moon if...' She bit her tongue.

'If what?' Anna couldn't work out what Grace was thinking.

'Never mind.'

'No, go on.'

'No. This is... This is not my business. I... Jon is... my—'

'Your what?' Anna said, fury creeping into her voice. Jon was what to her? Why was she getting so upset on his behalf? She was right; this had nothing to do with her. Or did it?

'He's my friend. And you're lying to him. And now I know that you're lying to him. About something *so* significant. So important. It puts me in a horrible situation. He needs to know. He deserves to know what you're doing!' She started to look angry.

'I don't think it's any of your business.'

'I know *you* don't want, might not want... No, no, I... I didn't sign up for this.' She ran her fingers through her hair. She looked stressed, out of her depth.

'What did you sign up for, Grace?' Anna's face was stony.

Grace took a sharp intake of breath. That question hit her harder than it should have done.

'I...' She faltered. 'I wanted to get to know you better, both of you. And...'

'And do you? *Know* us better?' Anna's voice dripped with sarcasm. Just how well did Grace know Jon, to be so shocked on his behalf?

'I... I don't know what you mean.' Her face flushed. She was clearly not enjoying this conversation. Anna, on the other hand, felt somehow more in control than she had done in a long time.

'I think you do.'

'Anna,' Grace said, fanning her hands out in front of her, 'I don't understand what you're saying but... you're making me nervous. I don't think this conversation is appropriate and I think we should stop talking now.'

'Agreed, I think we both should pretend that this morning never happened. I'll not tell Jon you're way out here, taking time

out of your job to run personal errands, and you'll not tell him...
Well, anything. This is between him and me.'

Would this work? Would utilising Grace's nervousness keep
her quiet? This was such a mess. She needed to fix it, and fast.

'I didn't sign up for keeping secrets,' Grace said.

'Really?'

Grace's face flooded red. She said nothing. Anna had caught
her, hadn't she? She hadn't said anything directly but it was now
clear that Grace was *something*. She looked suddenly guilty.

Check mate, Anna thought. *Two can play at this game. If you've
got secrets you don't want to tell, then you can keep mine too.*

'I'll see you back at the office then,' Anna said, and she strode
away as purposefully as her shaking legs would let her. She and
Grace had come to an understanding, it seemed, though Anna
was aware that Grace knew her secret, whereas Anna did not
know Grace's. She only hoped that she could work out the truth
and still have the upper hand.

17

Anna walked away from the pharmacy and into a local café. She'd not been able to face eating yet and suddenly she was absolutely ravenous. The only thing she wanted was a bacon sandwich. With lashings of brown sauce. And a huge mug of tea. She was surprised because she'd not eaten like that since she was a teenager. Thankfully there was no queue and soon enough, breakfast was in her hands. The saltiness of the bacon mingled with the melted butter on the soft white bread. Anna sighed with satisfaction. It was like she'd never eaten before and all her senses were on hyper mode. She relaxed and washed a big mouthful down with a glug of tea. She wasn't going to be sick. She was grateful for that in more than one way.

She would take a moment, have this breakfast, steel herself and head into the office. She was sure that Grace wouldn't tell Jon anything, at least not yet. That gave Anna time to work out what, if anything, she was going to tell him. Grace was withholding something from her, she was sure of that now. She didn't know what. She was trying hard not to take two and two – Grace with-holding something, and the scan and what Kate said – and make four hundred. She would need to wheedle it out of her, or Jon. Then she could decide what to do. The outright approach didn't work for Anna, clearly. Each time she'd tried, she'd bailed. She needed another plan.

Walking into the office, Anna tried to feel braver than she actually did. She didn't know for sure that Grace hadn't gone straight there and told Jon everything, or even her own version of 'everything', and whether she might be walking into an ambush. Maybe Grace and Jon were in on whatever it was together – they'd certainly been talking in hushed whispers lately. Jon had said it was just Anna's hearing, but she disagreed. Maybe it wasn't something that Jon knew about. Was it a baby? It was such a mixing bowl of lies – everyone withholding a secret from each other, no one telling anyone the whole truth. She screwed her eyes up tight at the thought of it. All the deception, the layers, the hierarchy of who gets to know the truth. It was too like her past. She had thought she'd escaped all that, but had she merely formed another version of it here?

'Hey, how are you feeling?' Jon said when he saw her, getting up from his desk and coming to take her coat. 'Did they help at all?'

Anna glanced at Grace, who was sat at her own desk. Grace looked down.

'Um, yes, they were really helpful. Yes.'

'Did they work out what the issue is?'

Was he playing with her? Had Grace told him? Was he stringing her along to see how she lied to him? Like all the other times she had lied?

Anna looked back up at Grace who shook her head almost imperceptibly. She hadn't said anything. She looked uncomfortable. Who was the cat here and who was the mouse? Who was the rock and who was the hard place? Anna felt quite dizzy with it all.

'They said my iron levels were maybe a bit low. I'm run down. They gave me some vitamins and said to keep my fluids up. Said there were a lot of colds and flu going round and to make sure I'm rested.'

'Ah, so the wine really didn't help then. Dehydration.'

'I should have had a Guinness instead.' Anna tried to laugh. She felt like she was having an out of body experience, watching herself flounder.

'Grace said she bumped into you.'

'Oh? Yes. Yes, she did. We had a chat while we waited, didn't we, Grace? Shared a few stories,' she said, catching Grace's eyes from across the room. 'Didn't we?'

Grace looked beyond uncomfortable, but Jon didn't seem to notice. Good. She'd come into the business and spoiled things. Turned up at the pharmacy out of the blue and now she was threatening everything. Or had she ruined things already?

'Yes,' Grace almost whispered. 'Yes. We did.'

'Are you OK, Grace? You've gone all croaky. Are you not feeling well either? Have we got some office illness going on?'

Grace looked hard-faced.

'Yes. Perhaps we have. Maybe we're all sick.' Grace threw a glance at Anna.

What did she mean by that?

'Well, how about I make everyone a cup of tea? That cures everything. Doesn't it?' Jon looked at Anna, then Grace, then back at Anna. He looked perturbed. There was an atmosphere. Surely he could feel it? Was he feeling nervous too? Was whatever he and Grace been whispering about, about to come to the surface?

Honestly, Anna couldn't keep up.

'Yes. Tea. That would be great,' Anna said. 'I'm still feeling like desiccated coconut. I can't drink enough.'

'No,' Grace said at almost exactly the same time. 'No, I think

I'm going to go home if that's OK, Jon? I feel sick. I think I shouldn't be here.'

She got up from her chair suddenly, making it shriek as it pushed against the floor.

'Oh, oh. Sure. Of course. Are you... Well, no, you said, you're feeling sick,' Jon said with concern. 'Can I drive you? You don't look like you ought to be walking home alone. You're as white as a ghost.'

What was wrong with getting Grace a cab? Surely if she was sick, Jon ought to try not to catch it? Or would it already be too late for that? Had the two of them just engineered some one-to-one time to get their stories straight?

'Yes, yes, that would be great actually. Thank you. I just think I need a break. It's all a bit much suddenly.'

What did she mean? Did Grace mean to take the opportunity to tell him what she knew about Anna and this morning? Were they going to come up with a plan without her?

It was all a mess, but suddenly one thing became crystal clear.

Baby scan or not.

Affair or not.

Grace telling Jon what she knew or keeping it to herself.

All of those things aside.

Grace?

She had to go.

18

Anna thought she would go insane in the hour between Jon taking Grace home and him walking back through their door. She had said that she still wasn't feeling well either but would take a cab back home, as it just made more sense than her joining Jon and Grace on the drive to her house. Part of her wanted to go along, to stop any discussion that might happen, but part of her felt almost self-destructive. This pretzel-twist of lies that they were all tangled in was too much and Anna almost wanted Grace to tell Jon the truth, to tear off the sticking plaster that she felt was holding everything together, just to see whether or not it would all fall apart. Would there be enough to keep them together when everything was laid out on the table? Would they be able to move forward? Would having no lies between them allow them to come back together?

Once home, Anna was suddenly overcome with a cold feeling. She went to the sofa and wrapped herself in the blanket that was draped over the back. She curled up into the foetal position, tucking her knees to her chest to keep all the warmth in. She had to try very hard not to go to sleep. She wanted to hear the car pulling up, to have a moment's warning of Jon's arrival. She had to be prepared that he might walk through the door, armed with the knowledge that she had been lying to him for most of their marriage, or worse – for him to come clean about his relationship with Grace. She couldn't be sleep befuddled when that happened.

When Jon arrived home, Anna was sat bolt upright, still wrapped in the blanket. She was staring blankly at the wall, wondering how she'd got herself into this mess. She knew her childhood had been hard and her adolescence a bin fire but even taking those into account, her adulthood had been harder than she had anticipated. Looking back over her years with Jon, she could now see clearly how she had kept him at arm's length despite his repeated attempts to break down the protective wall that she had built around herself. He had just adapted to living with her as close as she would let him and she felt ashamed when she realised that. When she thought about how that might make him feel, she was close to tears. How hard that would have been for him, especially when he was building his new life on the ruins of his first marriage. Had they healed each other or had they kept each other broken? With someone as open and trusting as Grace, would Anna blame him if he had strayed?

At first, she thought that perhaps she ought to let him go. She loved him, so she would let him be happy with someone else. Then she changed her mind and decided that she would fight for their marriage, fight for what they could have if she would let them and for that, Grace had to go.

'Hey, you,' Jon said as he walked into the living room, dropping his work bag onto the chair. 'I thought I'd come and work from home, keep an eye on you. Seems you and Grace probably have the same illness. You both look washed out.'

That'd be the lies, Anna thought.

'Thanks.' She bit her lip. Jon wasn't going to like what she was about to say.

She took a deep breath and slowly let it out, girding herself for the row that would likely ensue when she spoke.

'You're not feeling sick still, are you?' Jon said, turning towards the kitchen as if he might suddenly need a receptacle.

'No. No, I just need to say something and I'm not sure how best to go about it.'

Jon looked quizzical as he sat on the arm of the sofa. 'Go on...'

'It's about Grace.'

He shook his head in confusion. Anna took a second to look at his expression in case he gave anything away. If there was anything there, she couldn't catch it.

'Yes?'

'I think... I think we ought to let her go.'

Jon's eyebrows shot to the ceiling. 'Um, what? I... Why?'

'Something isn't right. There's something she's not telling us.'

Or not telling me, at least.

'I don't understand what you mean. Do you think she's lying about something?'

Did he look nervous? Did he look like he was about to get caught out?

'Yes. Yes, I do. She's odd, Jon. She's weird and stilted around me. She's been going through the office things – yes, I know you think you've explained that one,' Anna said, waving away his attempted re-explanation. Anna didn't buy it then and she didn't buy it now. 'She turned up at the exact same pharmacy as me, at the exact same time as me on a mid-week morning. Don't you think that's weird?'

'Why would that be weird? We bump into people all the time in random places. Coincidence is a thing for a reason.'

'Why would it be *weird*?' Anna said, shocked that Jon didn't get it, 'Because it was a pharmacy miles from here! Why on earth would she be there?'

Jon wrinkled his brow. 'Why did *you* go to a pharmacy miles from here? There's one just around the corner?'

Shit. She hadn't thought that one through.

'Because I don't like the pharmacist at the place near us. He's of the "take a paracetamol and come back in two weeks" type regardless of what might actually be the issue. Your leg could be falling off, you could walk in with clear symptoms of bubonic plague, and he'd still be pushing paracetamol and sending you home. That's why.'

Saved.

'Well, perhaps Grace was the same?'

'She was collecting a prescription.'

'So maybe that's where her aunt gets it sent.'

'Patricia? She lives miles in the other direction!'

'She has more than one aunt, Anna.'

'Oh.'

'Why are we even having this discussion? So, she happened to be at the same place as you—'

'So you don't think she followed me?'

'Why on *earth* would she be following you?' Jon scoffed. He wasn't taking her seriously. She could feel rage bubbling up from within. He was *her* husband; he was supposed to taking *her* side in this.

'Because she's weird! Because something isn't right, because... I don't know, OK? Something is just off.'

'You want me to fire someone, for no solid reason, just "because".' Jon held his hands up to do quotation marks.

'Don't mock me.'

'I'm not! You're being completely unreasonable! We can't fire Grace.'

'Why not? Because you like her?' Anna could feel tears coming and had to fight hard, the pricking sensation at the base of her nose distracting her. 'You'd miss her? Working with just me isn't enough for you? *I'm* not enough for you?'

'What the hell? No. Nothing like that. Don't be preposterous. You sound utterly unhinged. You sound like some jealous house-wife who can't bear a pretty young woman anywhere near her husband.'

'So you think Grace *is* pretty?' Anna threw at him.

'Don't you? We've both got eyes, Anna. She's clearly an attrac-tive woman. I'm not going to lie when it's true.'

'*I* can say that. *You're* not supposed to!'

Jon tipped his head back in exasperation.

'Seriously? No. Don't be ridiculous. Yes, I can see she's attrac-tive, but am I attracted to her?' There was a pause. He looked at the floor, before looking up at Anna, directly at her. 'No, I'm not.'

He looked down at the floor again. Was he lying? Was he protesting too much?

'Is that all you've got to say?'

'I don't see what else there is to say. You're being ridiculous. You're over-reacting. You're being hysterical! Grace is a hard worker, a fast learner, she's had some wonderful ideas about the business. She's keen, she's talented, she's an asset.'

'I don't *like* her. I don't *trust* her, and I think she has some hidden agenda, but you are too dazzled by her pretty to see it.' Anna crossed her arms in disgust.

He really couldn't see it, could he? Men – show them someone young, pretty and compliant and they'll overlook anything.

'That's insulting, Anna.' Jon's jaw muscle twitched. It always did when he was angry, though he wasn't often angry. He'd been more so since Grace had started than he had been before.

They sat there in silence while they both considered where

they were and what they wanted to say next. This had not gone how Anna had wanted. She had wanted Jon to show his loyalty to her. He hadn't. She considered giving him an ultimatum. Not necessarily to get an answer but to see how he would react, which way he would fall. Was that fair? Setting him a test that she mostly suspected he would fail?

'What would you say if—'

'What?' he snapped.

'What if I said she had to go? Or else.'

Jon looked appalled. 'Or else what? Are you saying that it's you or her? Are you seriously saying that? You want me to choose between you, my wife, and Grace? My wife and the good of my business?'

Anna took a breath and then jumped off the cliff.

'Yes.'

She needed Grace gone. Mostly to be sure she wouldn't tell Jon what she now knew about Anna and her lies to him. If Grace were to tell him now, it would look like sour grapes, she would look like a spurned young woman lashing out, and Anna would be able to be deeply hurt by the accusation, especially due to her unexplained infertility. Anna could be the wounded party, and surely Jon would have to believe her? Even if there was something going on with Jon and Grace, surely he would not believe such a thing of his poor, cheated-on wife?

Anna also needed her gone because of all the reasons she'd just given Jon. Anna *didn't* trust Grace. She never had. There was something about her that put her on edge and although she'd not yet been able to put her finger on what, it was always there, always making the hairs on her neck stand out, always putting her body into fight or flight mode – and not knowing why was making her crazy.

Anna also needed Grace gone as she was now starting to

believe that Kate might have had a point. About the scan, about Grace and about Jon. Here he was, standing in front of his poorly and distressed wife, refusing to get rid of Grace, refusing to stick to the agreement that she and he had had at the start, which was if it didn't work out they would let her go. Why did he not want to let her go? Why not? Why?

'No.'

'No?' Anna's heart fell through the floorboards.

Jon paled. 'No.'

'We agreed!'

'Agreed what? That you could throw your weight around and be unreasonable? Honestly, Anna, I don't know what's been up with you these past weeks but you're not who I thought you were.'

'I'm not? Me? What about you? Sharing in-jokes that I can't be part of, giggling at stupid things she says, whispering in the kitchen and changing the subject when I come in? It's been like being back at school and the cool kids trying to make me feel left out.'

'You feel left out? *You* do? Anna, do you know how much of your life you keep locked away from me? Do you know how many times I've asked you to open up to me? How often I've said that I want to help with whatever it is that is clearly haunting you? And you never do. You never do.'

'You know what haunts me; you know I lost my child. You know I lost my baby.'

'As did I, Anna. I thought we were supposed to be helping each other deal with that, live with that. But you act as though you're the only one it happened to.'

'But I carried mine for nine months.'

'So what? Because I never got to see my baby, feel my baby, because he died before he was even born, that makes it easier, does it? *Does it?*'

He was furious now and Anna couldn't tell if his tears were from rage or sadness.

Anna stopped. What were they doing? Why were they trying to tear pieces off each other's hearts? What was Grace doing to them?

'Do you see?'

'See what?' Jon said, a calm in his voice that was chilling.

'This is what she wants! She wants us at each other's throats.'

'OK, Anna. I've heard enough now.' He shook his head and picked up his jacket. 'I can't listen to you like this. You're unhinged.'

'I'm not, you just can't see it.'

'I'm not firing Grace. We agreed that we would give it a few weeks to settle, and it's barely been a month. You need time to adjust. She needs time to get into the swing of things. And anyway...' he added off-handedly. 'She and I, we're...'

'You're what?' Anna said, breathless.

Was he *leaving* leaving? Was this how it was going to go?

'We're... nothing. Nothing. It doesn't matter.'

'It *does*,' Anna implored.

What was he about to say? What was he about to tell her? He and Grace were *what*?

'I'm not doing this now. You're riled up, I'm angry. I can't guarantee I won't say or do something I'd regret, or something I can't undo. So I'm leaving for now. I'm going for a walk. You, Anna, need to take some time to look at what you're saying. You're throwing accusations of all sorts around without any proof, without any hard evidence. You're...' He shook his head in exasperation. 'I'm going out now. Please try and be rational when I get back.'

He walked out into the hallway and through the front door,

closing it behind him. He didn't look back. He did at least leave the car, so Anna assumed he wasn't going to *her*.

Anna sat down and as she did so, her eyes rested on Jon's work laptop bag. The computer she knew had his messenger app installed on. They occasionally used it at work to communicate silently when one or the other was on a work call – mostly *do you want a cup of tea* or *what do you think to this offer?* so that they wouldn't be heard by the person on the other end of the line. Maybe if he also didn't want to be heard, he might message Grace too. And she him. After all, Grace lived at home with her parents and siblings; privacy would be hard to come by.

Feeling the abject terror in her heart, Anna unzipped the case and slipped the laptop out, placing it on the sofa beside her. She opened the lid, hoping that Jon still had the same password as he always had. A nod to where they went on honeymoon. If he had changed that she thought it might break her heart, even if it had been changed for security reasons.

Cautiously she closed the camera shutter, never wholly convinced people couldn't watch her unseen, then she typed in the password.

She let out a breath of relief when the screen popped into life.

She opened up the messenger app and scanned the conversations.

There it was. Grace.

She clicked on the conversation thread and gasped.

Message after message had been deleted. The whole thread was gone.

She sat back. What had they been discussing? Who did they not want to see it? What the hell was going on? Surely this was proof enough that something was?

She swallowed and blinked rapidly, not wanting to cry. She was too tired to cry.

Then the thread pinged to life with a message from Grace.

Is everything alright?

Anna gasped. Would she know that 'Jon' had seen it? She closed the window immediately. Worst case she would think Jon was ignoring her.

But...

She had to know.

She re-opened the window. While she was trying to decide what to do, another message popped up. Jon must be accessing it from his phone.

Jon
Hi

Grace typing

Are you ok?

Jon typing

Not really

Grace
I'm sorry. I don't want to cause trouble.

Jon
You're not. You know the problem isn't you.

Grace
Is she ok?

Jon

Not really.

Grace

Does she know?

Jon

No. It's better that she doesn't. Not yet anyway. It's not the right time.

Grace

I don't like lying. You know that right? All the sneaking around was sort of exciting in a way, at first but now it feels wrong.

Jon

Me neither but we will tell her. Just not yet. Just a bit longer, till we're sure it's going to work.

Grace

Then we'll tell her?

Jon

Yes. I promise.

Grace

Ok. Hope you're ok. Hope you're both ok.

Jon

You too.

Grace

See you tomorrow?

Jon
Sure.

Grace
Night

Jon
Night

Anna slammed the laptop shut. She felt like she'd been punched in the stomach. The core of her hurt and she could barely breathe. Then she couldn't stop breathing – too quickly, too hard. She was getting dizzy. She took such a gasp of air that it came out as a sob and then the dam broke loose and she sobbed and sobbed and wailed in despair. They were lying to her. They were sneaking around behind her back, talking without her, talking about her.

The scan. The scan must have been sent by Grace – and now Anna really began to believe what Kate had said. Jon had told her that she'd pushed him away. Grace was distraught about her lying to Jon, about there maybe being a baby on the way. *Another* baby.

Oh my god. The baby. Grace's baby.

All the pieces that hadn't fitted properly together before suddenly fell into place.

And as they did, the picture shifted and pushed Anna out of the way.

She would confront them. She would let loose her fury on them both.

But...

Then she would have to admit that she had been reading Jon's messages. That she had logged onto his computer. The Jon before wouldn't have minded. But that Jon wouldn't have been cheating on his wife. This Jon had not only cheated but had got his intern pregnant. Or rather had hired his pregnant mistress as his intern. This Jon was not a man Anna knew.

She would have to find another type of proof and then she would lay her cards on the table and watch them flounder as they tried to explain themselves. And then she would burn the table to the ground.

And she would sit, letting the ashes rain down and settle at her feet.

19

The ring tone rang and rang and rang as Anna paced anxiously around the garden. Jon was home and she couldn't make this call from inside the house, it was too risky. They weren't really talking to each other but that didn't mean he wouldn't be listening.

'Come on!' Anna urged quietly into the mouthpiece of her phone. 'Pick up!'

'You've reached Kate's voicemail. Please leave me a message and I'll get back to you as soon as I can! Thanks!'

'Ahh. I needed to talk with you. I think you're right. I think the baby is Grace's and I think something is going on with her and Jon. I... I just needed to talk with someone, with you. I feel like I'm going mad, to be honest. Call me back? When you can? Thanks.'

Anna clasped the phone to her chest in frustration. She had to go to work today and sit in a small room with her cheating husband and the woman he was cheating with. How would she do that and not lose her mind? She *knew* but she had no proof. She had the scan, which showed everything and yet also nothing. She couldn't admit to seeing the conversation between them last night without admitting to snooping – exactly what she had been so angry at Grace for doing. She needed something, anything that she could lay out in front of them. What on earth was she going to do?

The phone jumped in her hand, vibrating against her chest. She brought it down to look at it. Kate. Anna answered immediately.

'Hi.'

'Hey. Sorry I missed you. I was at Rob's house and driving back when you called. Is everything OK? You sound manic.'

'No. It's not OK. I think you're right. I think Grace sent me the scan and I think she and Jon are... I saw a message conversation between them last night and I think... they're hiding something from me. I don't want to believe it, but when I put all that I do know together, well, it looks like you were right.' Anna's voice broke. 'I can't believe it.'

'Oh, Anna. I'm so sorry. I'd never have thought it in a million years before, but it does look that way. What did they say?'

'Nothing. Just about sneaking about and not telling me the truth.'

'Ouch.'

'Exactly.'

'Where did you see it? How did you?'

Anna paused. She could feel she was blushing with embarrassment. 'I... I hacked into his laptop and read his messages. I feel awful, but what else was I supposed to do? I know something isn't right, and I had to find out what.'

'Ah. Yes. I see what you mean.' Kate sounded pained.

'So what am I going to do? I can't tell Jon I saw the message and all I have is the scan. I feel like I need something else, something *more*.'

'OK, so you watch them both. Closely. One of them will mess up. You're all too close to be able to pull the wool over each other's eyes if you're *really* looking and you know you're looking for something. They don't know yet that you know. That gives you power.'

'I guess. I don't feel powerful. Not this morning, anyway. Last night I was ready to burn everything to the ground.'

'You don't need to do that. Just watch them. For example, does Grace look any different?'

'Different how?'

'Well, if she's twelve weeks or more now, she may or may not be starting to show a bump. Maybe a bit soon. But aren't women's breasts supposed to get bigger this early?'

'I don't know – she always wears loose fitting stuff. That's fashion at the moment, so it's hard to tell. I can't exactly go in today and stare at her chest!'

'No, that's a fair point. But there's baby face?'

'Baby face?'

'It gets sort of puffy with some people. There was a woman at my work who had said various cryptic things and I said to a mutual friend that I bet she was pregnant. My friend was shocked and said I'd got nothing to base that on, but she had stopped dyeing her hair and her face was puffy. And sure enough, a few weeks later she announced her pregnancy. Baby face.'

'Right. OK. I can look for that.'

'And Jon?'

'What about him?'

'Is *he* different?'

Anna sighed.

'Oh. That's not a good noise,' Kate said.

'No, it's just he's been different for a while. We've drifted, I know we have. So it's hard to know if that's *because* of this and I've just not known for a long time, or if our distance is what caused this. What if I made this happen?'

*By not giving him what he wanted, by keeping him just far enough
away from me to not guess what I am hiding from him.*

'Anna,' Kate said firmly, 'this is not your fault. Even if you were
the hardest woman in the world to live with. Even if Jon was
unhappy and wanted to leave, infidelity is not the answer. He's a
Christian man; he should have gone to his faith to bring him back
to you. Not moved on with the newest version of you!'

Kate sounded furious.

'You're right. I just know that he wouldn't have done this
without reason.'

'To be honest, my love, I'm not sure it's his *reason* that has led
him here.'

Anna laughed a dry laugh. 'Yes. That's true.'

'So, proof. You watch them. You ask questions. Follow him,
follow her. They will slip up. People always do. I will also keep an
eye on them. Wait, be patient. Truth will out. It always does. Until
then, be strong. And I'm here, OK?'

Anna nodded even though Kate couldn't see her.

'Thank you.'

'I've got to go, I'm late for a meeting. But call me if you
need me?'

'Thanks.'

Anna walked back into the kitchen from the garden. Jon was
just finishing tidying up.

'Everything OK?' He looked worried. 'Bit early for a phone
call?' He was curt but clearly trying not to be.

'Yeah, just Kate. She... wanted to be excited about her new
fella. She's been by herself a lot so I'm excited for her.'

'It is lovely to see.' Jon nodded.

'We should invite them over to dinner. Couples night,' Anna
suggested awkwardly, not because she particularly wanted to, as

much as she'd like to meet Kate's new man, but to see what reaction it got from Jon.

'That's a bit soon in their relationship, isn't it? For double dates? And we're really busy at the moment. Maybe another time?'

'Oh. OK.' Anna didn't know what she was looking for. She felt so far out of her depth, which was ironic as she'd spent the most part of her early life being lied to or fed half-truths. She should recognise them more easily.

'Shall we go?' Jon said, indicating the door with his head. 'Ought not leave Grace alone in the office too long. She might, oh I don't know, do a hostile takeover while we're driving in.'

If Jon wanted to make amends, he was going the wrong way about it.

Not wanting to reply, she bit her tongue and nodded.

Grace was already in and working when they arrived. She looked up and noted Anna, but could barely look at her. She tried to smile but failed, the corners of her mouth refusing to lift. Then, at Jon, just behind Anna, it was like the complete opposite and a huge smile broke on her face.

'Morning,' Anna said flatly.

'Hi,' Grace said, before looking away again.

Was it guilt from all the lies Grace was telling or was it a refusal to acknowledge Anna with her own lies? Anna tried to look more closely at her, for changes in her countenance, this baby face. But without outright staring, she could see nothing. Maybe pregnancy was easier on her because she was so young. If you were that age, you could pretty much hide it from the world until you were about to drop, couldn't you? Grace was tall as well so an early pregnancy would have a lot of space to hide, unlike on someone short, where the bump could only go out.

'Anyone for coffee?' Anna asked. It was unusual for her to offer to make it. She had initially felt it anti-feminist to be the senior woman in the office and still making coffee, but she supposed actually insisting it was more suited to Grace was almost worse. Anyway, she wanted to see how much caffeine Grace might be happy with, wanting to make her interact with her in some way. 'Feels like a strong coffee morning to me.'

She meant to sound light-hearted but it came out dark. This was painful.

'It does that,' Jon added, his face grey. He was still angry from last night. They hadn't spoken when he had come home. It had been late, and both had been tired. They'd turned their backs on each other and gone to sleep. Both had slept badly.

'Not for me, thanks,' Grace said, raising her water bottle in response. It was one of those huge clear ones where you could check on how much you were drinking through the day. If it had been full when she started, Grace had already drunk a lot. Was being thirsty a sign of pregnancy? Anna shook her head – even if it was, she could hardly accuse them of an affair based on water consumption.

In the kitchen, Anna felt herself breathing hard. It was painful being in the same room as them. She wanted to scream and yell and throw things, and there they both were, acting as if everything was OK. Or as if it was Anna who was at fault.

She had just started the kettle when Grace followed her into the room.

'Are you OK, Anna? You look... flustered,' she said.

'I'm just tired. Thanks,' Anna replied flatly.

'So have you told him yet?'

'I beg your pardon?'

'Have you told him? About the... you know?' She tapped her abdomen.

Anna spluttered. She was speechless. Was Grace really doing this here? Now?

'What do you mean?'

Grace's eyebrows pinched together in annoyance.

'You know what I mean, Anna.'

'I'm not sure I do, Grace.'

Could she make Grace tell her about the scan? Could she get her to admit to it out loud by playing stupid?

'Don't do this,' Grace said firmly.

'Do what?' Anna asked, almost mockingly.

'I don't want to lie to him. I hate lies.'

'Do you really? Are you sure about that? You seem to be involved in a lot of them.' Anna scoffed.

Grace looked shocked. Then she went a shade of pink.

'I don't know what you're talking about.' She couldn't look Anna in the face.

'Yes, you do... *Grace*.'

Grace looked up at Anna. She was upset. She opened her mouth to speak, then paused.

This was it; she was going to tell her everything.

'Grace?' Jon called from the main office.

Both Anna and Grace's eyes shot to the doorway.

'Yes?' she called back.

'Could you come here a moment? I need to run something past you.'

'Sure!' Grace said, not looking at Anna as she snuck out of the room. Did she seem relieved? She had looked as though she was about to unburden herself. Anna briefly felt sorry for her – young and tied up in a horrible mess. Then she thought better of it. The mess was at least in part of her own making.

Anna delivered Jon's coffee, putting it down on his desk where he was showing Grace something, with as much derision as she could manage without it being obvious. She should have spat in it. She sat back at her desk and tried to lose herself in her work. She ought to get her head down and do some decent work. She'd been all over the place since the scan had arrived and shattered her life's equilibrium, but she needed not to let their business slide. It might be the only thing that she would have left to cling to in the wreckage of her life.

She was mid task when she noticed that both Jon and Grace were not in the room any more. She looked about. She couldn't see either of them in the meeting area and neither had said they were leaving or going anywhere. She opened the team calendar – nothing. Where were they?

She got up quietly and slowly, trying very hard not to make any noise, and walked over to the kitchen. What had she come to? Sneaking up on the very people she was supposed to trust. She stood behind one of the large pot plants in the corner, feeling ridiculous, like some evil cartoon character spying. She could just about see them both in the kitchen. Grace was by the counter, leaning against it, slouched slightly as she now cradled a cup of herbal tea, playing with the tag which draped over the side of the cup. Still no coffee, Anna noted.

She couldn't tell if the angle was just unflattering or if Grace was thicker around the middle than before. Jon stood upright, by the fridge. He was sorting the clean cups back into the cupboard while they spoke. Anna didn't see the point if they were just going to use them again but he liked order. He was a man with fixed views on things. Had he really refused to consider a life without children if she could not give him any?

'It's getting really difficult, Jon,' Grace said. 'She knows... something.'

'What makes you say that?'

'Haven't you noticed? She's... prickly. Asking me random questions. I can tell she doesn't trust me. Or like me, if I'm honest.' She sounded hurt.

'I get it, she can be difficult to work with. And with our current situation...'

'I know, you said before I started. You said she found it hard with new people.'

Jon nodded.

Anna baulked. They'd discussed her being *difficult*? Together? She hated being talked about as it was, but by her own husband? Though if all they had been doing was talking then things wouldn't be where they were now.

'When are we going to tell her? We can't keep hiding it. It's going to be obvious soon,' Grace said. She sounded worried. Was she concerned about how things were going to pan out?

Jon moved from the fridge and now the edge of the cupboard obscured Anna's view of him. He reached out for something. Or someone? Was he touching her?

Grace sighed.

'Soon. We'll tell her soon. The plan was never to keep her in the dark forever, after all, just long enough to get things in a place where she would have to get on board with it. I feel like we're nearly there.'

'I know. I just feel like I'm stepping on eggshells sometimes. I don't know what to say to her. I don't want to say the wrong thing.'

Jon nodded. He reached forward again, out of view, closer to Grace. Anna felt sick. She was trying to stay rational, to see only what she was actually seeing, to hear what she was actually hearing, but with Kate's voice in her mind, when Jon went out of her sight, her mind's eye imagined him stroking Grace's hair like he did hers when she was worried. She saw him caressing her shoulders or grazing her cheek with his fingertips. It was torture. What was going on in there?

'She can be closed off at times, that's just her nature. Not like you. You're an open book.' He laughed. Anna felt it in her stomach. She knew that laugh.

'Open to mistakes?'

'You think this is a mistake?' Now Jon sounded hurt.

'No, no, I don't think so. Not really. I just don't like the secrecy about it.'

'I agree. I believe in instincts. And my instinct says we should do this, we should go for it. See what happens.'

'I'm not sure Anna would agree. It's not her baby, after all.'

Anna turned away. She swallowed hard to stop herself from vomiting. *Not my baby*. Had Grace already told Jon about the pill? Or was she holding that in her hand in case she needed it? She was offering Jon what he'd always wanted; of course he was going to take it.

'She'll come round when she sees how it could work for everyone. Don't worry, my darling.'

'You seem so sure.' Grace's voice wavered. 'I don't want her to hate me.'

Oh, I already do, darling, Anna sneered in her own mind.

'No one could hate you, Grace. Don't worry about that. You're brilliant.'

Grace chuckled. Was she embarrassed or was she flirting?

Anna couldn't take any more. She moved from out behind the plant and called out, loudly.

'Where's everyone gone? Are you still here?' She walked into the kitchen. Did the two of them jump apart? Or did she imagine it? Anna was too wound up to know.

Grace looked white, as if she had been caught out. And then her paleness was replaced almost immediately by blush, her face and chest peppering with pink. She was looking at the floor but had her hands protectively over her stomach. Jon tightened his jaw like he always did when he'd been caught out. They were both hiding something.

'What are you doing?' Anna accused.

'Nothing, darling, just chatting while we get some water. Would you like some?'

Darling for her, darling for me. How dare he?

'Thank you, but no.'

She had to get out of here. She was going to lose her composure – either in rage or despair. If she had already lost her husband, she had to make sure she had the upper hand with everything else. If he was going to have a baby with another woman, then she would make sure that their house, this business, would be Anna's. He could not take everything. She would not let him. She had started over once, she could do it again, but this time she would not do it with nothing. She refused.

'I've a meeting to go to but I'll be back, not sure when.'

'Oh, OK,' Jon said, looking confused. 'I didn't see anything in the calendar?'

They usually put all their movements in there. But Jon had clearly omitted where he was or what he was up to on more than one occasion. Anna could do the same. He walked over to her, put his hand on her shoulder and moved to kiss her cheek. Anna flinched. Anna saw Grace notice. A look passed between them. Good. Maybe Grace knew she was on to them. Let her stew.

At that moment, Anna knew what she was going to do. She was going to set them up, set a trap and enjoy watching them walk right into it. She needed a bit more time, a bit more information, and then she would put all she needed in place.

She could play the long game. She had before. She would again.

20

At first, Anna wandered aimlessly around the streets, not wanting to go home. Home was her and Jon, except, was there a 'her and Jon' any more? He was having a baby with someone else. There was no coming back from it. She tried to work out what he had meant when he said 'get on board'. Had he some crazy scheme in his head where the three of them would do this together? Was he thinking that Grace would be a surrogate? Or had he gone Old Testament and thought he could have both of them? Whatever it was, Jon had clearly lost his mind.

She felt that she was losing hers. All the elements of her past that she had thought she had locked away were now running freely through her thoughts. Was she the problem? Had she caused this by being a bad wife? A bad boss? A bad person? She had thought that she had started again after all the pain and loss of her past, but now? Had she just pushed it all down and tried to ignore it, but by not dealing with it had allowed it to fester, to return and to spoil things all over again? She had thought that she'd made a fresh start in her life with Jon, but perhaps by allowing some small element of rot to remain, she had accidently poisoned the whole thing. Maybe it all needed pulling down.

Exhausted, Anna finally went home, her brain fizzing with all the knowns and unknowns, theories and hopes. She had lain on the bed, expecting to think through all the possible plans of action, but had instead fallen into a deep sleep. When she awoke to the sound of a delivery driver dropping off a parcel next door, she had settled on a single yet devastating truth.

Jon had to go too.

She felt this in her soul. They had disconnected. She had allowed this to happen, she had kept him at just enough distance, at just enough emotional separation that he had stepped back. She couldn't have let him stay as close as she wanted and keep the truth that she was keeping from him. Was this all her fault? No. There was withholding a truth from someone and there was walking away into the arms of someone else. Yes, both betrayals, but one was worse than the other, surely? The first was between just the two of them; it was still *theirs*. But to be... *collaborating* with someone else behind her back? That was cruel.

She went into the bathroom and washed her face to try to wake herself up. She was groggy from being awoken mid sleep cycle and from all the missed sleep that lay heavy on her. She splashed cold water on her face and looked up into the mirror. She felt old. She leaned in closer, checking the texture of her skin for the lines that had started to form. They were delicate at first, and she had embraced them as signs of life, of laughter experienced, but now she had started to see them as lines tying her down, keeping her stuck. She was stuck.

At the sound of the front door opening and closing, Anna grabbed a towel, patted her face dry, took a long drink of cool water straight from the tap, something Jon disliked her doing for some reason, and prepared herself to face him. She wanted desperately to go to him, tell him all of her secrets, demand that he tell her all of his so they could be close again, so she could feel known again. Seen and accepted. That was what she had felt like when they first met. She wanted that again. She ached for it.

'Hey, you, are you OK? You didn't come back after your meeting and you didn't answer your phone,' Jon called up the stairs to her as she walked down to meet him. 'I came to check where you were.'

'Yeah, I'm fine. Sorry. What time is it?' Anna asked, aware that she had no idea.

Jon glanced at his watch. 'Just gone four. I was worried.' He sounded annoyed.

'Sorry. I fell asleep.'

'Are you sure you're OK? You're sleeping at odd times at the moment.'

'I'm fine.'

'Are you? You're sleeping badly at night. I've woken up a few times and you've not been there. Or you are but you're looking out of the window. Something's bothering you. Isn't it?'

She said nothing.

He walked to the foot of the stairs and held out a hand to her.

'I know what it is. I think we need to talk, don't you?'

She was stunned. Was he going to tell her the truth? She swallowed. She wasn't sure she was ready for this. Not yet. While she was still gathering solid proof, she could let a tiny part of her hope, a small part believe that everything could still be alright, even as the main part of her told her that this section of her life was over. If he told her the truth then that illusion would shatter, as would the remains of her heart. Maybe it was better to live in denial.

'OK,' was all she could manage.

'I'll put the kettle on. Do you want usual or a decaf?'

'Just some mint tea would be great, thanks.' She felt sick. Maybe the tea would help.

'Righto.'

How could he be so flippant? Wasn't he about to destroy everything?

She sat at the dining table. An odd place for a cup of tea for husband and wife, but she felt that the formality of the conversation they were about to have required it. You couldn't discuss a separation on the sofa. It didn't hold you up straight enough as your world collapsed.

'Here you go,' Jon said, sitting down opposite her.

Once side by side, now opposite sides of the same dream. She felt her resolve waver, her hand start to shake. She wasn't ready.

'OK,' Jon started, sounding for everything as if he was starting an online business meeting. 'We need to talk. It's about, it's about the baby.'

Anna threw up a little in her mouth and grabbed at her tea to wash it back down.

'What baby?' Anna asked, the last of her hope dying, like the last petals to fall from a summer flower. She needed to find her strength again, her rage even, if she were to survive this conversation.

'Our baby. Or rather our trying for one.' He reached out across the table and gently took her hands in his. He looked up at her, earnest, his eyes shimmering. 'I think we should stop trying.'

'...What?' Her voice croaked, as though swallowing her own words.

'I think we should stop trying. It's been a strain – on both of us. You know it has. We stopped talking about it and then we just stopped talking. Didn't we? I know I did. I didn't want to make you feel any worse than you did, than I did. You focused on work; I focused on the church, and we forgot what should have been the focus. Us.'

Anna looked at the table, took her hands back and picked up her tea. She sipped at it while she tried to work out her thoughts. How to respond. What was he trying to do here?

'I miss you,' he said, leaning towards her across the table.

What?

Anna closed her eyes. This didn't make sense. Was he playing with her? Did he know about her still being on the pill? Was he messing with her as some sort of revenge? Or something else? She thought back to the scan and the quote. God's grace was given freely, undeserving or not, wasn't it? Was *that* what the message had been? That they could have a baby, regardless of her unworthiness? Her lies? Was he giving her a way out here? A start-over?

But... If he had wanted a baby with *her*, then what was the situation with Grace? None of this made sense. Where did she come into this? If *Jon* had been the one to send the scan, then he was also in the wrong. To know about the pill, he must have snooped on his own wife, looked for things deliberately hidden, followed her, listened to messages. None of these were honourable behaviours, she knew that all too well. And then, emotional blackmailing by post? No. Whatever he was doing here, it was not in her best interests. Something did not add up.

She decided to play along, to see what else he would say.

She chewed her lip. 'You really think we should stop trying? What about having a baby? Isn't that what you've' – she corrected herself – 'what *we've* always wanted? A family?'

'We are a family. You and me. We found each other at a difficult time in our lives. We see that in each other in a way no one else really can if they've not also experienced it. That loss. But the more I think about loss, the more I think maybe we should focus on what do have, rather than what we don't.'

She put down her tea and reached for his hands, as he had done hers. 'You really mean it?'

'I do mean it. It's too much pressure. We need to be kinder to ourselves, don't you think?' He paused, looked down, carefully considering his words. 'Besides, there's more than just one way to have a family, more than one way to bring a baby into it...'

She froze.

Oh dear God.

He was being cautious. *Now* he was being cautious. Two babies at the same time from different women wasn't a good look for a church man. He'd been hedging his bets, spreading his chances along with his DNA. He wanted them to stop trying so that there was only *one* baby. The scan baby. Grace's. He didn't want there to be a chance of getting a strike twice at the same time.

How could she be so blind? She had thought he was looking out for her, giving her a way out. He was looking out for himself!

Or, and she couldn't work out if this was worse or not, he had some bizarre plan about bringing the baby into their family of two? Would he bring Grace too? Had he gone mad? Did he really think that the four of them could muddle along somehow? Him, his wife, his twenty-two-year-old lover and their baby? It was insane, He had literally lost his mind.

'Darling, are you OK?' he asked.

Was she? She didn't know. This was spiralling. What had started as a white lie, albeit a big one about trying for a baby, or rather not trying, had snowballed into lies every which way from everyone. No one was telling the whole truth to anyone.

'I am, I am, yes. It's just a lot to take in. It's a big decision.'

'I know. We'll need to take some time. Let it all sink in. Let the idea of a new future, a different future, take shape. We can work on the business and see where that goes.'

She had to ask.

'What about Grace?'

'What about her?' he asked, looking confused.

'Is she part of this... plan?' She tried to keep the bite from her tone. She did not quite manage it.

He sighed. 'This again. Look, I know you're not keen on her, on having anyone around, but she's great. You know she is. She's one of us now. We can't just get rid of her, it wouldn't be right. We have a duty of care towards her, and I will not dismiss that without good reason.'

Like a baby?

She was more convinced than ever now that Jon was cheating on her with Grace. That the scan was real. The baby existed.

'OK.'

'OK?'

'Yes.'

'Great, that's my girl,' he said, and she shuddered. Girl? Was that what he said to Grace? In Jon's head were they interchangeable? Just baby providers? What had happened to the husband she knew and loved? Where had he gone?

Anna could not find any words, so she simply smiled.

Jon smiled back at her. He was clueless.

There was too much history, too much emotion, too much love and too much damage between her and Jon to be able to look him in in the eye and ask for the truth. She could feel her hard-won strength crumbling as her life did the same around her.

Despite all this, she loved him. That made it too hard. Whereas Grace – Anna did not know her and could focus her anger on her more easily. It is always the way, isn't it? The other woman gets the brunt of the fury, despite it being at best half her fault. Anna would go to Grace and *make* her tell Anna the truth. Grace wasn't stupid, no, but she was young, and Anna had practice of pushing back against those who wronged her and surviving.

Grace had no chance.

21

The church was one of those modern buildings, unfamiliar to Anna, with its sharply sloping roof and colourful modernist stained windows, which filled the wooden-clad interior with a rainbow of light. The effect made her feel like she was in a sauna, a disco, or some strange combination of both. She sat at the back, tucked away in a corner where she hoped no one would notice her. She was there to observe, not to be observed. She wanted to see Grace in a situation that was home to her. Watch her being herself, so Anna maybe understood her better. She needed that before any confrontation. She didn't want to get caught off-guard in any way. She couldn't exactly park up outside Grace's house and stake her out there, partly because she didn't trust herself not to hammer on the door flinging accusations. So, her church was the next best thing. Somewhere she felt comfortable. Somewhere that hopefully, a stranger wouldn't necessarily stand out. Somewhere that people could just be. This church was a sister one to her own, but the congregation, including Grace, sometimes went to either or both. Anna had to hope no one recognised her. She'd had to wait several days for this and her nerves were in a frenzied state.

Tucking herself away at the back next to a pillar, and pulling her giant scarf around her neck and her hat down over her brow, Anna observed the scene. She was happy that at this church, people dressed for Sunday service – her hat was not out of place; her flamboyant outfit, chosen for its ability to hide her face, was not out of place either.

She watched as people filed in, a mix of people in age and demeanour. Some quieter, here likely just to worship and go home. Some who were clearly significant members of the congregation, welcoming friends and family, catching up on the news, asking after relatives and asking how they were. She noticed when Grace's mother arrived, and quickly turned her face away, in case she recognised her from that day at the shopping centre. Then, after her, Grace.

She was there with friends. They were giggling and joking around, their peals of laughter echoing off the walls and ceiling of a building designed for its acoustic tendencies. It made Anna feel like she was being mocked. What were they laughing about? Grace's naïve boss who didn't know her intern was sleeping with her husband? No. Surely Grace wouldn't be sharing that information with her good Christian friends. She might have told one or two particularly close ones but Anna did not think an out-of-wedlock pregnancy to a married man was something that Grace would want to be laughing about, and in church at that. No, she was just having a fun Sunday morning with her friends, carefree.

Anna's jaw hurt from clenching her teeth so hard. She was already a night-time stress grinder – her dentist would not be pleased to know that she was doing it when conscious too – but rage was coursing through her; how Grace got to have her life whilst she destroyed Anna's.

'Tsk.' The woman in front of Anna made a disapproving noise, pulling her jacket collar straight around her shoulders.

'I know,' said her companion. 'I like that youngsters come along. I like that they're having a nice time, but really?' The woman in front agreed with her. 'All that cackling. It's a bit disrespectful, isn't it? I like Grace and her friends, but this new relationship... it's, well, not for *here,* really, is it?'

Anna's ears pricked up at the sound of Grace's name. She edged forward. Church people, well-meaning or not, could always be relied on to know the ins and outs of people's lives. There was a very fine line, after all, between caring and nosiness, between keeping an eye on someone and pushing your nose in where it didn't belong. Either way, Anna wanted to hear what these ladies were saying. She turned her head, as though reading the order of service, but tilted one ear towards the conversation. Which relationship were they talking about? Surely not Grace and *Jon?* Did *everyone* but her know about the baby?

'I know what you mean. Her family are wonderful. Lovely family...'

'Absolutely. Wonderful family.'

'Yes. I couldn't agree more.'

Oh, enough with the niceties. Stop pretending you're not gossiping and get on with it! Anna had no patience for those who trussed up their gossiping in more respectable terms before going ahead and blabbering anyway.

'Absolutely. But still. This is a place of worship, of divine contemplation, and it's difficult to do that when there's all this flirting going on!'

'Save it for the tea and coffee afterwards if you ask me.'

'Absolutely. Not all this laughing and touching, right in front *of the altar*. It's not appropriate.'

What flirting? Anna took a chance and lifted her head,

straining her neck in the direction of the sound of the laughter that these women were taking exception to. There was Grace, stood next to a young man of about her own age. He was smartly dressed, almost as though his mother had chosen his *good* outfit for church. Maybe she had. Grace was smiling widely as he said something to her that then made her throw her head back in laughter, as loud as before, and reach out her arm and drape it over him, whereupon he kissed her on the top of her head, wrapping his arm around her waist. Anna felt sick. She had three immediate and conflicting thoughts.

Firstly, what was Grace doing? Was she cheating on Jon? Or cheating on this boy *with* Jon?

Secondly, how dare she do that to Jon? Which, Anna immediately recognised as a bizarre reaction, although she took a moment to realise that it meant she still felt like her husband was on her side. A betrayal of him was a betrayal of her too.

Thirdly – if Grace was in a serious physical relationship with this boy, then how could she prove that Jon was the father? She couldn't, could she? She couldn't possibly know. Was this boy a cover for the situation she and Jon had got into? Was Jon a cover for this boy? Was she playing both of them? This boy and Jon? Was she using one against the other to get the best solution for herself? Was she trying to tie down someone with better financial means? Just how manipulative could one person be?

'Still,' the women continued, 'it is a nice thing though, after all the upheaval. Don't you think?'

'Upheaval?'

The first woman shifted a bit on the pew, perhaps realising she'd said too much, shared too much information, that she was either not supposed to or not meant to have even known in the first place.

Anna leaned forward again, this time flicking through the

hymn book, pretending to look for the pages for the service's chosen hymns.

'Well. Yes. You know.'

'Do I? I don't think I do. How do you know?'

'I'm sure Liane's mentioned it. You know. How Grace has had a few... difficulties of late. A few things that she's coming to terms with. You know, *family* things.' She practically whispered this last bit of information, as though it were something not to be spoken of.

Anna's stomach contracted hard.

'...Family things?' The other woman sounded scandalised.

The first woman looked around her, checking to see who was there. She turned and looked at Anna, but not knowing her, she only registered her, nodded a polite hello and kept on scanning the room before returning to her conversation.

Ice was creeping all around Anna's body. What *family things* did they mean? Was it common knowledge that Grace was pregnant? Surely not. But if she didn't mean that, then what did she mean? Was Grace having problems at home? Was she looking for a way out? From what Anna knew, her family was kind, supportive, loving. But who knew what went on behind closed doors? Anna's own family were outwardly respectable, seen as pillars of their community, but at home they had been cold, regimented, inflexible. Anna knew that it was entirely possible for people to talk so kindly about your own family, not truly recognising the people they described. The parents Anna knew and the people her church community thought they knew were strangers to each other.

'Yes... There have been some developments with the family, and I understand that Grace has been affected by them. Liane, her mother, said that she's finding it all very difficult and that her behaviour at home has been less than ideal. She's trying to be strong for her, you know, as you would be...'

'Of course.'

'But it's hard. Liane is dealing with the fall out. And it's challenging her. Her faith.'

'Her faith? Really? You surprise me.'

'Everyone has their own personal desert to go through. We don't know when it will come nor how we will cope when it does.'

'That's why we have our church community, our faith family. Mm-hmm.'

Anna had not found her old church family to be any more supportive than her own family, but she tried to push that thought away. It wasn't relevant.

'True.'

'So I suppose the fact that Grace is here is a good thing. Liane is here too. Perhaps we should be a little more understanding of Grace right now.'

At this, there was another cackle from Grace's group and Anna turned to look again. Grace didn't look troubled. She was stroking the arm of the boy. There was definitely something going on between them. How did this change things? *Did* it change things? Was this what her mum and Grace were arguing about? Was it about Jon? Was it about a baby, *the* baby?

There were too many scenarios here. None of it made sense, none of it was the standalone obvious truth.

What Anna knew was this: there had been a scan posted. There was a connection with Grace. Grace was not as innocent as she had first made Anna think, or as Anna had assumed. Twenty-two wasn't fifteen, after all. She was an adult, albeit potentially an emotionally immature one, sheltered by her family. People were multitudes. It wasn't sinner vs saint, Madonna vs whore, guilty vs innocent. People could be both.

* * *

The service started and Anna took the opportunity of the first hymn, when everyone would be standing and singing, shielding Grace from seeing or hearing the back door open and close – to leave. She could hear the wonderful sound of all those voices singing together in praise as she walked away from the church, and she tried to feel the joy in it, to stop the dread that was churning inside her.

Anna walked around the corner, and she waited. She tried to look casual, sitting on the hard brick wall there, but her legs went numb and she stood up, stamping her feet to try to get the feeling back in them, when she saw Grace and her family and the boy coming round the corner.

She got her phone out, pretending to be looking through the news, when Grace approached.

'Anna? What are you doing here?' she said, dropping the arm of the boy and gesturing to him and her family to go on without her. She didn't look pleased to see Anna.

'We can all wait for you, love,' Liane said, looking tensely at Anna. She nodded a hello but was not exactly effusive in her greeting. Anna nodded back.

'No, it's fine, honestly, I'll catch you up. You go ahead.'

Her mother looked tense but agreed, walking slowly away with her husband, Grace's siblings and the boy, clearly not wanting to leave Grace there with her. Did Liane know why Anna had good reason to be furious with her daughter? Enough to make a scene in the street, right outside their church? Was Grace close enough with her mother to tell her everything, good and bad? Anna envied her that if it was the case.

'Hi,' Anna said, her voice high and unnatural. She swallowed, trying to hide the shake in her hands, putting them both around her phone. This was harder than she thought it would be. 'I'm just waiting for a... friend to pick me up.' She waved the phone about. 'She's late, as always!'

'I'd thought you'd be at your own church. Why are you here? You checking up on me?'

Anna waited for Grace to laugh this last comment off as a joke. She didn't.

'I went to a service yesterday,' Anna lied. She hadn't thought this through properly. Grace was suspicious. She had got Anna's intentions spot on. Anna needed a reason and fast.

'My friend's having... a difficult time at the moment so I want to be there for her,' Anna said, surprised at where all these lies were coming from. They were spilling out of her mouth like air. Did Jon find it as easy to lie too? Did Grace?

'Oh, that's kind of you,' Grace said flatly. 'You're a good friend.'

'Good friends don't let each other make bad choices.'

Grace looked confused. 'I guess not. No.'

'Do you have a good friend, Grace?'

If Grace was Anna's friend in this situation, Anna would be there to listen to her, to advise her and to tell her to get out before she got hurt. But Grace was not her friend. Grace was potentially the person who was blackmailing her, who was trying to break her family. Or she had already betrayed her, taking away the only solid thing in her life, Jon, and trying to take him for herself. Her heart hardened.

'I... yes.'

'Good. You should talk to them.'

'Um, OK? Anna, are you alright? You seem...'

'What?'

'Just, not well. You don't seem well.'

'I'm fine.'

Grace started to get out her phone. 'Look, let me call Jon for you.'

'I don't need you to call *my husband* for me, Grace.'

Grace looked annoyed. 'Anna, you're not making a lot of sense. I'm worried about you. Let me help you.'

'That matters, doesn't it? Looking after people? Kindness? Do unto others as we would do to ourselves? Or to the Lord?' A brief moment of guilt for the lies she had told Jon flickered into Anna's consciousness before she pushed it away with her anger.

'It does. Yes. Look, are you sure I can't call him for you?' Grace was talking to her as if she was a child. Anna didn't like it. She had to make sure Jon didn't hear of this. She was in enough trouble with him as it was. Though, really, wasn't it him who was in trouble?

'Sure. Like I said, I'm meeting my friend. Truly. I'm OK.'

'If you're really sure.' Grace didn't look sure.

'I am. You can go.'

Grace glanced up at the road, at her disappearing family. 'I should. Mum has invited Nathan to Sunday dinner today.' She blushed. 'He'll think I've left him.'

'For another man?' Anna asked archly.

'What?' Grace said, taken aback.

'Nothing!' Anna laughed. She felt like she was losing her mind.

'Right...' Grace's tone became guarded. 'Look. I'm going to go, I should catch up with my family. I'll see you tomorrow at the office?'

'Of course. Where else would I be?'

'Ok then... Bye,' Grace said, looking wholly unsure about what had just happened.

Anna waited until Grace had walked to the end of the road and then she turned left, out of sight.

Left.

Anna knew from checking her address on her contract that Grace's house was to the right from here. Where was she going?

Anna hurried down the street after her. She knew she must look insane, but she didn't care. She was going to catch her out. She *was*.

As Anna neared the corner, she hung back, tipping her head to see round the curve in the road. Grace was talking on her phone, oblivious to her surroundings. Anna crept after her, trying to look normal, feeling anything but. As they walked down various roads, it became clear to Anna where Grace was going. To the office.

Anna continued to follow her until Grace arrived at their office and knocked on the door. Jon opened it and immediately ushered her inside, closing the door behind them. Anna felt like she'd had the wind knocked out of her. Grace had said she was going home; Jon had told her that he was going to be at church this morning.

Both of them had lied to her.

Raging, she stormed across the road from where she had been following at a distance, right up to the front of the office, ready to swing the door open and catch them in the act of whatever they were doing, give them both hell. But at the door, she hesitated. She needed to see with her own eyes, but she also didn't want to. She reached for the door, but the handle held firm. They'd locked the door behind them.

She looked in her bag for her keys – they weren't there. Frantic, Anna had to hold herself back from banging on the door, demanding to be let in. No, she had to be strategic about this. She had to be clever. She needed the upper hand here, though in all honesty she had no idea what she would do with it. She had already lost.

Stalking the building perimeter, Anna found a window and, tucking herself close to the wall, she peeked into the office. She couldn't see them. She tried further round at another window, and there they were. Grace was sat on the edge of the desk, looking serious. Jon was standing, listening to her talk, nodding. His face was ashen.

He knows I'm on to them.

Then it happened. Grace stood up, Jon leaned forward and put his arms around her. She looked upset. Had Jon just called things off?

Anna strained to hear through the window, putting her ear as close as she could manage without being seen.

'I can't do this,' Anna heard Grace say.

Was *she* the one calling things off?

'Oh, Grace. I'm so sorry. I... We're so close to being able to tell her. It will be OK then, I promise.'

'I'm not so sure. We've lied to her. She won't take that well.'

'She'll come round. I know it.'

Grace sighed.

'Just give it one more week, OK?'

'Fine. One more week. Then we tell her. Promise?'

'I promise.'

Anna stepped back, pushing her back flat against the outside wall. She needed to feel its solidity as her knees were giving way. She needed something, anything to keep her upright.

She had seen enough.

They thought they had a week.

Anna would not give them that.

'Are you sure? You're absolutely sure?' Kate asked.

'As sure as I can be. I *saw* them. I heard them talking about telling me. About lying to me. They're *lying* to me.'

'OK. OK.' Kate nodded calmly, handing Anna a large glass of white wine which she took and gulped down. 'Woah, slow down, sweetie. That's not going to help!'

'What will? My husband is lying to me, colluding with Grace, and there's going to be a baby. And her poor boyfriend. He can't know about all this either. They're messing with everyone. It's not fair.' Anna took another large gulp of wine and sat back in her chair, tucking her legs up. She let the warmth of the wine work its way down, hoping it would relax her. She was so taut, her jaw hurt. Her hands were sore from clenching. There was a tight knot in her stomach. She felt as though the fibres of her body were tearing apart. She was overly stretched, and nothing could keep her together.

'I wanted to... I wanted to kick down the door and I... I wanted to yell and scream and... I didn't know what to do. I still don't.'

Anna held her hand out in front of her; it was shaking. She wrapped it round the wine glass and took another long sip.

'You need to talk with him.'

Anna nodded. 'What about *her*?'

'Right now, she has nothing to do with you. He is your husband, and he is the one who has broken his wedding vows. He is the one who has betrayed you. He is the one who needs to start to fix this.'

Anna took a shaky breath. 'I don't think he can. Fix this, I mean. Fix us. How can he if he's having a baby with someone else?'

Kate nodded grimly. 'Are you absolutely sure?'

'You don't believe me?' Anna roared. 'I *saw* them. They hugged. They talked about lying to me. I am completely sure.'

'I do believe you. You know I do. It's just so out of character for him, though those rumours... Have you and Jon talked any more about the stopping trying thing? I mean, that's huge from him, right? That's all he's ever wanted in life. To be a good man and a good father. That's his whole point of being, and for him to just... stop trying? It doesn't fit.'

Anna wasn't sure how much she liked Kate assuming that she knew Anna's husband as well as Anna did. Kate had known him far longer, that was true. Recently, there had been times when Anna couldn't say with absolute certainty that Kate didn't still hold a candle for Jon, but then, she'd be back to platonic in the blink of an eye and Anna would convince herself she was being unreasonable. She drank again, the alcohol stinging her lips where she had bitten them through nerves. The pain buzzed into her mind where it fought with her now woozy brain.

'But that's why I'm sure. Because the not wanting to try any more doesn't fit. But if he already has a baby on the way then it *does*.'

'Unless...'

'Unless what?'

'Unless he knows about your being on the pill?'

'How would he? Did you tell him?'

'No!' Kate said, holding up her hands in defence. 'That's not my business. It's between you and him. I wouldn't do that to you. You have your reasons, whatever they are.'

Anna crushed her anger down. Kate was not the enemy here. If Jon and Grace were an item, then without Kate on her side, she was utterly alone. She did not need to be dismissing allies on a mere paranoia. Kate had never given her any solid reason to really believe that she was after Jon, interested in Jon, that she was in any way out to oust Anna from her position as wife, that she'd take his side over hers. Unlike Grace, who had apparently moved into their business, and from there, almost immediately or even beforehand, into Jon's arms. And his bed. Their bed? Anna sat forward and retched, her whole body reacting to the mere thought.

'Shit. Anna, are you OK?' Kate slammed her own glass down too fast, slopping wine over the side, spilling it onto the glass tabletop.

Anna sat up, straight backed, and swallowed. She nodded, being cautious not to open her mouth until the feeling passed, breathing in deeply through her nose.

'Let me go get you some water,' Kate said, pushing herself up and heading out to her kitchen. Anna heard sounds of the cupboard and refrigerator being opened and closed and Kate returned with two glasses of chilled water, beads of condensation already rolling down the sides. She placed one onto a coaster and passed the other to Anna.

Anna took it and downed the water, letting the cool feeling settle the urge to vomit.

'Better?' Kate asked, having sipped her own water.

The nausea passed and Anna placed her glass down onto the table and sat back, closing her eyes briefly. The room started to spin. She opened her eyes again.

'Yes, thanks. Everything is just too much at the moment. I'm not looking after myself properly. I need to.'

'You do. I can't imagine what this feels like. I'm sorry.'

Anna's heart dropped. She felt the burn of tears again at the back of her throat.

No. She wouldn't shed them.

She was done crying for what people had done to her.

'I can't make everything make sense otherwise. You know? The scan. The quote with the scan. How they are in the office together, always whispering in corners. The messages I saw. The conversation yesterday. How Grace is with me, like she's got a hidden agenda. Jon suddenly no longer wanting the one thing he's always wanted.'

Kate leaned forward, eyes wide with anticipation as to what Anna would say next. Was she *enjoying* this?

'I could throttle him for you.' Kate was getting angry.

Anna felt relieved. No, Kate wasn't enjoying this, she was getting furious on her behalf, angry with those who were treating her badly, as if she didn't matter, like she was a vessel to be discarded when no baby had been forthcoming. Kate was on her side. She hated that there *were* sides, but if that was how things had to be, she was glad to have someone in her corner.

'But then what about the boy?' Anna said, asking both Kate and herself. 'At church this morning. Nathan? I assumed he was Grace's boyfriend. She was flirting and laughing and... and he was going to her family for Sunday lunch. But then she went to Jon...'

'Maybe he's just a friend? Or a decoy?'

'A what now?'

'A decoy. You know, the nice polite boy you take home to meet your parents, to throw them off the scent of the guy you're actually seeing? Maybe he's her gay best friend? Maybe she's *his* decoy? Who knows? Just because you've seen them laughing together, doesn't mean they're a couple. If they're a couple and he is the father of this baby, then why would she even bring you and Jon into it? I think he's a red herring.'

'How can you be so flippant?'

'Sorry. I didn't think I was.'

'I... Sorry.'

'It's OK. I didn't mean to be if I was. Just, I don't think that this Nathan has anything to do with anything. He's the bit that doesn't make sense while the rest all paints a picture. Don't you think? You know, like he's a bit of a jigsaw that's made it into the wrong box and doesn't fit with the rest of the pieces.'

As miserable as this made her, Anna couldn't find any reason, any element of what Kate was saying, that didn't resonate with her. She took a moment, pressing into the web of skin between her thumb and forefinger, pushing hard until it hurt. When that pain wasn't enough, she shifted until she was pinching it with the nails of her other hand. It didn't work – nothing stopped the pain at her centre as the realisation that the life she had, the life that, despite its flaws and difficulties, she had loved, was about to be over.

'So... What do I do? My marriage is over? We share everything – a house, a business, a life. Everything. There's no escape here.' Anna's voice cracked as despair inched its way into her, seeping through her pores, joining with the rage that was simmering, waiting to be unleashed. She leaned forward, desperate for someone to tell her what to do, what to say, where to go from here. Her life was so intertwined with Jon's that to lose him would be to lose everything – her husband, her house, her business and her best friend. All in one fell swoop.

The business and the home were in both their names, but they'd have to split them, wouldn't they? Or could one take one and the other have the remainder? Which would she take? She could feel her world wobbling, as though she was a on a boat and someone had just untied the mooring rope and pushed her out to sea with no engine, no rudder, no oars. She was floating, directionless, waiting for a storm to sweep in and capsize her, sending her down.

'Do you want my advice?' Kate asked.

Anna wrinkled her nose in confusion. Of course she did – that was why she'd called her in a panic after seeing Grace. She nodded. 'Are you going to tell me to stick with him? In sickness and in health, in bad times and in good, till death do us part etc?'

Anna wanted Kate to say yes. She wanted Kate to tell her that it would be OK to forgive Jon, to forgive Grace and somehow find a way to move forward. But did Jon even want that? If he'd found a woman to give him a baby, wouldn't he want to keep her? Would she fight him on it? How could she?

'Pssht, no! He promised to forsake all others, didn't he? He broke the vows first. What happened to "let no man put asunder"? No. I am not going to tell you to stick with him. How could you? With a baby on the way. What, the three of you are going to live together in a weird, Old Testament multi-wife scenario? No. I think you should confront them, both of them, and ask them what the hell they think they're playing at. That's what I would do. Invite her over, sit them down and ask them to explain themselves. Get everything out in the open. That's the only way to know what the hell is actually going on, and once you know that, only then can you work out what to do about it from here. Information is power after all, right?'

Kate downed the last of her drink.

Anna did the same, despite the acidity biting into her throat and burning all the way down. She needed courage, she needed strength. Kate was right. She would get them all together and demand to be told the truth. At the very least they owed her that. And she would make them give it to her.

'You're right! They've treated me like I'm nothing, and I'm not. I'm *not* nothing!'

She had felt for years that she was, but eventually she had seen her own worth. Ironically, it had been Jon who had helped her see that and now it was Jon who would have to cope with the results of his hard work. She would *not* be treated like this. She wouldn't have it.

'Atta girl. Like I said, I love Jon, but this is too much. I'm furious with him and I'm absolutely Team Anna here. Jon needs to explain himself.'

'Yeah. He should.'

'They both should. This is a joint effort, after all. She's not a child.'

'Exactly.'

'Make them admit what they've done and explain themselves. Watch as they try to somehow justify this sordid situation.'

'That's it! Sordid. I...' Anna felt the flicker of something in her gut, but she pushed it away. No one was perfect, no, but this was a low. Kate was right. Jon and Grace owed her this. And she would make them pay it.

23

When Anna turned the key in the lock to her home, she could feel that she was wobbly on her feet. That wine had gone straight to her head and she needed a large glass of water and to sit down somewhere quiet for a bit. Maybe try to eat something. She tried to think back as to whether she'd had breakfast, but she couldn't remember. She'd been so intent on getting to see Grace, she'd just felt sick from the moment she got up and it hadn't abated during the day.

'Hello?' she called out nervously. Part of her wanted to have the house to herself, to be able to think, to work out what her next move should be without having to face Jon, but she also felt her stomach drop when she realised Jon wasn't there. She would have to get used to coming home to an empty house. To a life without him.

She walked through into the kitchen and ran the tap until the water was cold. She placed her fingers underneath the stream to check the temperature, and the memory of Jon caring for her when she'd burnt her hands came to her mind. The floodgates opened and with it came memory after memory of good times she and Jon had had together. The difficulties they had faced together. The life they had built, the ambitions they had shared. Anna felt herself get hot with rage. Grace had ruined everything. She had waltzed into their world, and she had torn it to pieces.

Anna looked at her pale, shaking hand under the water and something snapped. She picked up the glass that she had been planning to drink from and threw it with force into the sink where it shattered with satisfying destruction. It felt good. She flipped her head from side to side, looking for what she could tear apart next – something, anything to dissipate this anger that was coursing through her. This picture-perfect room with all its matching colours was a sham, a lie, like everything else in this house. She pulled all the tea towels from the rail onto the floor, spilled the contents of the fruit bowl over the countertop where they rolled and fell, bouncing as they came to rest all over the place.

She continued through the house, through the hallway, knocking pictures off walls and enjoying listening to the glass smash as they landed. *Let it all go to hell,* she thought. Passing through into the living room, she stopped. She was face to face with a photo from her wedding day, in a heavy pewter frame that had been a gift from Jon's parents. It had represented family to her, support, a network. A life. Now? She was back to being alone, like she had always been, only perhaps this time, even lonelier for having experienced not being so. She reached her hand out to smash the picture but stopped just before she did so. No. It was Grace who had done this. Grace who had spoiled everything.

Reaching into her pocket, she pulled out her phone and dialled. Her brain had switched off and she didn't know if she could bring herself to care. She was just feeling now; no logic was available to her. She was feeling her way through the darkness of fury.

'Anna?' Grace sounded surprised to hear from her.

Anna couldn't speak. She was incandescent with rage.

'Anna? Are you OK?'

Still nothing – Anna was trembling, a volcano about to erupt.

'Is anyone with you? Anna? Talk to me.'

Anna was taking deep breaths. She wanted to speak but she couldn't.

'Anna? Talk to me. Is anyone else there? Are you safe?'

Why is she talking to me like that? Does she think I'm some sort of incapable idiot? What does she think I'm going to do?

'You...' Anna managed to say. 'You... you whore.' Anna was shocked at the words that fell from her mouth. She had opened the floodgates. 'You scheming, cheating whore. You home-wrecking, selfish little bitch. You... should be ashamed. Shameful, that's what you are. You ruined *everything* and you *don't care!*'

Anna's whole body was convulsing, as though she was possessed. She felt demonic. She was shocked by opening her mouth and hearing her own mother come out. Words that Anna had never said but had heard many times before. Words that had been flung at Anna to deliberately hurt her, now being used by her to hurt someone else.

'I...' Grace said in shock before bursting into tears.

'You... you know. You know where this is coming from. You *know* what I'm talking about. You and Jon. The sneaking, the hiding, the *lies*. He's *my* husband and that meant *nothing* to you. Nothing! You waltzed in and destroyed it all. Everything. You've destroyed everything!'

Anna could hear Grace sobbing on the end of the line. Good. She had to know what she had done, what damage she had caused. She should have to feel some of the pain, some of the horror, some of the despair that she had inflicted on Anna through her selfish, wanton behaviour. It was always the same, allegedly God-fearing people hiding their shitty behaviour behind their faith. Claiming to be devout and then behaving in a way that was anything but. She'd seen this before; she'd grown up with it and she was utterly sick of the hypocrisy.

'What do you have to say for yourself? Huh? Nothing?' Anna yelled.

'Anna,' Grace said finally, her voice shaking as she tried to regain some composure. 'Anna, I don't know what you're talking about. I don't know what you mean.'

'I mean you and Jon, sneaking around behind my back. Lying. Secret meetings. All of it.'

'It's... You need to talk to Jon.' Grace's voice firmed as she found her composure.

'No. I want to hear it from *you*. I'm talking to you! You are the one who took my husband away from me. You are the one who is having his baby, you are the harlot who thought it a good idea to post your baby scan to me. You are the hussy who didn't have the decency to tell me to my face. You, Grace. You. If you can't handle these truths, then perhaps you should have kept your legs closed!'

Anna gasped for breath. Who was this woman who was raging at Grace? This was not her; she did not talk like that. She had rejected the idea of ever talking like that when she had left her childhood home. She did not speak of harlots and heathens and decency, nor did she accuse women of all the sin that men shared. Jon had his part in this, so why was Anna throwing all of her hurt of the betrayal at Grace? She had tried so hard to escape the cycle that her family had set for her, and yet here she was, finding her parents' words in her mouth, their thoughts in her brain. She was reacting, falling back on the only imprint that she had, that had been passed to her by them.

Grace was silent on the other end of the phone, apart from the sound of shaky breathing and the phone rattling against her earring, perhaps being held in trembling hands.

Anna pushed back against the wall and slowly slid to the floor, her rage spent, her energy drained. She slumped against the side table and closed her eyes. Everything was ruined. Everything was spoiled. Her mother had been right – she was worth nothing and would come to nothing. Everything she had tried hard to build was crumbling through her fingers. The room was silent, other than the now oppressive tick of the clock, marking each second of the wasteland that was Anna's life.

Suddenly she was aware of there being a voice in her ear, another voice on the line that wasn't Grace.

'Hello?'

'Hello,' Anna said, confused as to who it was.

'This is Liane. Grace's mother. Who is this? Is this Anna?'

'Yes.'

'I think you and I need to have a talk. Now.' Her voice was stern.

'Really? Isn't Grace old enough to speak for herself?' Anna's voice dripped with disdain.

Who was she? Why was she being like this? Anna knew from experience that mother and child weren't one and the same.

'Really. I understand why you're so upset but you can't behave like this. Is Jon there? Can I speak with him?'

'No. And I don't need him to speak for me either.'

'That's not my intention. We all need to talk together. And urgently.'

'About the baby?'

Liane inhaled, as though she was trying to keep calm, be patient, measured. 'Sort of.'

'I don't want to hear it.'

'I think you need to. You have to,' Liane insisted. She was

clearly protective of both her daughter and her grandchild. No matter how they had come to find themselves in this situation, it was clear that it wasn't going away.

'Fine. Grace knows where we live. I'm not going anywhere.' Anna could hear the petulance in her voice but could not stop it.

'We're on our way. I suggest you call Jon to be with you.'

And with that, Liane hung up.

Anna closed her eyes as she sat on the floor, her bottom going numb from the slight chill in the floor. How on earth had everything gone so wrong?

She didn't know how long she sat there, but soon the sky was darkening, so it must be early evening. There was a sound of a car pulling up outside and headlights reflected in the windows at the front of the house. Anna knew that she ought to move and yet found that she could not bring herself to do so. She had no energy, nor incentive. She just wanted to cease.

The front door opened and closed.

'Anna?' Jon called out as he switched the light on in the hallway. He gasped. He must have seen all the broken picture frames that scattered the floor. 'Anna?' he called again, this time with worry in his voice. 'Anna, are you home?'

He quickened his pace, his feet crunching on broken glass as he went through into the kitchen. He flicked the light on there and saw the destruction equal to that which he had seen in the hallway.

'Anna?' he called out, desperate as he ran through the rooms. He stopped in his tracks when he found her, staring into space.

'Anna, thank goodness. You're OK,' he said as he dropped to the floor to meet her. 'What on earth happened here? Are you all right?'

He knelt down beside her and scooped her up into his arms. She was passive, as though she were a rag doll. Jon pulled back to look at her, aware that she was unresponsive. He looked confused, then worried as he looked at his wife, there but not there at all.

'What happened? I've had a call from Grace, upset, not really making any sense, talking about a baby. And you. And then her mum said I ought to go home, that she was on her way over and everything would make sense when they got here. What's going on? I don't understand.'

Anna lifted her head, tipped it to one side and smiled.

'You've been caught.'

Jon shook his head.

'What do you mean? Caught? Caught doing what?' he started, but then realisation began to dawn in his expression.

'Anna... It's...'

'It's what, Jon? It's not what I think? It's not what it looks like? I've got the wrong end of the stick? I've put two and two together and got forty?' she asked sarcastically. He would not pull the wool over her eyes again. The truth was coming out whether he liked it or not. The chickens were coming home to roost and his goose would be getting cooked.

'Yes. Yes, there's a very simple explanation.'

'I'm sure there is. You lied. Grace lied.'

'Well...' Jon looked embarrassed. 'Yes, but for your own good, for the business's good. It's all going to work out well.'

'Business? What on earth does this have to do with the business? You carrying on with Grace?'

'I'm what?' Jon's face paled.

'You. And Grace. And the baby.'

'What baby?' Jon asked, looking more and more distressed by the moment.

Anna threw back her head and laughed. She sounded unhinged. She *was* unhinged. She had been cast adrift.

'Anna, what are you talking about? What baby?' His voice was serious now. 'Are you... Are you pregnant?'

'Me? No! Never going to happen. Not me. Grace.'

Jon looked like he'd been slapped. 'Grace is pregnant?'

'Don't act dumb, Jon. It doesn't suit you.'

'Eh?'

Sickened by his continued insistence on playing dumb, Anna looked at him with disgust.

'She hasn't told you?'

'Why would she have told me? She never said a word.'

'Because it's yours, Jon. The baby is yours.'

He sat down heavily next to her, looking as if he'd been shot.

'What on earth are you talking about?'

She was just about to start shouting at him, about to tell him to stop messing with her head, to stop trying to wriggle out of this, to stop all his lies, when the doorbell rang.

'That'll be Grace and her mum,' Anna said, pushing herself up from the floor and dusting herself down. 'Let's get this show started, shall we?'

She smiled at him strangely. After all the lies and the deceit, part of her was just relieved that all the dirty little secrets were about to come tumbling out, hers included.

24

Anna walked to the front door and swung it open. On the doorstep was Grace, looking pale and terrified, Liane looking furious, and a man who Anna recalled seeing at Grace's church, so must be her dad, looking as if he'd rather be anywhere but here. Anna felt strangely calm as she invited them into her house, knowing the conversation they were about to have would change everyone's lives irrevocably.

'Come in, do go through,' Anna said, suddenly switching into hostess mode, despite having nothing but accusations to serve.

Silently, all three of them filed through into the living room, where Jon stood, utterly confused, in the middle of the room. He looked to Grace, who shook her head and looked at the floor, then back up to Anna, to Liane who looked as though she wanted to slap everyone in the room.

'Can I get anyone a... a drink...?' Jon started to say before realising it was an inappropriate suggestion. There was clearly a lot of talking to be done but drinks were not to be part of it. This was not a party.

'I think we'd best get straight on with things, don't you?' Liane snapped.

'I'm sorry,' Jon started, 'I'm not really sure what's going on. I really think that...'

'Oh, for God's sake, Jon, give it up! You've been caught. It's done. Let's all at least give each other the decency of just telling the truth,' Anna said derisively.

'Anna, I really...'

'Stop. Enough,' Liane said suddenly. 'It seems someone here has to be the adult, the grown-up, and if none of you want to be that person, then I will.'

Without any delay, she turned to Anna.

'Firstly, Anna. How *dare* you. You have treated my daughter, my Grace, appallingly. You have been dismissive and rude from the start, and what on earth do you think you're doing, accusing her of... of being the other woman? When I calmed Grace down enough to find out why she was so distraught, I was horrified. I honestly didn't know what to say.'

'I don't think I'm the one in the wrong here, Liane. Your daughter posted a baby scan through my front door. Your daughter is having my husband's baby. And you think I'm the bad guy in this scenario?'

'She did what?' Liane said, turning to face Grace with a question in her expression.

'Mum, I... I wanted her to *know*.'

Liane's face softened as she faced her daughter.

'Wanted Anna to know what?' Jon said, becoming aware that there were strands of various conversations going on here and he had absolutely no clue as to what anyone was talking about.

'You see? Who does that?' Anna said.

'What baby scan?' Jon asked. 'What baby?'

'Oh, don't play the fool,' Anna sneered. 'Like I said, you've been caught.'

'OK, so I admit that perhaps this isn't the best way to go about all this,' Liane said, trying to calm herself down, holding on to Grace who was physically shaking. 'This is not how anyone would want to find out.'

'Find out what?' Jon yelled. 'Will someone *please* tell me what on earth is going on? Everyone seems to have lost their damn minds!'

Anna turned to him.

'Like I said, Grace is pregnant. And you're the father. That's what's going on.' She kept her face stony. The betrayal hurt so much that she could only cope with it by shutting out all emotions completely.

'You keep saying that but, I... What?'

'You heard me.'

'Yes, my love, I heard you, but I have absolutely no idea what on God's green earth you're talking about. You think Grace is pregnant, and you think *I'm* the father? How on earth did you get there?'

'Jon...' Grace started to say. She was so quiet that no one heard at first.

'How do you think?' Anna snapped. 'All the secret meetings, conversations, messages. And the scan!'

'I don't know which scan you're talking about. Grace?' He turned to her. 'Are you pregnant? You know that we'd understand if you were, as employers, that is.'

Grace started to cry again.

'See?' Anna said.

'No. Enough from you,' Liane said, pointing her finger at Anna. Anna stopped.

Grace swallowed hard and then tried to speak. Her voice came out as a squeak, so she cleared her throat and tried again.

'I'm not pregnant. I've never been pregnant.'

'Exactly,' Liane said, taking Grace's hand.

'You're not?' Anna said, confusion on *her* face this time.

'No. And though I shouldn't have to justify this, I am not having an affair with Jon. He's been nothing but kind and appropriate with me.'

'You're lying,' Anna stammered. 'I know you are. I *know the truth*! We all just need to admit it!'

'Anna,' Liane said, her voice firm but kind. 'She is *not* lying. You are wrong. You are so wrong. You need to stop talking now and listen. Just listen. Please.'

'Thanks, Mum. Anna, I would never do that to you. Jon would never either. It's really not what you think.'

'So...' Anna was trying to piece things back together, now the picture she had built had been taken apart again. 'If you... then who... who sent the scan? It said... Wait, I'll get it.' She went to her bag and took out her book, bringing the scan out from the back.

'What is...' Jon said, coming to take it from her, looking at it intently as though that would be enough to make it make sense. 'I am trying to stay calm here and try to understand what's going on. It might take me a while to catch up, but please, please Anna, let me process this. OK?'

'Fine. Go ahead.' She crossed her arms.

'This is a baby scan.'

'Yes.'

'And you thought that it was a scan of my baby. Of my baby with Grace?'

Anna felt sick.

'Yes...' she said, trying to stop the tears that were pricking at the back of her eyes. She swallowed, her throat feeling as if it was closing up.

'Right.' Jon nodded, pursing his lips. 'And how did you come about this scan?'

'It was posted through the door.'

'Our door?'

'Yes.'

'When?'

'A few weeks ago.'

'Weeks? You've had this for weeks and you've not said anything?'

'No. I...' Anna stuttered. Her assurance that she was the wronged party here was starting to be chipped away. Jon did not look like a man caught out, rather a man trying to work out what on earth his crazy wife was talking about.

'OK. So, this was posted through our door, by someone. Do you know who?'

Anna shook her head.

'I thought it was Grace.'

'But you didn't *know* that? Just that someone posted this through our door, and you went from that to deciding that I, your husband, who promised before God to be faithful to you, was cheating, with Grace – our twenty-two-year-old intern – and had got her pregnant? Am I right?' His tone was mostly kind, but with an increasing amount of outrage creeping in at the edges.

'Not immediately, no...'

'So... what?'

'I...' The guilt of her lying to him about why they hadn't ever conceived stuck in the back of her throat. She hadn't thought this through. How could she explain how she'd found them out, or at least thought that she had, without outing her betrayal first?

'Anna, can I say something?' Grace said meekly.

Anna jumped. She'd almost forgotten she was there.

Jon interrupted. 'Sorry, Grace, can we just take a minute first? I just want to know why, Anna, why you'd assume such a thing?'

With no answer to give to Jon, Anna shook her head and then turned to Grace.

'I'm going to be blunt here. Did you send this to me?' Grasping at the straws of what she thought she knew, Anna grabbed for the scan and turned it over. 'There. The note. It means Grace. *Grace!*'

Grace looked at the floor.

'So?' Jon continued as though Anna had not blanked his question. 'You took these two pieces of information and ran a marathon with them? I know you've been stressed lately, and I know you've an imagination on you. It's why your ideas are always so good, but really? Did you really believe I'd do that to you? That Grace would? I *love* you. We've been through a lot in our lives, but together? We're invincible.'

'No, we're not! We've been fighting, a lot. And I haven't given you a child,' Anna said. Her legs were jelly. She had been prepared for a huge fight, and now that it hadn't come, she was exhausted. She sat down.

'No... We haven't been blessed that way yet, no. But I would never do that. You're my wife. I only have eyes for you, and I don't mean to be rude to Grace but she's half my age. Do you really think that of me?'

'No. No. It was something that Kate said and then I couldn't get it out of my head and then... with you two whispering and working late and...'

'Kate? Oh goodness, I know you two are friends, but she is well known for her gossiping. She takes something someone mentions, halves the sense, doubles the drama and spreads it about. She doesn't mean it, she's not malicious, she just takes too much interest in other people's lives. She's a good person, we all have flaws after all, but we know to take what she says with a pinch of salt.'

Anna deflated, like a balloon that someone had let go of. She'd rushed all over the place, from accusation to accusation and now she was spent. Her theories were lying in tatters on the floor. What had she done? She had allowed her own guilt about lying to Jon to convince herself that *he* was the villain in the piece, that she was the victim of betrayal and lies. She had always worried that in not giving Jon a child, the one thing she could not give him, that she would push him into the arms of someone else, and when she had the smallest flicker of a suggestion that she had been right, she clasped on to it as if it was a life preserver and she was drowning.

She had been so wrong. How on earth would he ever forgive her? Would he?

Anna's face fell. All those awful things she'd said, all the horrible names she'd called Grace, and she was wrong? She was utterly mortified as well as being wholly confused.

'I'm so sorry,' she whispered towards Grace. She repeated it to Jon and half-heartedly reached out for him, not thinking that he would want her to.

Jon stretched out his hand and took hers in it. He was strong, warm. He turned to her, putting his other hand over theirs.

'Anna,' he said gently. 'I'm sorry too.'

'For what?'

'You know how much I want a family with you. I just hadn't realised how much pressure I was putting on you. For you to think I would do this, to cheat on you to get a child, well, I assume you felt it's what I wanted more than anything else.'

'Well, isn't it?'

'No. I want you, us, a good life together. Helping others, creating good things. If we're blessed with a family then wonderful, amazing. I'd like that. But if it's not going to happen, if that's not God's plan for us, then OK. Who am I to question that?' He smiled. 'We're in this together, always. Right?'

The relief that flooded through Anna was short lived.

'I love you.'

'Good.'

'But...'

Jon stiffened. 'But what?'

'If it's not your baby, and Grace isn't pregnant, then... whose baby is it?'

Anna turned to Grace. Her face was white as a sheet.

Liane whispered to her. 'You don't have to do this, love. Not now, not like this. We can just go home if you want to.'

'That's right love,' her dad added.

Grace shook her head.

'Grace, did you post this scan?' Anna demanded. Even if Grace was not pregnant, Anna was sure that it was her who had posted it. She had gone through who else it could have been and no one made any sense. Not that this made sense either.

'Yes,' Grace whispered.

Anna nodded. She felt justified. She had thought that she had jumped to a terrible conclusion and dragged poor Grace into a mess of lies and deceit that she was too young to really be dealing with. But she *was* involved. But how?

Be kind, Anna told herself, reminding herself that the animosity she felt for Grace had been based on a falsehood. She was not a vixen, seducing Jon at work. She was not trying to steal her husband. She was a young girl who may have done something stupid. Haven't we all been that person at some point in our lives? Anna knew she had been.

'Grace, lovely. Are you in trouble?' Anna said quietly, as if it was just between the two of them.

Had she lied about not being pregnant? Or was it that she was no longer pregnant now? Had something gone wrong?

Grace was picking at the skin around her nails and Anna could see how raw they were. Grace was anxious and had obviously been anxious a lot lately.

'Are you sure?' Jon said, with warmth in his voice. 'You wouldn't be the first and you won't be the last. You can tell us the truth and we'll help you.'

He turned to Anna and she felt a wave of love return for this kind, gentle, understanding man she had married. She decided there and then that once this had all blown over, whatever it was, she would tell him the truth. All of it. He would forgive her. She was sure of that now. They could start again with a clean slate.

'I'm sure. I'm not pregnant. But...'

'Grace, my love. Are you sure you want to do this?' her mum said again quietly.

'Yes?' Jon coaxed.

'It is my scan.'

Now it was both Anna and Jon's turn to be confused. They looked at each other, then to Grace, to the scan which was lying in the middle of the table where Anna had slammed it down in anger, and then back to each other.

It was Jon who spoke first.

'I'm sorry. I don't understand.'

'It's *my* scan,' Grace repeated.

Anna's and Jon's faces stayed blank. Anna shook her head from side to side as she looked at Grace.

'I don't understand. You're not pregnant, you're not in trouble, but the scan is yours. *Were* you pregnant?'

Grace looked pained as though she didn't want to have to spell this out. 'No. I'm... *I've* not ever been pregnant. But *you* have,' she said, almost a whisper, towards Anna.

'So...' Jon said, his face screwed up as he worked through the options. 'The scan is yours... the baby is... you? The scan is *of* you?' he said softly.

Grace said nothing but nodded.

'God's benevolence on the undeserving – Grace.'

'That's my handwriting. I wrote that,' Liane said, beaming, pride on her face.

'When we decided that's what we wanted to call you when you were born,' David, Grace's dad said, smiling at his daughter.

'That's... lovely,' Anna said, trying to slot all this new information into place. Why had it not occurred to her that the scan might not be new? It was pristine, it didn't look twenty-something years old. It had clearly been looked after. A cherished memory. That was one thing about getting older, Anna thought, things that seemed new and groundbreaking in a way had actually been around way longer than you realised. Or not even that, just that you'd forgotten that decades had happened while you were busy trying to work your way out in life. 'But I don't get it. Why post it to me? What did you want to tell me?'

Grace looked as though she was about to be sick.

'I didn't want to do it like that. Or like this. But I didn't know how to do it. I... No time seemed right. No way seemed appropriate. We tried to... but they said it wasn't a good idea. I wanted to know. I...'

Anna shook her head in increasingly inpatient confusion.

'The scan. It's me but it's also you,' Grace said, looking directly at Anna. 'It's your scan too. You're my mother.'

Anna felt the floor fall away from beneath her as the words sank in.

Jon suddenly got angrier than Anna had ever seen him.

'Now just you wait a minute. I don't know what you think

you're doing, I don't know what your plan is, but this has gone too far.'

'Jon. Don't.'

'Enough shouting. Stop it. Now,' Liane said as she turned to face Grace.

Anna had not taken her eyes off Grace since she'd said it. *Mother.* She said she was her mother. It didn't make sense. How? Grace would be the right age but...

'Anna?' Jon said before stopping. He caught the look in Anna's eyes. She wasn't angry. She wasn't denying it, the impossibility of it all. There was a question. She was in the room but also miles away, years away.

'How?' Anna said to Grace. 'I don't see how this is possible.'

'Exactly. I mean...' Jon interrupted.

'Jon. *Please,*' Anna implored. He stopped.

Grace picked up a sofa cushion and held it in front of her protectively, her hands shaking as she did so.

'Well, you've done it now, love. Tell them everything,' Liane said. 'But if you want to go at any point, you just say, OK? I'm here.'

'We're both here for you, love,' David said, breaking his silence.

Grace nodded at them both, breathed out shakily and then began.

'I was born on the twelfth of October, twenty-two years ago. My mother couldn't keep me. She was young, unmarried, from a highly regarded and religious family. I've been told that she wanted the best for me, but she couldn't keep me. She was only fifteen. My parents' – Grace gestured towards them – 'had been happily married for years but had been unable to have a baby. They wanted to adopt but frankly, the whole system scared them. It was too overwhelming so they'd not started the process. Then, a woman at church mentioned a situation she'd heard about, then introduced them to this girl's parents. And, well, they came to an agreement.'

Anna's face drained of all its colour.

'But... You *can't* be here. It's not possible... It's... not...' Anna felt her breath being squeezed out of her.

'But I am.'

'No, not like that,' Anna said as she felt her vision flicker. 'You can't be here because you... You're dead.'

'What?' Jon and Grace said at the same time.

'You...' Jon said, looking at Anna in shock. 'You had a baby when you were... what, fifteen? You... you never told me. I mean, I knew you'd lost a child, but I didn't know...'

Anna opened her mouth to speak but the words wouldn't come. She was trying to process too much. Her brain couldn't cope. How could her child be here, sitting in front of her? Her child died, years ago. Two decades ago. Two decades Anna had kept that pain inside her, knowing that she had failed her child, knowing that she was supposed to have kept her safe and hadn't, knowing that she had paid for the sin of getting pregnant in the first place by carrying all this pain around with her ever since.

She grasped hold of the arm of the chair she was sitting in. She couldn't hear the others, couldn't see them. She was no longer there. She was back in her childhood bedroom. She was lying, curled up in the foetal position, her back to the door, facing the window where the thick, heavy curtains had been drawn against daylight since she had come back from the hospital. How many days it had been, she could not have said for love nor money. Occasionally her mother would come, try to speak with her, receive no reply and leave again, only leaving a tray of food that Anna barely picked at. If she could sleep, she slept.

She was soul tired. From the fear, from the hidden pregnancy, from the terror when she had been found out, too late to 'do anything about it' despite her being sure her parents would never have even considered an abortion as an option, from the panic of going into labour when she was home alone, not knowing who, if anyone, she should call. From when her parents came home and took her to hospital where the staff were cold and judgemental at her sin, ensuring maximum pain and minimum care as her penance. Until the moment that her baby girl had been born. The moment Anna heard her tiny lungs belt out their first cry and something inside her blossomed against her will. She had refused at first to hold her, too scared that she would love her, knowing the baby would be someone else's daughter. Then she relented and had that one moment she thought she would cling to, that small pocket of time when she held her, when it was the two of them against the world and it felt like it would be OK.

Then she was taken away and she was gone. To where, Anna didn't know and no one would tell her, no matter how much she had asked.

Back home, Anna had wanted to die. She had prayed for it. She had asked to be taken but then assumed she had not been because God didn't want sullied girls like her, sinful women like her. She had not had time to atone and so he would not spare her suffering now.

Then that day, her father had strode into the room, swept back the curtains, letting in a light so blinding that Anna felt her eyeballs would burn.

'Right. That's enough. Enough now. No more wallowing. What's done is done. Get up.'

Anna sat up, shielding her eyes.

'I have some news of the baby.'

Her heart leapt then stopped.

'Is she OK?'

He coughed.

'No. No, I'm afraid not.' He looked at the floor, then back at her mother who nodded, holding the crucifix at her throat and crossing herself. 'No. She was too small, she'd not had proper antenatal care, no medical attention. She developed an infection. In, um... in her lungs. She was too little and I'm afraid she has passed. She is with God now.'

Anna felt the core of her crumble away, every fibre of her being falling apart like an old leaf, crushed into dust and blown away on the wind.

'What?'

'Don't say "what". Say pardon,' her mother intoned from the doorway, as though this was a conversation where correcting someone's grammar was appropriate.

'What?' Anna repeated.

'She died. So... Now you can get on with your life and put all this nonsense behind you. A new life starting today,' her father said, unaware of the cruel irony of that statement. 'It's sad obviously but it's for the best. Now, dinner is downstairs in fifteen minutes. I expect you dressed and at the table. No more of this tray nonsense. It's time to move on.'

And with that he left.

Anna's mother hovered a little longer in the doorway, as though she had something to say, some sympathy, some love to offer. But then she coughed and followed her husband downstairs, leaving Anna on her bed, alone, the magnitude of what she had just learned, and how she had just learned it, seeping into her understanding. That was the moment she locked it all away – her heart, her mind, everything – into a box where no one else could ever hurt her. She wouldn't heal there but she would not survive anything else and so to protect herself, broken and destroyed, she shut herself away. Jon had partially unlocked the box, but Anna had still kept a piece of her, the piece that belonged to her daughter, hidden.

Now Grace was trying to claim that piece as her own.

'No,' Anna said tonelessly.

'Pardon?' Liane said, as Grace stared in shock.

'You're lying to me. You must be. My child, my daughter... She died. My parents told me. I saw the death certificate. I went to her *funeral*. As much as I might want to believe that she is still here, I know that she is not.'

'Anna,' Liane said gently. 'Anna, I know this must be a horrible shock. I... I don't know what to say. We thought, we understood that...' For the first time, Liane was rattled.

'Your parents told us you weren't well and that you weren't able to care for the baby,' David said, picking up the thread where his wife was unable to continue. He took her hand in his. 'It was our understanding that you were aware of Grace's adoption but not well enough, mentally, to be involved in any way. A breakdown, they said, and...'

'You're *lying* to me!' Anna stood up. 'I want you to go. Now. I don't know what you're playing at, but this is cruel. I want you to leave.'

Grace looked at her mother, unsure of what to do. Liane's calm returned as she stood up to face Anna.

'I understand why you would think so. I think we have all been lied to but not by who you think,' Liane said. 'I met your parents when Grace was born. They told me that you were mentally ill, that you were incapable of parenting her and incapable of making a decision about the future of your baby.'

'They did what?'

'You saw a death certificate? Well, we saw medical paperwork that declared you unfit to care for your baby, signing parental control over to your own parents. I still have it, if you want to see it. We kept everything. Because we didn't do this through an agency, we were not wholly sure that we were doing it right but... We trusted your parents, their priest, the church, the court's decision. It... seemed the best thing for everyone involved.'

Everyone was silent as the truth of what had happened started to sink in.

Eventually Jon broke in.

'So, you're saying that Anna's parents lied to you about having the right to sign Grace over to you? And that they lied to Anna about her baby having died? That their priest and a doctor falsified paperwork to support those lies in court?' He sounded horrified.

'It would seem so.' Liane nodded. 'We'd never kept it from Grace that she was adopted. She's seen her scans, seen the documentation. We've talked about how sometimes babies are born into one family but become part of another and how love isn't necessarily determined only by blood. We always said that when she was older, if she wanted to know more about her birth family, we would let her know, help her find you. As far as we knew, Grace's mother was from a church-going respectable family who had done the best in difficult circumstances. But then, well...'

'Well, what?' Anna said.

'When we approached your mother to say that Grace would like to meet you, she was incredibly defensive. She said that you had never recovered fully, that the death of your father had caused your condition to worsen, that you were still mentally unstable and that it would be a bad idea for everyone if you were to meet. She shut the whole idea down. Let bygones be bygones and that was that.'

'And yet you tracked me down?' Anna said, still disbelieving. It was not sinking in that this was true. It couldn't be. Her daughter was dead, Grace was an interloper. A different kind to the one Anna had imagined, but an interloper all the same.

Grace spoke up for the first time.

'When they said we shouldn't meet you, I wanted to find out something about my birth mother, anything about her. I was scared. I was scared that I might have what you have. What she said you had. A mental health disorder. I didn't know anything about my biological family at all. I've seen my birth certificate. No named father.'

'You don't want to know.'

'But I *do*. I did. So I googled you. And you were really easy to find. I had your name, your date of birth and frankly, I look like you. Don't I?'

Anna couldn't look at her.

'I found your wedding pictures, on your church website. And it was like looking at me. I was so sure that it was you. And you... you looked fine. Not ill at all. Normal. I looked up your business and it was what I wanted to do too, design. And I knew of your church through mine and so... I asked my aunt.'

'Patricia.'

'She doesn't know,' Grace said quickly. 'I didn't tell her why I wanted to meet with you. I didn't tell anyone.'

'No. You didn't,' Liane said gently. 'You should have told me, lovely.'

'You were told to stay away and yet you stalked me. And got your feet under the table.'

'It wasn't like that. You're my *mother*,' Grace implored, 'my biological mother,' she corrected, looking anxiously at Liane who shook her head, smiling that she understood. 'I wanted to know you. I *want* to know you.'

Anna was silent, her mind trying desperately to make all this fit with what she had been told, what she had known, what had tortured her for the past twenty years. Trying to undo all that had been lies, trying not to let what had been true get destroyed amongst all that had not been. She was raging but unsure how to let that out.

'I'm not lying,' Grace said, fear on her face.

Her voice brought Anna back to the room. She blinked in shock as she re-registered where she was, who she was with.

Anna stood up and walked round the table and sat down again next to Grace. She adjusted herself to face her straight on and looked into her eyes. Was it even possible that this was true? Did she want this to be true? She scanned Grace's face for clues, trying to recall the face of the man who'd fathered this child but then wanted nothing to do with her, trying to see if she recognised anything of him or of herself in Grace's pale and nervous expression.

She took Grace's face in her hands, one either side, over her ears and she *looked*. For something, some flicker of one soul recognising a part of themselves in the other. Something, something biological, at a cellular level, that would tell her that Grace was her daughter.

To everyone else, it seemed like an age, Grace, sitting right in front of Anna, trembling under the stress and the scrutiny. Even from within her own turmoil, Anna was painfully aware that even if this wasn't real, she had to do this right. She had to remember that she held someone's child, her biological child or not, between her hands at this very moment and it was her human responsibility not to crush her. People are gentle with babies, their fragility easy to see, but they forget that all humans need gentle care. That we're all fragile in our own way.

Anna was holding this thought in her mind and then she saw it – a flicker in Grace's eyes, something in the way the flecks of gold spread out from the pupil across her iris, that brought back a long and deeply buried memory.

It was the middle of the night. She was cold, despite the room in the hospital being warmer than average. She was terrified. She was alone. Well, almost alone. She had laboured for what felt like days, what could have in fact been days. No one had really spoken to her much throughout it. What words she did receive were coated in disapproval, in judgement, in disgust. She had sinned. And she was now paying for that sin through pain, through child-birth. She had given birth to her baby, a girl, and there was this one moment, the briefest of moments, but one which she had locked up in her memory so tightly to keep it from hurting her, but also to keep it from slipping away. The one moment that she got to hold her daughter. She got to look into her unfocused eyes as this small, squashed, red-faced, perfect human being clasped hold of her mother's finger, holding tight. *Don't let me go.*

Tears rolled down Anna's face as she looked at Grace and accepted the truth of what she was saying to her, against the lies that she had been told by those who were supposed to have loved her then.

She knew that she was looking into the eyes of her daughter.

'I know,' Anna whispered. 'I know. It's you.' She let go of Grace's face and sat back, exhausted.

Grace started to cry, swallowing hard to try to stop the heaving sobs that were wracking her body. She couldn't do it. She couldn't keep it in. It all came tumbling out in a torrent. She reached for Anna but Anna flinched.

'I can't do this,' she said, getting up and leaving the room.

She picked up her coat, opened the front door and walked through it, leaving everyone else in the house in shock, unsure of what to do. Anna walked into the night, as though the darkness could shut everything out.

25

Anna's mind was filled with too many thoughts and her phone wouldn't stop ringing, shattering any ability to think straight with its incessant beeping breaking her train of thought. She took it out of her pocket and clocked the missed calls from Jon and from a number she didn't recognise, which she assumed was Grace's mother. *Mother.* She held the button down and felt a release when the screen went black. She needed time.

It was getting chilly, and Anna's toes were going numb as she wandered aimlessly. She was trying to make things fit right in her mind and she couldn't. The lies and the truth were all tangled up together. She couldn't work out what to believe. Looking into Grace's eyes, she had felt the truth of what she and Liane were saying, but even knowing what her parents were like, what her childhood had been like, she couldn't quite believe that they had done such a terrible thing. Had they thought that they were doing the right thing in the circumstances? By Anna? By Grace? Or had they just been trying to hide their daughter's shame in order that they themselves were not tarnished by it? How had that not ruined their lives as it had ruined hers?

She needed to talk. With someone neutral. There was only one place she could go.

'Yeah, yes, I'll call if I see her,' Kate was saying into her phone as she opened the door to a broken-looking Anna. Kate raised her eyebrows in question and motioned to the phone. Anna shook her head. 'No. I've not heard from her,' she continued, 'but I'll let you know as soon as I do. Try not to worry, I'm sure she's fine.'

Kate shuffled her into the living room and sat her down, immediately draping her in a thick blanket. Wordlessly she went to the kitchen and returned a few minutes later with a hot water bottle and a cup of tea, both of which she handed to Anna before sitting down opposite her.

'So I gather something has happened.'

Anna nodded.

'Is it what I think?' She tipped her head to the side sympathetically.

Anna shook her head. She sipped at the tea, grateful for the warmth that it spread through her. She hadn't realised how cold she had got. She had been grateful for the numb feeling.

'No?' Kate was surprised. 'I guess that's... good?' She clearly didn't want to press Anna but obviously wanted to know what on earth was going on.

'Honestly? I don't know,' Anna said finally.

'Why don't you tell me what's happened? Jon sounded so worried. I'd really like to let him know you're safe. Can I let him know that?' Kate lifted her phone up in a question.

Anna nodded.

Kate quickly sent a brief message before turning her phone on silent, putting it down and looking back at Anna.

'Right. What's happened?'

'The short version? Grace isn't pregnant. She and Jon are not having an affair. The scan is mine.'

'Yours? You said you weren't pregnant?'

'I'm not. But I was. Twenty-two years ago. With Grace.'

'With Grace? I don't understand. What are you saying?'

'That's the long version.' Anna took a sip of tea. She was so tired. All she wanted to do was to slip down on the sofa, curl up under the blanket and go to sleep. Except she couldn't. Her mind was running at a million miles an hour. That was why she was here; she needed to talk this out, straighten out her thoughts before she could even think about going back. She knew walking out had not been the best reaction, but she also knew it wasn't the worst. She didn't want to lose her shit in front of Grace, nor blame her or Liane for things that were not their fault. She needed to get her own feelings ironed out rather than releasing them straight away, still all crumpled and messy.

'Grace says she's my daughter. The scan is mine, of her.'

Kate's eyes widened in shock.

'Exactly,' Anna replied.

'So... But... I...'

'Exactly,' Anna repeated.

'Is she? Could she be? I thought you said that...'

'My baby died. Yes. I did say that. Because I thought she had. Because my parents told me that she had. Because I went to her funeral, saw the smallest coffin that no one should ever have to see, watched my priest bless her, and yet...'

'Yet?'

'I think Grace is telling the truth. I think she is my daughter,' Anna whispered.

Kate was silent. She wanted to let Anna say what she needed to say.

'I think my parents lied to me. I think the priest and the doctor, and my parents, were all in on this together. That they were doing it "for my own good" by telling me that she had died, and that perhaps they honestly thought I would be better off with a clean slate. A fresh start. Only it was never that. I was dragging the pain of that loss around with me, and it was only growing heavier with words unsaid, as I tried to move forward with it always pulling me back.'

'Dear God.'

Anna nodded.

'I keep thinking, *Who is lying to me? Who lied to me? Who does it profit to lie and who does it not?* And I keep thinking that Grace and Liane have no reason to do that. If they wanted to scam some random woman, then why would they pick me? It's not like I'm some super successful billionaire. They have details that they shouldn't have had otherwise. They know about my parents. They know about my church. Where would they have got those details from? This was not reported, this was pre any social media, websites were new. But my parents? This fits in perfectly with what I know of them, how they were, how my mother was when I went to see her. The fact that when Liane approached her about me now, she lied to them again. They had no care for *me*. Just their own reputation in their little church bubble. I looked at Grace and...' Anna's voice dwindled and stopped as her mind went back to the moments she had with Grace before she had walked out.

'And what?'

'I *felt* her. I know that probably doesn't make any sense but, that one time I held my baby, before they took her from me, I... There was a connection. She was me. I was her. And when I looked at Grace, really looked at her, all grown up and so, so different to the baby I once had, I felt it again. Like she was a part of me.' Anna's shoulders started shaking as the tears came. 'I think she's telling me the truth. I think she is my baby. She's my baby.'

Anna then collapsed in on herself, her breathing ragged as her tears fell. Kate moved next to her and put her arm around her as she cried.

'It's OK, it's OK...' Kate whispered.

Anna snapped her head up. 'How? How is it OK? She's the innocent party in all of this and I accused her of adultery. I called her a whore!'

'Ah.'

'I phoned her and I yelled all sorts of things, vile things, at her. I think I lost my mind, I think I'm losing my mind. I was just so convinced that I had the answer to all the questions. It made sense.'

'To be fair to you, how were you supposed to know that she was who she was? You thought you had no living children. And I'm sorry, I didn't help with all this; I was convinced of it too.'

'You didn't know either. God, this is such a mess. I've been horrible to Jon, convinced our marriage was over. I've not ever been nice to Grace. I didn't trust her from the moment she stepped into the office and I haven't hidden it. Something was off but I couldn't ever put my finger on it. I've been nothing but hostile this whole time. What must she think of me?' She held her face in her hands.

'I mean, she is an adult, albeit a young one. Surely she will be able to see that you had no idea this scenario was even possible?'

'I can only hope that. I... I literally walked out on her. I left her. Again. Like I left her before.'

'She was *taken* from you before, that's not the same thing.'

'I can't walk back in there and face her.'

Kate rubbed Anna's back supportively. 'Anna, love, I think you have to. But what do you want?'

'How do you mean?'

'I mean, Grace came looking for you for a reason. She came

into your life for a reason. She wants a relationship with you, to find out about you. To be part of your life, I assume.'

'Yes? And? I don't understand what you're asking me.'

'Do *you* want that? You don't have to. Not every adoption reunion is a happy one. Not every family wants to go back to the past or forge a new future. She wants to be in your life. Do you want that too? Putting aside what in theory a parent should want from their child if you take out the greys, what do you want? Do you want to get to know her? Do you want a relationship with her, whatever that might be? Or would you rather have the past be the past and move on? I'm not judging either way, mind, I'm just asking what you want. For you.'

Anna looked at Kate, her eyes wide in surprise. 'I think that's the first time anyone's actually asked me that. What I want.'

'Well, it matters. You matter.'

Anna started sobbing again and Kate held her until she calmed down. She took deep breaths, trying to get herself back under control.

'I do,' she finally managed to say.

'Do what?'

'I do want a relationship with her. I'll admit, when I was pregnant and terrified, and the only thing I wanted was for none of it to be happening, I would have happily wished her away then. But then when she was real, she was here, I wanted nothing more than to be her mother. That I had let her down, that I had not protected her and that she had died was the worst thing imaginable to me. I would have swapped places with her in a heartbeat.'

'Then you need to go back and fix this.'

Anna put her head in her hands again.

'I don't know if I can.'

'You can. Just go and tell her the truth, your truth. Apologise for the behaviour that you're ashamed of. Just be you, and let her in. You know how you struggle to let people get close to you, but now is the time. OK?'

Anna nodded. 'OK.'

'Right, give me two minutes and then I'll drive you back over.'

'Now?'

'Anna, you walked out in the middle of a conversation. If you want to continue that conversation, you need to go back. Delaying now only gives Grace time to change her mind, or to fill in the blanks of what you're not saying with her own version. Now is when you lay all the cards on the table and work out together how you're going to do this.'

Anna nodded, grateful that someone else was taking charge. She was going to have to be the adult soon but right now, she felt so out of her depth that she wished that she had a parent. Not her actual parents, but someone who could guide her through this.

On the drive on the way over, Anna couldn't stop her knees from jiggling. Nerves were zipping through her body uncontrollably. She was going to meet her *daughter*; she was going to rescue this mess. She felt hope creep into the dark place that she had kept hidden from everyone; she felt gratitude start to fill the void that she had carried inside her for so long.

As the car pulled up outside her house and Anna could see that Liane's was still there, she felt fear too.

Was it all too late?

26

'Do you want me to come in? Or wait here? Or...' Kate asked as she sat with the engine running outside Anna's home.

'What do I really want? I want you to drive me away and drop me back in six months when this is all cleared up and tidy.' Anna laughed nervously.

'Would if I could, love. You know that.'

Anna nodded. 'I do know that. And it means a lot. Thank you.'

'Honestly, I feel part of this mess is my fault, so whatever I can do...'

'It isn't, really. It's not like you stole my child and told me they were dead, is it?' Anna laughed darkly.

'God, Anna. It's so, so awful.'

'It is. And yet... frankly, it doesn't surprise me. Which is awful in a whole different way, I suppose. I was not blessed in the parent department. I don't even know if I know *how* to be a mother, I just know I don't want to be anything like mine.'

'You and Grace will find your own way.'

Anna nodded again, trying to convince herself. 'OK. I'm going in. You don't have to wait. Thank you.'

'If you're sure? I'll just be at Rob's house if you need me. Let me know how you go?'

'I will do. Thanks.' Anna reached across and squeezed Kate's hand before getting out of the car and closing the door with a slam. She knew as the sound reverberated around the evening air that those in the house would know she was back. She hoped they were pleased about it.

She closed the front door quietly behind her, took off her coat and took three deep breaths, trying to steady herself. She then opened the door to the living room and stepped in. All eyes turned to her. She scanned their faces, expecting to find anger there but she felt her heart calm when she saw nothing but relief. No one spoke as they looked at her.

'I'm sorry. For walking out. It was all too much, all information I needed time to process. I'm sorry. I... I know it's the same for everyone, but I just needed to walk.'

Liane spoke first. 'I think we all understand that,' she said, looking around the room for confirmation. 'I didn't think we were handling this well even before we found out what your parents had told you. I'm so sorry. I hope you can forgive us.' Her face settled into a pained expression.

Anna wrinkled her forehead in confusion. 'Forgive you for what?'

'For... taking your child when you had not given her up to be taken. We truly didn't know.' Pity flooded Liane's face, the idea of a parent doing that to their own child clearly incomprehensible to her.

Anna's eyes went to the floor as her emotions threatened to overwhelm her. Already Liane was showing her more compassion than her own mother had done all those years ago. How much of your life and your self-worth is made by the love of those who raise you? Anna had never felt worthy of anything, of anyone. She felt a wash of gratitude that this woman had raised her daughter, when she herself had been deprived of the chance. If anything, it was obviously to Grace's benefit and she was happy for that, for Grace, if not for herself. Was this what being a mother was about? Putting your child's happiness above your own?

Anna kept her eyes down, disgraced, embarrassed by what she had accused Grace of being, of doing. She forced herself to look back up. She had to fix this.

'Thank you,' she whispered to Liane. 'Grace.' Anna turned to face her. 'I'm sorry. I... I should never have made such a disrespectful assumption about you and I'm sorry. I... I was in fear of losing everything and I let rumour and panic drive me. I want you, all of you, to know that. I'm... I'm really embarrassed about it. I feel awful and I—'

Liane interrupted her. 'We understand.'

Anna looked at her, confused. 'You do?'

'Yes. I mean, I was appalled that you'd think that of Grace. I was horrified when she told me what you'd accused her of. What you thought Jon had done. But then I realised it's because you don't *know* her. You've not had the chance to know her. She's a stranger to you and, well, then my heart broke for you. Now we've all had a chance to calm down, things look different. Don't they?'

Grace nodded.

Anna opened her mouth to reply before realising she did not know what to say. Liane was speaking the truth.

'I'm sorry that we arrived all guns blazing, shouting and making a fuss. I had wanted to come and say thank you, but my defence of my child took over.'

'Thank you?'

'For Grace. For giving her to us. I understand now that it wasn't your choice or decision, and that your parents behaved abominably towards you, but I want you to know what a blessing you gave to our lives. You started our family. So for that, I want to thank you. After Grace, we were unexpectedly able to conceive with her siblings to have our family as it is now.'

She looked both worried and like she wanted to grasp Anna into a hug. Anna could see that Liane's maternal instincts wanted to mother her and for a moment, Anna wished that she could let her. There had been so many times when she had needed her parents and so many times when they not been there, both before she left home and since. She'd had to hold herself up for so long and she was tired. Feeling so separate from Jon lately too had taken a big toll on her. Feeling utterly alone in this world was too much.

Anna didn't know what to say. Yes, her parents had taken Grace from her, not given her any agency or say over what happened to her child. They had told her that she was dead, presumably believing that this would give her peace, an ending of sorts, so that she did not spend her life pining for what she could not have. She spent her life grieving instead. Was that better?

'I want to thank *you*. From what Grace has told me and from what I have seen, you have loved her the way that I would have wanted my child to be loved, have given her the family she deserved.' Anna's voice cracked as she spoke. She paused to compose herself. 'I... I don't think I could have given her better. I wasn't in the right place, I didn't have my own life together, and I certainly wasn't ready to bring up a baby. I won't say that it didn't ruin a part of me but that's not your fault. And I'm grateful for you loving her and I'm grateful for you supporting her now. For giving her space to find me.'

'We agreed that we would never try to keep you apart. It was just when your mother told us that you had never been well, that it wasn't wise to contact you, we weren't sure what was best to do. Which is why we waited. Except, obviously, Grace didn't.'

Grace looked sheepish.

'I was right though, wasn't I?' Grace said to Anna. 'To find you.'

'You were. You were,' Anna nodded. She glanced at Jon, worried how he was feeling about all this. She had lied to him, kept him at a distance, accused him of adultery and then landed him with all this. He'd be within his rights to walk away.

Jon's eyes were kind as he walked around to join her. He gently placed a hand on her shoulders, before reaching for a chair to pull towards him and sitting down.

'I'm so sorry for keeping all this from you, Jon. I... It's just...'

'I think I get it. At least in part,' he said, taking Anna's hand in his. 'Can you tell me now? Help me to fully understand? All the things you've kept hidden from me?'

Anna nodded. 'I'll try,' she said, looking between Jon and Grace. 'I owe it to both of you.'

She took a deep breath and began. 'I was a child of a deeply religious family. You both know that. I was the last surprise gift, long after they thought those years were done for them. They were an older generation, and they were tired by the time I arrived. A lot of my parenting was simply them assuming that, somehow, I would learn what I needed to learn by osmosis rather than directly. They forgot to actually pass on knowledge to me that they had already imparted to my older siblings.'

'You've siblings?' Jon asked. 'I didn't know that either.' He looked ashen.

'Five. The oldest two wanted nothing to do with my parents and I barely knew them. The strict upbringing had pushed them away. The younger three were very much caught up in the family way of thinking and when all this happened, I was disowned by them all. I'm sorry not to have some loving, extended family to offer you,' Anna said to Grace.

Grace shook her head. It didn't matter.

'By the time I was a teenager, I was pulling away from the church, from the strict and puritan way of living that my parents tried to keep me in, keep me locked up in. I was rebelling, trying to find some freedom. I had taken to slipping out of the house in the evenings, as my parents were early risers and were often sleeping by nine thirty. My siblings were older, wrapped up in their own burgeoning lives, and no one noticed I was gone. I would go to clubs, to music bars and meet other people, much older people who thought my naivety was amusing. Attractive, even.' She scoffed bitterly. How quickly their actions had made her grow up. 'I was not... aware... of how things happened. Biologically. I just knew that affection meant I was worth something. I was wanted. And I met... your...'

'Dad?' Grace asked, hanging on Anna's every word.

'I'm not sure he is worthy of that title if I'm honest. But yes, your biological father. He was a doorman at the local club. He always let me in, and we'd have chats every night and he'd get me a drink from the bar. He'd let me stay after the club was closed and we'd talk more, about everything. He was older and knowing and funny. He wasn't necessarily a bad man as such. Though he knew how old I was so maybe he was. We had a friendship, I thought. He looked out for me. No one else looked out for me, other than to remind me how sinful I was being, how I was supposed to honour my parents with my behaviour and how anything other than complete and total obedience was a failing on my part. I looked forward to our conversations. He asked my opinions. Something about him spoke to a part of me that no one else did, that no one else even admitted existed. And then we got closer. It didn't happen much, the sex. Maybe two or three times, but being young and hyper fertile, it was enough. I didn't know about contraception. I wasn't aware that it even existed. As far as I knew, you either got blessed by God or you did not. And I was told often enough that I was a sinner, that I was bad, and I assumed that God would not bless me because of that. I was too young, too trusting to question why, if you were blessed with a child, it was sinful to have a child out of wedlock? If sex was a sin, then how were blessings born of it? Too many contradictions. Too much that seemed like control rather than logic.'

'They really hadn't told you anything at all? About sex?' Grace looked shocked. 'I mean, my family is religious, and I am fully informed about it.'

'I'm glad of that. My parents didn't want me, or any of their children, to have any power. They'd have less themselves if they gave any to us. Or maybe I'm being mean... Maybe control was the only way they could cope. I've thought a lot about it over the years and have tried, really tried, to forgive them for what they did. Until today, until I learnt the extent of their control. I can never forgive them for that.'

'There's a question, something I've wondered over the years since I found out I was adopted. Why didn't you fight to keep me? Why didn't you want me? What did I do wrong?' her voice wavered.

Anna's heart cracked to hear it. She wanted to envelop Grace in a hug and the emotion surprised her.

Liane's dad spoke up.

'It's like she said, love, she wasn't allowed to. She thought you were gone, nothing left to fight for. You know that now.'

'Yeah, I know but... I just...' Grace looked so young suddenly. Anna felt it was like looking at her as a child.

'Oh, my darling, nothing. You did nothing wrong. You were perfect, pure – a true blessing. I think I fell in love with you the first second I saw you. You were this perfect, warm little bundle with your tiny toes and your dark eyelashes like a shock against your blue eyes. I wanted to keep you. Even though I knew I couldn't, that I wouldn't be allowed to, I wanted to, but I couldn't and then when they told me you'd...' Anna's voice faded as the memory overtook her. She jumped as Jon squeezed her hand in support. She placed her hand over the top, grateful for its warmth, its familiarity, the connection, which he was reminding her was still there.

The sorrow hung in the room. No one knew what to say.

'How long did it take you to find us?' Jon asked, breaking the silence, and everyone turned to him as though they had forgotten he was there.

'It wasn't hard. We knew Anna's name from my birth certificate.'

'You have it?' Anna asked, snapping her head up. 'I didn't get to register you. I was told as you had died so close to birth that it wasn't needed.'

Liane was gentle as she replied. 'That's not true.'

Anna scoffed. 'Of course it wasn't. Of course. What... what did they name you?'

'The name was listed as Miriam,' Liane replied. 'It means *wished-for child*. They said it was an encouragement to know that her new family had much wished for her. Which was true, we did.'

A lump came to Anna's throat. 'That's... actually quite a beautiful thing to do. I... I'm surprised.'

'It was one of many things that convinced us we were doing the right thing and taking you, willingly, from a good, truthful family.' Liane's voice cracked. 'I'm so sorry we didn't know. We should have asked to meet you.'

Anna didn't respond. 'But you changed it to Grace. Why?'

Liane breathed out through pursed lips, regaining her composure. 'It was for you.'

'How do you mean?'

'Anna means Grace in Hebrew, a version of Hannah. Our darling daughter was God's favour on us, but her name tied her to you at the same time. We named her, partially, for you.'

Anna put her head in her hands and drew them across her face to cover her mouth. This was so hard. Every aspect of this was so hard.

Grace continued. 'It wasn't difficult to find you from the information we had. We knew how old you would be – my age plus fifteen years. I put the facts into a search engine and there you were. I thought it would be harder, if I'm honest.'

'I wasn't hiding. My family disowned me, and I thought there was no one left to look for me. I've spent all this time thinking you were gone. I've grieved the loss of you over and over and over. I felt that it was my punishment. To have had you for so little time but to grieve you forever. But the thing that really hits me now?' Anna pushed the tears off her face, pulled her hair back behind her neck and held onto it as though she was literally falling apart. 'How could they do that? If they felt even the tiniest bit of love for me, compared to the love I felt for you, then how could they take you from me and then tell me that you were dead? How could they think that it was right?'

Grace suddenly became angry. 'In my adoption paperwork there's a letter, supposedly from your doctor, outlining your mental health breakdown and subsequent inability to parent me, along with more documentation assigning the parental responsibility for me to your parents. So that they could agree to allow my parents to adopt me. I thought you had a breakdown because you didn't want me!'

'I should be angry too,' Anna said flatly.

'You should!' replied Grace. 'For all the lies. And the pain they caused you. Caused us.' She was indignant, in that way the young can be. The world outlined in black and white, so clear, so obvious, greys and nuance no match for the surety of youth.

'I've spent years trying to move forward from this and failing. I left the very minute I felt strong enough and never looked back. My parents lost a daughter and a granddaughter through their belief that sin was stronger than love. They were kept small and beholden by their faith. That's not what faith is supposed to be,' Anna said. 'It's strength and joy and love. Losing you gave me the strength to leave and to find my own path. You, you have a wonderful family, who are loving, supportive, kind. You've grown up to be a wonderful woman, brave, and imaginative. You've had siblings and family and love. That one night in the hospital, when I got to hold you before they took you away, *this* is what I wished for you. And I was scared that I would not be able to give it to you. Would I have kept you if I had been given the chance? Yes. Would your life have been as good as it has been?' Anna paused while she considered the question. 'Honestly, I don't know that it would. I was young and stupid. I made a lot of mistakes out there by myself. I had one foot out the door at most times. My life was unstable, a mess. Unhappy. For a long time. Would I have been better with you by my side? Was the unhappiness caused by the lack of you? Maybe? Who can say for sure?'

'You're being very forgiving...' Grace said, almost petulantly, as though she felt that Anna wasn't angry enough.

'No. No, I don't forgive them. I'll never forgive *them*. I just feel that I have wasted enough of my life being destroyed by their hand. I don't think I have any more to give. They wanted an obedient, chaste and God-fearing daughter. They do not have one. I wanted my freedom. I have that. And now?' She reached out for Grace. 'Now I have *you*. I thought I had lost you forever, only to find that you're still here and you *found* me. My *daughter*.'

Anna smiled as a love she thought was long dead and buried flooded through her. Her daughter was alive. She was here.

'I... What do we do from here?' Grace asked nervously. 'I have my family, I love my family, but I want to be part of your life too. And you to be part of mine. Both of you...' She looked at Jon, as if asking for his approval, asking him to let this happen.

Jon ran his fingers through his hair.

'I'm sorry. It's a lot to take in. I... I'm going to need a minute.' He turned away and Anna's heart dropped. What was he thinking? They had moved so far apart and she had pushed him away. Would he come back to her now? Would he come back to her at all?

27

'Look, I think we're all tired,' Liane said, surveying the room of drained-looking people. 'Why don't we go home, leave you and Jon to it for the moment? We could come back tomorrow? Later in the week? And talk more. There's still lots to be said, I'm sure.'

'I think that's sensible,' Jon said in a tone that Anna couldn't place. Was he tired, or angry?

'Can I come back tomorrow?' Grace said, sounding like an eager child.

'Sure. Yes. Of course,' Anna said, feeling unsure what their standing was with each other. The lines of the relationship were being redrawn and she didn't know what to do or say.

Liane stood up. Grace followed.

'We'll call in the morning?' Liane asked.

Anna nodded as she accompanied them out of the room.

Liane took her coat, opened the door and turned to Grace, who was stood in front of Anna. There was a brief shuffle of feet as neither woman knew what to do, before Anna grasped Grace into a hug and Grace hugged her back. Neither said anything with words but the closeness of the embrace, the length of time before either of them wanted to let go, said more than words could have done. Grace stepped back and Liane stepped forward and hugged Anna too.

'See you tomorrow,' Grace said as she stepped through the door, a hopeful smile on her face.

'Bye. Till tomorrow.'

Anna closed the door as slowly as she could manage, keeping Grace in her sights. She rested her forehead on the door for a moment, bone tiredness seeping through her body. She was emotionally drained, but she knew more needed to be said between her and Jon. What had she broken by distrusting him? And how could she fix it?

Walking back into the living room, Anna looked at Jon, who was slumped back on the sofa, deep in thought. He was quieter and paler than she'd ever seen him, and she suddenly wondered if he was wishing he'd never met her. She was not turning out to be the ideal wife, was she? Not giving him a baby but then bringing a fully grown adult child out of the woodwork like this. She had ruined everything.

He wouldn't look at her. He sat up, hunched over, elbows on his knees looking at the floor. What was going on in his mind? Was he wondering where the way out was? For him? For them? A way out or a way forward? Tears began to stab at the back of Anna's throat. Things still felt like a tangled mess.

'Jon?' she said, hesitantly, quietly, as though she didn't want to scare him off.

He looked up at her, his eyes brimming. He said nothing but stood up and opened his arms. She ran to him, into his embrace, and as he held her, she cried, and he kissed the top of her head.

Should she come clean now about why they'd not conceived a child of their own? Now he might understand why she had not been able to even consider trying for another baby. Maybe getting everything out in the open, now she could discuss the why as well as the what, would be the fresh start they would need to move on from here. Could she tell him? Would he understand? Or would it be the thing that broke him? Broke them?

* * *

Once her tears subsided, Jon broke away, but did not let go, holding her shoulders so he could look at her.

'Why didn't you say? Why didn't you tell me?' he asked, looking pained. 'I'd have understood.'

'Would you? When everyone else who was supposed to have loved me pushed me away because of it? When my own parents disowned me and, as it turns out, told me the worst of lies based on their disgust of me? How could I risk that?'

'Because I'm not them?'

'I know that now. We met and married so quickly. I was so happy. A new life was in front of me for the taking and after all the hurt, I just wanted to close the door on it all and move onwards. I did mean to tell you, but there was just never quite the right time. I tried but you... you represented all the good in my life. I didn't want to sully you with my past. And I was scared. I wasn't that person any more. It changed me. And you loved the new me. Why bring the past into it? Especially as I didn't ever think this day would come. I thought she was dead.'

'I know. I can't see how they could do such a thing.' The line of his jaw tightened as he ground his teeth. 'You knew what I'd been through when we met. Losing her, losing them and trying to find some way to keep going. You helped me. I told you everything, and you? You told me half of nothing. I knew you'd lost a child, but you'd never talk about it. I had no idea you'd been so young. You had a whole other life you didn't even ever mention to me.

Sure, I knew there was something, I guessed some sort of abusive relationship from the way that you were with me.'

'How was I with you?' Anna was suddenly defensive.

'Like you didn't want to rock the boat. Any sign of a row and you shut down, closed off to try to stop it happening.'

'Fighting isn't good though?'

'No, *fighting* isn't, no. But disagreements? Arguments? That's normal. That's healthy. Stops things from festering into more than they are. But you never want to, you shy from it and, well, here we are.'

'Where?'

'Where? With me furious with you. Or at least wanting to be. But then you've gone through so much and you had to do it alone that I feel like a shit for being angry with you as well. But then *that* also makes me angry because that's not fair on me and then, well, what the hell am I supposed to do with all this? I...'

Anna was frightened. He was angry. With her?

'Jon...'

He looked at her, the anger leaving his eyes almost as soon as he did. 'Yes?'

'I'm sorry.' She felt so small. She had made such stupid assumptions. 'I should never have thought that you and Grace were... that you would do that to me. You're a good person, the best person I know.'

Jon breathed in, mouth closed, trying to keep things calm. 'I won't say that I'm not hurt. I can't quite believe that you honestly thought it possible of me. I thought you knew me. Adultery is not something I would ever do. Ever.'

Anna could sense him pulling back from her. She wouldn't blame him if he walked away. 'I know. I think I lost my mind if I'm honest.'

'Lying? Sneaking around behind your back? It's not *me*, Anna.'

'Isn't it?' Anna arched an eyebrow at him. Yes, most of the lies had been hers but Jon and Grace *had* been sneaking around, talking behind her back, lying to her face. Jon's face reddened at the truth of this.

'Ah, well. Yes.'

'So? Are you going to tell me? Now that it's not an affair? What is it?' Anna asked, her throat feeling dry as she recalled the deleted message thread, the sneaky conversations, the meeting at the office that morning after church. There *was* something they were keeping from her.

'Well, I think Grace ought to be here so we can tell you together. You have to trust me, Anna. It's not bad, I promise. We did it with you in mind, not in spite of you. OK?' Jon looked at her encouragingly.

She had no choice.

She had to wait. She had to trust him. To push him away on this would mean to keep him at a distance from her still and she didn't want that. 'OK. I can wait,' she said.

Jon nodded. 'Thank you,' he said, pulling her back into another hug.

* * *

They stayed like that for a while, before Jon suddenly tensed. Anna could feel the question creep into his mind, affecting how he stood, before he opened his mouth to talk.

'How do we move forward from here? I'm trying to understand why you kept this from me. I know we've been bickering lately. I know that we've drifted. Now I wonder if it's because of this secret between us. If it's in part due to my keeping things from you too then I'm sorry. I'll admit, my mind is all over the place.' He half-laughed. 'Is there anything else you haven't told me?'

Anna's stomach dropped. There was more. So much more. But would telling him add to this same storm that they could ride out together? Or would it turn into a tidal wave that no one could survive? She wanted to trust in his love for her, she wanted to believe that he would still stay if she just told him everything and they could start over in the morning. A new day. But... her scars were too deep. They'd caused too much damage. She was too used to self-preservation, to only relying on herself. She would swallow this last untruth, about why she had not got pregnant, and she would take it with her to her grave. He would never know. He would never need to know. She would take this last lie, lock it up and be done with it.

'No, there's nothing else.'

'OK,' Jon said resolutely. 'I love you. You're my wife. We promised to stay together through bad times as well as good and, well, honestly, though this is a shock, I can't say it's necessarily bad. You've kept a lot of your past from me, a lot that would have helped me to understand you, to support you. I've always known there was something you were keeping from me, but I felt you would tell me when the time was right. But you haven't committed adultery. You haven't committed a crime. You haven't lied to me.'

Anna flushed with guilt at this last statement.

She looked up him, into his still-loving face, and she knew keeping this one lie to herself was for the best. She couldn't bear to see that love fade as she spoke the truth. She *had* lied to him, time after time, month after month, for years. On one level, their whole relationship was a sham. But it wasn't, not really. It was just this one part, this one piece of her that was so broken, had been broken all her adult life. Maybe now, now that she knew the truth, that some part of her was not dead but was *here*, maybe that part could heal, and she and Jon could move forward together.

'No. I've never lied.'

She lied for the last time.

From now on, truth.

'Anna,' Jon said gently, 'I want you to know that I did not marry you so that you could give me a baby. I married you because I love you. You know how hard things had been for me before I met you. You healed me. Let me do the same for you? We can work this out, how everything will fit together. And we will do it together. OK?'

'OK,' she whispered.

She closed her eyes for a moment, just a few seconds, as she tried to hold on to the feeling of peace. She had married a good man, a kind, strong, forgiving man. She would remember that, when he and Grace revealed whatever it was that they had been keeping from her. She opened her eyes again.

'Still, I want you to know how sorry I am. I'm sorry I didn't believe in you, in us. I'm sorry that I took all the badness I have known and attributed it to you. I didn't trust you and I should have.'

'Forgiven. From what I know now, I can see how you came to that conclusion. Wrong, *so* wrong that it was. Honestly, I like Grace, she's great, but she is young enough to be my daughter. Heh, I suppose she is now, in a way?'

Anna smiled. 'I suppose she is.'

Maybe she had given Jon a family after all. Just not how they had both imagined it. Maybe this would be enough for them both. Or maybe one day, in the future, she might feel ready to look again at the idea of having another child now that Grace had been returned to her. This still terrified her but now there was a question mark where before there had been a full stop.

'An extended family of sorts?' she said.

'My darling, we already have everything. Anything else is a bonus.'

28

Anna had slept badly the night before, all the possible ways this could go wrong winding in and out of her mind all night, all the possible reasons that Jon and Grace might have had to lie to her. Eventually she had given up in the small hours of the morning and sat, watching the sun rise as the day began.

With everyone now back in their living room, she was regretting not even resting if she couldn't sleep. She could feel her eyelids were heavy as she looked around the room at Grace and her parents, at Jon. She blinked, closing her eyes for just a millisecond longer than was polite. Everyone was being so terribly British, so quiet and courteous. Not quite saying things how they wanted to say them, perhaps not saying things at all. It was exhausting.

What were they doing?

There was a stilted silence following the usual niceties. No one wanted to say or do the wrong thing and so they were confused into not saying or doing anything. Five adult humans with no idea what to do for the best. They needed someone to guide them. Anna thought there must be organisations who could help with reuniting families. She had never looked because she thought her child was gone.

She looked across the room. She smiled and Grace smiled back. If they just kept Grace and her needs at the forefront, then surely they could negotiate a new way forward? Respectful, with agreed boundaries. No one treading on anyone's toes or over-stepping the mark. A step-family of sorts?

There was the sound of an escaped giggle and Anna looked up again and across the room at Grace. She was trying very hard not to laugh, holding her hand over her mouth, but you could see the amusement in her eyes. They were shimmering. Anna was trying to work out if she was happy or laughing with nerves. She wasn't being cruel, was she? At how awkward this suddenly felt? Anna felt empty as she realised how little she knew her daughter. Her *daughter*. She had barely had time to let it all sink in.

Grace let another loud laugh escape and Liane turned to look at her. Then she laughed too.

'Honestly!' Grace said as she managed to bring her breath back under control. 'You all look so serious! This is a good thing, isn't it? We're all here! Why does everyone look like they're going to a funeral? We're all here to work something out, aren't we? We all want this to work, don't we?' There was just a hint of concern in the solid assurance of her voice.

Her mum took her hand. 'I think so, lovey. I do. We're all just a bit scared, I think. I know I am. We've no idea how to do this and honestly, since you and I started all this, I've been worried we did it wrong. I feel, well, a bit like we ambushed you... Anna. It was a one-sided way of going about it.' She turned to Anna and Jon. 'And with Grace joining the business without saying who she was. I'm very aware that we've not done this well so far and we want to make sure we get it right from here. Should we get advice before we do this even? Are we here too early maybe?'

'I know what you mean but in all honesty, I've waited twenty-two years already. I don't think I've the patience to wait any longer,' Anna said.

'So how are we going to do this?' Grace said, looking expectantly at her four 'parents' around the room.

'How do you want to?' Anna asked. 'I mean, I'm still catching up. A few hours ago, I wasn't aware of who you really were to me, that you, my daughter, were even alive. What did *you* want, when you decided to track me down? What do you want that I might be able to give?'

This seemed the best way to start.

'What do I want?'

'Yes.'

Grace sat back on the sofa, her initial assuredness draining away. Liane took her hand on one side of her, and David rested his hand on her knee. She was utterly protected. From what? From who? Had Anna's voice been sharp? She found it so hard to tell. This whole scenario was so messed up.

'I don't know.'

'Yes, you do,' Anna said gently, smiling to show this was not an attack but a confirmation of what Grace was thinking was OK for her to voice. 'You tracked me down. You got a job working with me. You've been in my life for weeks now. You must have some idea, some ideal scenario of how this will go? If I promise to just listen, will you tell me what questions you want answered? What dreams you had of this situation, of us meeting and knowing each other? What you thought about when you knew you were adopted and that one day we might meet?'

Anna knew Grace must have thought about this. Surely you would. Even thinking her child was dead and buried, when thinking about her, Anna had envisioned what her life would have been like if she'd lived. If they'd been together. If she'd survived and been adopted, what her life with her new family would have been like. Anna had pictured scenario after scenario, first to comfort herself, then to punish her, then to torture her until it was too much, and she had to block her from her mind entirely.

'I...' Grace looked uncertainly at her mum.

'I don't mind, lovey. If I didn't think getting to know your birth mother was a good idea, then I would have said so before now and I wouldn't have done this, I wouldn't suggest you be here now. You can say. This isn't about me right now so don't worry. Go ahead. We can pop out of the room if it helps?'

'No, I want you here. Just... I love you. I'm not trying to replace you.'

'I know. We're all about adding here, not losing anything. Everyone's lost something already, haven't they? We're here to build it back up.' Liane nodded, as though trying to pep talk herself too.

'God, you're so good,' Anna said without realising it.

Liane snapped her head up, unsure if Anna was being sarcastic or not. She looked hurt.

'No, I mean it. You're so good.' Anna smiled to show her true intention. She was awful at tone. She often got it wrong. 'You're being so kind, supportive. Like a proper parent should be.'

'Well, this is partly my doing, isn't it? I adopted her, albeit not with the true information in my hands. Did I ask enough questions then? Or was I too busy getting what I had wanted for so long that I didn't look past what I was being told? I've spent all of Grace's life thinking of you. Every milestone I had that you didn't get to see, every birthday party, every little handwritten note. I thought of you and what you had lost for me to gain it. I was grateful. I was sad. I was happy. But was I fair? To you? Probably not.'

'Now come on,' David said, 'we were led by professionals, with the correct documentation. It was all above board as far as we were concerned.'

'I'm sure it was,' Anna said. 'My parents didn't cut corners when it came to doing things the way authority set them up. They would have made it look right, like they believed it was right. Look, I don't blame you. Really, I don't think I blame anyone. I have no plans to confront my mother about what she did. I'm done with her. I just want to know what we're going to do from here.'

'I want to ask you a million questions, that's what I want do,' Grace blurted out.

'About what?'

'Everything. Anything. I want to know what you were like, what my dad was like, my *biological* dad. Where is he now, do you know? Were you happy at all when you were pregnant? Did you ever think of me like I did of you? Did you remember my birthday? Did you ever wonder what I looked like, what I was doing, where I was...?' She trailed off, then laughed. 'Yeah. I've a lot of questions.'

Anna tried not to feel overwhelmed. 'You do.'

'But also, now? I just want to hang out. I want to know you. I... I don't need another mum, I have one. I have a family. But... but I want to be part of your life. If you'll let me.'

Anna could do that. 'I'd like that.'

Jon shifted in his chair and Anna looked at him. She raised her eyebrows, hoping he could read her thoughts, her asking him permission to make this work, for all of them.

'I'd like that too if I can be part of it with you. Would you like to keep working with us? As it's going really well. In fact, is now a good time to tell Anna?' Jon looked sheepish.

Anna's stomach contracted. Despite the assurance that the secret was not a torrid affair, her imagination had still drummed up countless scenarios that she did not want to be true. She wanted to know what had been going on, partly only to drive these out of her mind.

'The meetings Grace and I had. The ones you... misunderstood.'

All the whispering in corners, the secret meetings. These still hurt Anna, whatever it was about. She had still been excluded.

'Tell me,' Anna said shakily.

'Grace and I have been working on an entry to the local business awards. It's a portfolio of work, along with an entry to a design specification. We've come up with ideas, created them, gathered together elements of the company's work and submitted them. We've made the next round. We've got to do a presentation next. It's going... really well.'

Anna exhaled. She paused while she let this sink in. Then, she was appalled. They lied to her for *that*? She'd lost her mind for some stupid business award? This was ridiculous! She was not some harridan who refused to consider such things. She opened her mouth to rail at them but then bit her tongue. They had not been cheating, they had been trying to grow something, together, for her. She reformed her thoughts before speaking. 'What? Why on earth did you keep that from me? That's... that's great, isn't it?'

Jon looked wryly at his wife. 'I did tell you, but you refused to consider it.'

Ah, perhaps I am a harridan who refused to consider such things, Anna thought.

'You said we weren't ready. I thought we were, but I needed a design eye.'

'So, you asked Grace.'

'So, I asked Grace. We've had to have a few meetings and discussions without you, obviously. It's been difficult, keeping it to ourselves. I just wanted to show you how far we'd come and how far we go could go.'

Grace's face broke into a relieved smile.

'I'm so pleased we don't have to lie any more. I felt awful. Like an interloper in the business. But I wanted to show you what I could do, what we could achieve together. To make you...'

'Proud of you?' Anna whispered.

Grace nodded.

Anna closed her eyes. What on earth had she been thinking, taking this beautiful truth and twisting it so badly? She had known she was hard-wired to see the worst, but this made it clear quite how much so. No more. She pushed all of that down.

To gain things, sometimes you have to let things go.

'This all sounds great. I am proud of you both. It sounds wonderful.' Anna nodded.

'Thanks. I wonder if I get my artistic eye from you. Neither Mum nor Dad have any artistic skills.'

'Oi! Thank you very much!' Liane laughed. 'You've got a wider family to draw from now, haven't you then? Lucky you.'

'You could be like second parents? Godparents? Stepparents?' Grace asked Anna before turning to her parents for their thoughts.

Liane and David nodded.

'Something like that,' David said. 'Part of the family.'

Family.

Something Anna had never quite managed to feel that she was part of. In her early life, being the outlier, the disappointment. Then having her baby taken from her, and after meeting Jon, never quite feeling that she'd got it right. Something still missing. Was this her finally getting to put all the pieces together?

Could they really make this all work?

29

The garden was full of laughter and the sound of clinking plates, cutlery and glasses as the party took place under the shade of the trees at the end of the lawn. Anna had laid out a long wooden table underneath an umbrella with all her brightest plates and glasses. She decorated it with bowls full of freshly cut flowers from the garden and candles scented to keep away the bugs. It was a happy jumble of colour with plate after plate of food. She had gone all out for this party – a 'happy sort-of-birthday' party that she and Liane and Grace had agreed to throw, to mark the day that this new family of a kind was founded.

'You really mean it?' Anna had said when Grace stood next to Liane and laid out her suggestion the day before. Everyone was exhausted and wrung out, confusing themselves over details, and yet the answer seemed somehow so simple.

'I do.' Grace had smiled. 'Like I said, I don't *need* another family, or more siblings. I have been *strongly* blessed in that department already!'

'Oi!' Liane had said, a little hurt.

'I'm not being sarcastic, Mum!'

'Oh. Sorry. Thank you, love.' Liane beamed.

'But what is *need* when it comes to love? We all need love and' – Grace shrugged – 'more is good. Right? I want to know you, to know where I came from. To know about you, what you're like and if what you're like is why I'm like it in some ways too. You're... me and I am part of you and... I want that to be how things are.'

Anna blinked her happy tears away. 'And Jon?'

'Me?' Jon had said, hovering in the background, wanting to be involved but not wanting to push into a conversation that was not about him.

'Well, who else is gonna teach me about the mechanics of the printing process! And who else is as geeky about pigment particles as me? I want someone who gets that.' Grace tipped her head to the side, as though asking permission.

Jon stepped forward and awkwardly put his arm around her. She relaxed into it and Anna could hardly breathe. Everything looked so right. She looked at Liane to check how she was feeling but she had a genuine massive smile on her face too. Like she knew that things were right as well. Everyone finally where they were supposed to be.

The party was in full swing. Grace, her grandparents and her siblings were here so the place was filled with all generations, from young to old. Kate had been invited along, as well as some others from the church who were the first to be told about who Grace really was. Anna couldn't face telling everyone, one by one, about her child from the past, and so she and Kate had picked a few close friends, and one or two less close ones from those who liked to spread the word. The church gossip network had its uses. Keeping an eye on its members but also for disseminating news. Anna told these people and let them do the rest. The community would accept things. A gift from God in any form was to be welcomed. And soon enough Grace and Anna and Jon would be allowed to just be. No explanations needed.

Anna thought back to the first time that she knew. To the first moment she had accepted she was pregnant. Wave after wave of sheer terror. The knowing there was no undoing this. The knowing of what was to come and the knowing that it would be hard and painful, and for what? To be alone? To have lost everyone and everything. To be cast aside into her own wilderness for years and years. Would she have continued if she had known just how hard it would be?

But now? Now she was with all these people, all choosing to be part of her life despite none of them having any reason to have to. No assumed unconditional love here. Just love, given freely. If only Anna had been able to tell her younger self what happiness might be brought to her, to keep going because you never know what might be around the next corner if you just hold on. That one day you would be stood in your own home with your child, who had been lost to you forever but then one day miraculously returned to you, with your husband who had chosen to be with you and chosen that over and over again despite the truths you had kept from him, with a wider family who were not yours, but had shared their family with you as you had once unwittingly done with them. Anna felt that her heart just might burst with joy.

There was a shock of laughter from underneath the table umbrella and Anna looked over to see Grace smiling. They locked eyes and Grace walked over to her.

'Hi, Mum. I mean, Anna. Or Mum Anna? I'm not really sure what to call you,' she said, looking a little shy.

'Hi. You can call me Mum if you'd like, so long as your *mum* is OK with that?' Anna said as her heart fluttered.

'Yeah. She knows you're not taking her place. It's all good. Is it... good with you?'

'It is. It's really good.' She took her hand. 'I am going to tell you all you want to know, OK? Everything.'

'I know this isn't easy for you,' Grace said, compassion on her face.

'No, but I owe it to you.'

'You owe me nothing. You gave me everything.'

'You know what I mean. I don't want to keep anything from anyone any more.'

'Really? Anything?' Grace's eyes clouded a bit. Like the sun had gone behind clouds.

'What do you mean?'

'I think you know.'

Anna ran possibilities through her mind. What was Grace talking about?

'I... I don't.'

Grace looked down at the ground. She jiggled her foot anxiously before looking up again. 'Yes. Yes, you do.' She stared at Anna, her face hardening.

Anna couldn't think what she meant and her panic was rising as she could see the hostility in Grace. Their relationship wasn't going to be all sunshine and butterflies; it was going to be complex and complicated at times. She knew that; she wasn't an idiot. She had given Grace away, had not wanted nor been able to keep her.

Anna shook her head, confused.

'Oh, come *on*!' Grace said, grabbing Anna roughly by the elbow and guiding her towards the open kitchen door. 'Look. I understand that lying has been what you've done for so long that it's second nature to you now.'

'I beg your pardon?'

'I'm not trying to be rude...'

'You're not succeeding.'

'I just think that now you know about me, Jon knows about me and we're all trying to work out our new blended weird little family, that it should be all out in the open. No secrets, no lies, nothing to trip anyone up.'

'I agree.'

'So, you've told him then?'

Anna tipped her head to the side, confused.

Grace sighed. 'You've told Jon. About why you've not got pregnant. About still taking the pill.'

All the colour drained from Anna's face, and she thought she was going to be sick. She couldn't breathe and she felt as though she had suddenly been plunged into deep, cold water. Eventually she managed to spit out a word.

'What?'

Grace looked angry again. 'Stop it. *Stop* it. You know what I'm talking about. That day in the pharmacy.'

'So...' Anna's breath returned, her brain flooding back with air, allowing her to think. 'You followed me? You were following me?'

'No.' Grace shook her head. 'Truthfully, no, I was just there to collect my aunt's prescription. It really was just coincidence, fate, whatever. But with what the pharmacist said about the contraceptive pill, and with Jon saying you'd been trying to have a baby for years with no luck, well, it suddenly fell into place. *He* was trying for a baby. You? Not so much. I guess the trauma of me meant you didn't want to.' She looked down, as though this was her fault.

Anna took her hand. 'Hey. Look at me.'

Grace looked up, her darkest fears in her eyes.

'I can't,' Grace said, shaking her head. 'OK? I can't do this if I know something that Jon doesn't. About you. About the two of you. I know I shouldn't know and I guess you have your reasons for lying, but if you're going to *keep* lying, then I can't do this.'

Anna's throat closed up. 'You mean, this? Be my daughter again?'

'Yes. I have to look after myself. I can't and won't get mixed up between you two. Especially when he clearly still wants children of his own. I am not a consolation prize, an add on, an all grown up kiddo. I won't be that.'

'I'm not asking you to be.'

'Good. So, you'll tell him?'

Anna felt her hands grow clammy.

'Anna?' Grace asked, growing impatient.

'It's complicated.'

'How? You stop lying to him. He deserves better.'

'He does. I know. He does. Just...'

'Just what?'

'I don't know if I could have another baby. I've spent my whole life avoiding that possibility.'

'After your first one ruined your life?'

'No. No!' Anna said firmly. '*You* did not ruin my life. What my parents did and the choices I made are what made my life hard. Getting a second chance with you is all I want. I just don't know if it's fair to bring another child into this. I don't know if I can be that mother as well as a try-again mother for you. And you're here. This' – she waved her hands about to indicate a lack of something – '*baby* is not.'

'So, tell him that.'

'It's not that simple.'

'You're scared he won't forgive you?'

Anna could barely get the word out. 'Yes.'

She had, after all, mere hours ago promised him that there

were no more secrets. No more lies. To undo that now would surely ruin his trust in her forever.

'I get that. It is a huge lie. I have to admit, it made me think.'

'Think what?'

'Well... whether it was a good idea, trying to reconnect with you.'

'Ouch.' Anna winced.

'Sorry. It's true though. Like, what sort of person lies like that?'

'It's complicated,' Anna said again.

'I just think you owe him the truth. The chance to know if he might actually ever be a father or not. That's not fair to take from him. Or at least to let him know it's off the table. You know?'

'How did you get so wise so young?'

'Good parents,' Grace said, deadpan. 'Seriously though. You have to. You really have to. Because either you do or I will. I won't be part of any more lies. I won't do it.'

Anna swallowed. Her throat was dry. Grace was right. She'd spent so long lying that she almost didn't know how to stop. When to stop. Well, she could learn.

'Would you go and get him for me?'

'What? Now? You're gonna tell him now?' Grace's eyes widened.

'Yes. Else I'll lose my nerve. It has to be now. Please, could you go and get him?'

Grace leapt to her feet from the arm of the sofa where she had been sitting.

'OK.' She walked to the door before turning back. 'It will be OK you know. I really think so.'

Anna could only hope she was right. If she wasn't, then Anna was about to take a sledgehammer to her marriage.

Grace returned mere moments later with a confused-looking Jon in tow.

'What's going on? Are you OK, Anna? Grace said it was urgent? I've left David doing the grill but I shouldn't be too long. He is our guest, after all.'

Grace squeezed Anna's hand and left the room, subtly closing the door behind her.

Anna took a deep breath and was suddenly overcome with a huge wave of nausea. She flushed hot, her skin pricking with needles, acid hitting the back of her throat. She was going to be sick.

'Anna? Anna, are you OK? You look awful.'

She was too scared to open her mouth to respond for fear that she would vomit all over the place. Not the best opening for such a difficult conversation. She shook her head as vigorously as she was able and ran from the room, clutching her hand over her mouth, hoping against hope that she would make it to the bathroom. She ran upstairs, jumping two steps at a time, and threw herself into the bathroom, flinging up the toilet seat, slumping to the floor and vomiting copiously into the bowl. Wave after wave hit her and she retched until she felt utterly empty, and even then her body decided to really make sure by making her heave and gag until her stomach muscles hurt and her throat was raw.

'Anna?' Jon called up the stairs. She could hear how he was looking back at the garden filled with guests as he spoke.

'I'm OK. It's fine,' she managed to croak out.

'You sure? I... I can come up?'

'No! No, I'm OK.' She hated being seen sick and Jon was great with many of life's moments, but vomit was not one. She needed a moment. She had to regroup. What was happening? She'd been fine one moment and the next, it was like her whole body wanted to invert itself.

She placed the seat down, flushed the toilet and then rested her arm on the side, her head on her arm. She was cooling down, no longer flushing with heat. Her breath was returning to normal. She closed her eyes for a moment and when she opened them again, she found herself staring across the room to the cabinet next to the bath. It was a bamboo one, with a glass top on which sat a trailing string of hearts plant and a coaster. She loved to sit in the bath with a cup of coffee or a glass of wine and read, and this was her table. Underneath was where she kept her sanitary products and spare bathroom necessities. It was this that caught Anna's attention, or rather, drew her mind to inattention.

She took a long slow intake of breath as her mind raced. What was the date? When had she had her last period? Things had been so crazy, so emotional, full of such life-changing moments that she couldn't immediately recall.

Think!

She tried to grasp a memory, which she could line up with a date, or the passing of time, to work it out. She grabbed at one memory – meeting Kate shopping. It had been hard because of such bad stomach cramps. That can't have been the last time. That was *weeks* ago. There must have been another. There must have been. She'd noted these things down in her diary – she'd go and look.

Anna opened the bathroom door and, looking down from the hallway window, seeing that the party was in full swing and fine without her, she skipped across to her bedroom and retrieved her diary from her bedside table. She flipped it open and skimmed the pages as she went back in time, looking for the 'P' that she noted when her period arrived, or a PE for when it ended. Page after page after page. Nothing. Her heart rate flickered up. Shit shit shit. No, it was fine. She was on the pill – she was literally just about to tell Jon that, wasn't she? She had been taking it for so long, like clockwork, at the same time every day, midday, just to be sure that lie ins or late nights didn't derail her. She was always awake and lucid at midday. There had been that one time but she'd got the morning after pill. That was really effective. Wasn't it?

Throwing her diary on the bed, the pulled the nightstand drawer right out and reached into the back. She had a set at the office and a set here, in the same place, wedged up against the very back of a drawer in the little cardboard box they came in. She pulled the packet away and opened it up. There were lots in there. Shit. No, she would have taken the ones at work then? Though, Saturday? She'd been home. But the days wouldn't line up anyway because of the two packets. It was fine. It was *fine*.

She took a deep breath in and let it slowly exhale.

It wasn't fine.

She couldn't remember last taking the pill and she couldn't place her last period She wracked her brain but the pill taking was so clockwork as to no longer register and so she couldn't be sure. Not really.

Anna sank down on to the bed and laid her head on the pillow. It was pounding. She was getting herself all worked up over nothing. She had managed not to get pregnant her entire marriage. She and Jon had barely had sex lately anyway with everything that had been going on. Firstly, she had been too suspicious of him, and then, with all the revelations about Grace, she had been too emotionally wrung out to do anything other than sleep the moment her head hit the pillow.

She was being ridiculous. She was tired, overwrought, and that was making her sick. She closed her eyes. She tried to read her body. Maybe she was just late, and the hormones were mimicking pregnancy. That's how she had given Jon false hope in the early days – her breasts got sore, she was tired and cranky, but the blood always came. She had wasted so many pregnancy tests on symptoms she knew weren't true.

Pregnancy tests. She still had a box of them!

She jumped off the bed and went back to the bathroom, closing and locking the door behind her. She rummaged in the back of the cabinet and found them. They were old but maybe they'd still work? They might be less sensitive but still, it might calm her mind down long enough for her period to start. She ripped open the packet and sat down on the loo, leaning forwards to try to convince herself to pee. Imagining waterfalls and flash floods and trickling streams eventually did the trick and she managed to wee on the right bit.

She put the stick down and washed her hands and waited. Three minutes. And then she could tell herself to stop being an idiot and go back to the party. She'd have to tell Jon about the pill, but maybe now with all their guests here wasn't the right time. There was never a right time, but there was a bad time, and this was it.

Two minutes.

She'd tell him tonight, when they'd gone. When he could react how he needed to without an audience of people.

One minute.

Her stomach growled now that it was empty and the smell of food wafting in from the window overlooking the garden made her hungry. She was suddenly ravenous.

Thirty seconds.

Then she could bin the test. Go downstairs and eat with her newly extended family. It was a day of celebration, and she was being stupidly dramatic.

Ten seconds.

Five.

Done.

With shaking hands, she picked up and looked at the test.

Two lines.

Two clear and distinct lines.

Anna's knees gave way beneath her, and she crumpled to the floor. Tests can give you a false negative, if they don't detect enough of a hormone to show up, she knew that. But a positive result needs the hormone present, the one that's only present when you're pregnant. And there were two lines.

Anna held her breath, waiting for that moment of absolute terror to hit, like it had done before, when she had held the test in her fifteen-year-old hands, in the public toilet of the local shopping centre, away from her parents' prying eyes or the chance of a sibling crashing into the bathroom. She had sat on that dirty floor that had smelled of other people and had sobbed until she had been sick, the all-encompassing knowledge that her life was ruined spreading out in front of her like discarded toilet paper.

It didn't come. The terror she had carried around with her for so long. It wasn't there.

Something else flickered inside her, where fear had once sat. Joy.

A spark of joy that grew as she looked at the test again. A baby. Hers, Jon's. Together. The more she thought about it, the more the smile on her face grew until she was grinning like a Cheshire cat. This was not the reaction she had expected but she knew that her instinct never let her down. She was happy about this. This was right. Her first baby was here, back with her, and she and Jon would have their family too with this baby, and Grace included. Suddenly it all made sense; it all felt right.

A smaller realisation came to her also. Jon would never have to know that she had lied. She didn't have to tell him about why it had not happened until now. It hadn't happened because it hadn't been right, she hadn't been ready. Any child that had been conceived before now would have had the shadow of her missing first child hanging over it, a heavy weight for a child to bear. Every step of the pregnancy would have been shrouded in trepidation, bad memories and lies. That's no way for a life to begin.

Now, things were better, clearer. Still in the process of being worked out, but better. And all Jon needed to know now was that he was going to be a father. Everything else was just detail and Anna could live without him having all the details. Grace would not need to know what conversations had or hadn't happened. She would just need to know that Anna was no longer lying. There was the chance that she would tell Jon, but unless Grace was deliberately trying to cause problems, and Anna didn't think she would be, that was a very small risk.

Anna would take that chance.

She stood up and wrapped the test in some paper and put it to one side. She'd show Jon later.

Straightening her clothes, she rinsed out her mouth and fixed her make-up, which had smudged when she had been retching earlier. The past half an hour had felt like a lifetime. Now everything looked different.

As she walked back into the garden, Jon caught her eye and came over to her.

'Are you OK, darling? You've been gone ages. Are you all right?' He leant to kiss her on the top of her head, and she took his hands in hers.

'I'm good. I'm great, actually. Really great.'

'I was worried. Glad you're all right. Let's feed people!' he said as he turned with a flourish and indicated to everyone to sit down.

Anna took her place next to him and looked over at Grace. She wrinkled her nose at Anna and mouthed, *Did you tell him?*

Anna shook her head but smiled and mouthed back, *No. I will tell him today. I promise.*

What she would tell him she did not specify, and she looked to the heavens and hoped that God would forgive this one last white lie, to straighten things out. She hoped Grace would too. She didn't want to lie to her, but also telling Jon now gained nothing for anyone. Telling him the good news would cancel things out, she was sure of it. Karma would be in balance.

Grace looked put out but nodded in agreement.

I love you, Anna mouthed at her, and Grace spontaneously broke into a wide smile. Anna put her hand gently on her stomach. It was all going to be OK.

Anna sat back and looked around her. Sometimes life has a way of working things out in the strangest of ways. While you're making plans or coping with one thing, something else falls into your lap, or swerves your path and you have to roll with it. Those moments where everything feels just as it should be are fleeting moments of gold.

At a peaceful moment, when everyone else was chatting amongst themselves, Anna gently prodded Jon next to her.

'Jon?' she whispered.

'Yes?' he said, leaning in closer to listen.

'I've got something to tell you.'

'What is it?' he whispered back.

Anna took his hand and laid it gently on her stomach and looked up at him. At first, he didn't get what she was saying, but then his face lit up as realisation hit.

He looked at her, a question on his face. 'Are you...? Do you mean...?'

'Yes.' She beamed at him.

'Are you sure?' He looked panicked almost, as though he didn't want to let himself believe.

Anna was sure. She knew. 'Yes.'

'Oh my god. I... I love you.'

'I love you too.'

'This is perfect. Everything is perfect.'

Anna looked up at Grace to find her looking at them both, she had been watching. Anna saw in her face the moment she understood what Jon's huge smile meant. Grace raised her eyebrows in question, in confusion, surreptitiously crossing her arms, briefly moving them into a cradling position and back again, asking Anna to confirm. Anna nodded and Grace looked shocked, then confused, and then happy acceptance spread across her face.

Grace had been taken away. Grace had been returned to her. Grace had brought them all together.

A new family, made from all the broken pieces of the past.

ACKNOWLEDGEMENTS

As always, writing a book is a group enterprise, with so many people to thank for getting this book completed.

To start, thank you to the families who shared their stories of adoption and of child loss with me. Thank you for your generosity with your time and for your openness about such emotional moments.

To my lovely editor, Emily Yau, who helped craft this from a very early draft to the finished product, with encouragement all the way.

My wonderful agent, Marianne Gunn O'Connor, who is always supportive, and a much appreciated voice of experience.

To the wonderful #TeamBoldwood – to Jenna, Ben, Claire, Issy, Nia and everyone who makes it such a joy to work with them.

To Jennifer Davies, my copyeditor, for helping me get my love of the word 'just' under control! To Rose Fox, my proofreader, for helping me make sure there are as few errors as possible.

To Aaron Munday for yet another striking cover design, thank you!

This book was written during a whirlwind of a year, both the highs of publishing my debut and a follow up novel, and the lows of a difficult personal few months. I am beyond thankful for the support of those who held me up while I tried to get this book completed. To my amazing friends, the Wonder Women, Katharine Oldak, Michelle Perrott, Mark Wood, Heather Bell,

Delia Slucutt and more I cannot name here. My gorgeous neighbours, Richard Horan and Sasha Garrett for support, cake and help with parcel deliveries! My book groups for standing with me and cheering me on.

My Cambridge Literary Festival friends and colleagues for being part of the journey with me.

The wonderful Lucy Cavendish Fiction Prize community for their support.

To fellow writers such as Julia Laite who helped me wrangle out the story from the initial idea with the baby scan scene. Emma-Clare Wilson for your support when life fell apart and Georgina Skull for being such a good listening ear. Thank you.

To the Debuts groups 2022 and 2023 for going through your debut years with me and propping each other up, and my Faber group for your amazing encouragement and support.

To the wonderful booksellers, especially Heffers Cambridge, David Roberton, Sarah Whyley and the team and Amy Crawford at Cambridge Waterstones.

To Bookstagram and Book Twitter and the wonderful bloggers who give so much of their time to help readers find books. It is always appreciated.

To the wonderful readers for your encouragement and support for my first two books. I hope you enjoy this one as well. Thank you for spending time with my stories.

To my wonderful family, especially Malcolm, Beatrice and Madeleine who share me with my characters and with the writing process and inspire me to keep going. Thank you for everything.

And lastly, to my own beloved mother, Lynn Mulford, who died during the writing of this book. I want to include her here so that she will always be a part of it. Writing about motherhood for *The New Girl* made me think about my own experience of being mothered and allowed me to realise how grateful I am for the love and support that I was so lucky to have had. Thank you, Mum. Love you always.

ABOUT THE AUTHOR

Alison Stockham has worked in TV documentary production for the BBC and Channel 4, and is now the Events Coordinator for the Cambridge Literary Festival. Her debut novel The Cuckoo Sister, was longlisted for the 2020 Lucy Cavendish Fiction Prize.

Sign up to Alison Stockham's mailing list for news, competitions and updates on future books.

Follow Alison on social media here:

    facebook.com/AlisonStockham-Author

    x.com/AlisonStockham

    instagram.com/astockhamauthor

ALSO BY ALISON STOCKHAM

The Cuckoo Sister

The Silent Friend

The New Girl

THE

Murder

LIST

**THE MURDER LIST IS A NEWSLETTER
DEDICATED TO SPINE-CHILLING FICTION
AND GRIPPING PAGE-TURNERS!**

**SIGN UP TO MAKE SURE YOU'RE ON OUR
HIT LIST FOR EXCLUSIVE DEALS, AUTHOR
CONTENT, AND COMPETITIONS.**

SIGN UP TO OUR
NEWSLETTER

BIT.LY/THEMURDERLISTNEWS

Boldwood

Boldwood Books is an award-winning fiction publishing company seeking out the best stories from around the world.

Find out more at www.boldwoodbooks.com

Join our reader community for brilliant books, competitions and offers!

Follow us
@BoldwoodBooks
@TheBoldBookClub

Sign up to our weekly
deals newsletter